High Praise for
Hot Legs

"Versatile author Ms. Johnson adds a new element to her terrific writing as *Hot Legs* shows. Her mix of pop and sizzle blends expertly with a zany plot and charismatic characters. I enjoyed every minute." —*Rendezvous*

"A perfect ten as a story not to be missed this year. Susan Johnson's writing is exceptional, and I plan not to miss any more of her releases." —*Romance Reviews Today*

"Funny, romantic, steamy, sexy! A great read!" —*The Best Reviews*

Hot Pink

"The sassy, bold heroine of this fast-moving book . . . will appeal to fans who like their tales geared more toward women of the twenty-first century who go after what they want and aren't afraid to get it. I loved it from beginning to end." —*Rendezvous*

"This erotic contemporary romance shows Susan Johnson at her hottest, which means that the lead couple generates enough thermos heat to keep the Northeast warm in winter." —*Midwest Book Review*

"This one lives up to its title." —*People*

Praise for the Novels of
Susan Johnson

"Smart . . . sexy . . . sensuous . . . Susan Johnson's books are legendary!" —Robin Schone

"Johnson delivers another fast, titillating read that overflows with sex scenes and rapid-fire dialogue." —*Publishers Weekly*

continued . . .

HOT SPOT

SUSAN JOHNSON

BERKLEY SENSATION, NEW YORK

THE BERKLEY PUBLISHING GROUP
Published by the Penguin Group
Penguin Group (USA) Inc.
375 Hudson Street, New York, New York 10014, USA
Penguin Group (Canada), 10 Alcorn Avenue, Toronto, Ontario M4V 3B2, Canada
(a division of Pearson Penguin Canada Inc.)
Penguin Books Ltd., 80 Strand, London WC2R 0RL, England
Penguin Group Ireland, 25 St. Stephen's Green, Dublin 2, Ireland (a division of Penguin Books Ltd.)
Penguin Group (Australia), 250 Camberwell Road, Camberwell, Victoria 3124, Australia
(a division of Pearson Australia Group Pty. Ltd.)
Penguin Books India Pvt. Ltd., 11 Community Centre, Panchsheel Park, New Delhi—110 017, India
Penguin Group (NZ), Cnr. Airborne and Rosedale Roads, Albany, Auckland 1310, New Zealand
(a division of Pearson New Zealand Ltd.)
Penguin Books (South Africa) (Pty.) Ltd., 24 Sturdee Avenue, Rosebank, Johannesburg 2196,
South Africa

Penguin Books Ltd., Registered Offices: 80 Strand, London WC2R 0RL, England

This book is an original publication of The Berkley Publishing Group.

First edition: June 2005

Library of Congress Cataloging-in-Publication Data

Johnson, Susan, 1939–
    Hot spot / Susan Johnson.—1st ed.
        p. cm.
    ISBN 0-425-20257-7
    1. Comic books, strips, etc.—Collectors and collecting—Fiction. 2. Women booksellers—Fiction.
3. Comic book fans—Fiction. I. Title.

PS3560.O386458H69 2005
813'.54—dc22

                                                                2005041139

PRINTED IN THE UNITED STATES OF AMERICA

10 9 8 7 6 5 4 3 2 1

ONE

 THE DATE WAS CIRCLED IN RED ON THE CONAN calendar behind the cash register.

Lumberjack Days.

Only a week away.

Stella groaned.

She must have been crazy to say she'd hand out campaign literature with Megan. Since when was she the type to walk along with the Lumberjack Days parade and hand out leaflets to parade watchers who didn't want them?

Since never. That's when.

Even if she and Megan were good friends, there were limits to friendship. She was capable of manning phone banks, addressing campaign literature, even designing campaign signs . . . signs that had turned out to be hotter than hot if she did say so herself. Megan had inadvertently become "The Green Lady" in her state senate campaign, the designation compliments of the various green hues on her campaign signs. The media had picked up on the phrase and had made Megan a real contender against an incumbent from an old Minnesota political dynasty.

So really—whether one more person handed out leaflets during the parade was incidental. Right?

Aaargh.

As if Megan was going to let her off the hook that easily.

Damn. Why couldn't she think of a way out—you know . . . something really plausible and polite—maybe even an excuse that would elicit sympathy.

A funeral wouldn't work. She was more or less a relative—less except for her grandma who was either at the casino playing the nickel slots or running a marathon and was healthier than God, and her parents who were pretty young and lived in town besides, which made a fictitious funeral tougher to carry off. And outside of them—there had been only Aunt Martha who had died and left her this great house and the wherewithal to start her own comic book. But a second funeral for Aunt Martha was probably not going to fly because Megan had attended the real one.

Could she fake a sprained ankle?

A sudden attack of the flu?

PMS that affected her ability to walk?

Chewing on her drawing pencil, Stella glanced down at the page one sketch she was roughing in. How would her heroine, Marky B, handle such an ethical/potentially wimping-out situation? She'd kick butt of course, face the challenge, and come out on top. Which was the beauty of creating comic books. It had nothing to do with real life.

"Are you open?"

Stella looked up from behind the counter, and suppressing a small "Wow" she would have put in caps in a balloon for Marky B, her gaze lighted on the man entering her bookstore. "Ah—sort of—I guess," she said, like some dolt instead of uttering some clever, witty, perhaps sophisticated comment that would show him instantly she was worldly and accomplished despite her teddy bear pajamas and uncombed hair.

"Your hours are on the door . . . I'm early, but"—he shrugged faintly—"I saw you inside."

For a man who looked like he did—lean, toned, darkly handsome in a Tolkien hero sort of way—she was tempted to say, "Your time is my time." But then an otherworldly-movie-star-type guy probably heard that a lot. "I live upstairs, so my hours are flexible," she said, trying to sound cool. Trying not to notice the really long lashes and dark bedroom eyes that Tolkien had never had the good sense to describe.

"Nice place."

Ohmygod . . . a sexy smile, too. But she managed to say, "Thanks. It's my little piece of paradise," in a near normal tone. And a guy who looked like that was used to fawning women, she reminded herself. That was neither her style, nor her personal ambition. "You're looking for Marvel, right? I usually can tell," she said, relegating his charismatic face and bod to the fantasy dustbin.

"I hope your psychic powers are confined to comics," he said with a grin.

"Are you hittin' on me?"

"Wouldn't think of it."

"Good. It's way too early." Or just inopportune. She looked like a bag lady.

"I could come back later."

Was that a wink? Yes? No? She should tell him right now that she never dated customers. "Why don't we deal with the comics," she said, giving herself a little more time to drool before having to make one of those principled decisions. "Am I right or not about Marvels?"

"Definitely psychic."

"In this business, it's sometimes psycho, too."

"What the hell." He grinned. "Anyone can be normal."

"That's my mantra." The comic book world was sometimes more appropriately written in caps, and the people who lived and breathed comics tended to be a little more out there than the average bear. "I see all kinds in here, present company excepted. You look pretty sane."

"I have my moments. Speaking of fringe though, Buddy Morton told me about your place."

"I suppose anyone who's into Japanese underground stuff like Buddy is has a quirk or two." She preferred that her action heroes concentrate on saving the world, rather than chopping up people with their samurai swords and having kinky sex, but Buddy was a *real* good customer. "The Marvels are in the back," she added, pretty sure she didn't want the conversation to veer in the direction of Buddy Morton's interest in underground comics and kinky sex. At least not until she changed her rule about dating customers.

Sexy Guy moved away from the door and walked toward her—all lithe grace and animal magnetism—and she found herself sketching him in her mind. This guy would make one bomb-ass super hero.

"Buddy tells me you're doing cutting-edge stuff with your *Marky B* comic."

"I'm just starting out. It's fun if nothing else." She slid out from behind the counter and started toward the back room, thinking fun with him would entail a large bed or, what the hell, twenty minutes anywhere.

"Give me a heads up on your favorite *Marky B*'s, and I'll buy some."

"You don't have to do that." She gave him a glance over her shoulder. Jeez, he was right behind her—all that hard muscled male swagger up close and personal.

"But I want to."

Startled at his deep, husky rasp, she stopped, turned around, and met his gaze with what she hoped was an I'm-in-charge-here look. "Just for the record, we're talking about comics."

"Sorry." He pointed at his throat. "Something caught in there."

If he hadn't been smiling, she might have bought it. "It's too early to deal with wiseasses. I have something you want, not the other way around, so watch yourself."

"Gotcha. Comics." That tousled, just-out-of-bed look was hotter than any Victoria's Secret ad, but he got the message.

She gave him a look. "Just so we're on the same page."

"Gotcha. Comics, pages, stop, do not pass Go. You're the boss."

"Very funny." She tried to glower, but her mouth twitched.

"If you smile your face might break."

"What are you, five years old?"

"Most people who own stores smile at their customers, that's all," he said, looking innocent as hell. "Customer service 101."

She'd like to do a whole lot more than smile at him, but the modicum of reason she possessed—not always to be relied on but apparently on the job this morning—cautioned her against throwing herself at a relative stranger no matter how much he looked like a Tolkien hero. "I'll smile, okay?"

"Hey, that's nice."

"Thank you, and now what Marvels do you need?" It probably wasn't wise to stand too close for too long to this sexy man who was definitely hitting on her.

He almost said, "Great tits," 'cuz that was what he was thinking. But he backed up his brain, replayed her question, and said, "*X-Men*," instead.

"Which *X-Men*?"

"*The Uncanny X-Men*, issue ninety-four," he said, trying to keep his eyes off those teddy bears dancing across her boobs.

"You and everyone else. That one's pricey."

"I figured."

He didn't bat an eyelash. Did that mean his gray T-shirt, worn jeans, and shredded sneakers were urban chic instead of poverty? Or had he robbed his piggy bank? It happened in her business—the fanatic collectors, young kids especially, would spend their last penny for a special edition. "I have two copies." She pointed. "One is mint, the other is poor but readable." She turned to take them off the shelf.

He gave Stella the once-over—from her bare feet past her great ass to her blonde curls. Definitely nice. Buddy had said Stella Scott was worth making the trip to Stillwater, and he hadn't been wrong. She could be a stand-in for a comic book heroine—slender, shapely, tawny blonde hair with a wide-eyed look that gave out innocent and sexy vibes at the same time.

According to Buddy, she was unattached. And according to his radar, she was interested.

He'd seen that look—the once-over, the approval. He was guessing if he asked, she'd say yes.

But with a store like this, one he was sure to patronize from the looks of her large inventory stored on floor-to-ceiling shelves, asking her might make more problems than it was worth. Casual dating was his strong suit; hooking up with her once or twice might mess up what could turn out to be a perfectly fine business relationship.

"Here's the mint one." She held out a comic in a clear plastic dust cover. "It's the best *X-Men* 94 in the country." The pride in her voice was obvious, her real passion for comics momentarily overriding even bodacious hunks at close range.

Taking it from her, Danny whistled softly. "What a beauty. How much?"

"Five and a quarter. The other copy is eighty bucks. Even without a decent cover, the inside is good reading."

"I'll take the prime one."

No hesitation. Not even a scintilla. He was either rich or into collecting before eating. "It's a good price," she said.

He smiled. "I know. Show me your other *X-Men*."

In the next ten minutes, he bought enough comics to make a real dent in her total weekly sales. She was hoping like hell he didn't want to pay with a check, because she couldn't take a chance on a personal check that large. But he paid with a credit card—thank you God—filling all the gaps in his *X-Men* collection to the max.

As she was putting the comics into bags, one of the neighborhood kids walked in, his skateboard under his arm, gave Stella the high sign, plopped down in a chair near the door, and shut his eyes. She ran baby-sitting central in the summer time—wall-to-wall kids from sunup to sundown.

When the door opened, Danny had turned, exposing in all their flagrant grossness the words on the back of his T-shirt: FREE MUSTACHE RIDES.

She should have known.

He had way the hell too much going for him to be humble.

Screw him and all the men like him who think every woman is waiting to get laid. "There you go," she said, plunking his bags down on the counter. "Have yourself a good day."

He swung back, his brows drawn together. That wasn't "Have a good day." That was one pissed woman. "Something wrong?"

"Uh-uh." She gave him a tight smile. "Enjoy your comics."

"Thanks, I will." Grabbing the bags from the counter, he walked away. But there was something about her beyond the obvious that hit some kind of quirky nerve center in his brain, and when he reached the door, he hesitated. What the hell. He turned back. "Would you like to go to dinner sometime?"

"No thanks. I don't date customers." She lifted one shoulder in a faint shrug and took great satisfaction in saying ultra-sweetly, "It's just business."

"Too bad," he said, pulling open the door.

Did he mean too bad for her or him, she wondered as he walked out. And what was with that casual tone? Didn't he notice that she'd cut him off at the knees? Where was the satisfaction in blowing off a FREE MUSTACHE RIDES guy if he didn't even get it? Particularly when she found herself feeling as though *she* might have missed something when she shouldn't feel anything of the kind about a guy who wore that sexist, chauvinist-pig T-shirt.

* * *

STELLA HAD SCORED a direct hit though, even if she didn't know it.

Danny hadn't been turned down since—jeez—he couldn't remember when.

As he descended the long bank of flagstone steps to the street, he reminded himself it wasn't about winning or losing. Sometimes things worked out, and sometimes they didn't. Not that he'd ever been on the "not working out" side when it came to asking someone out, though.

But maybe it was true. Maybe she really didn't date customers.

Not that it mattered—he'd had no intention of asking anyway.

He should thank her for saying no.

STANDING TO ONE side of the parlor window so she wouldn't be visible from the street, Stella watched him get into a nondescript white pick-up truck. His chauvinist-pig mentality aside, it was a crying shame she couldn't have checked him out. He was about as close to perfection as she'd seen off the pages of a hunks calendar. But discounting the macho sentiments on his T-shirt, he'd also spent too much money in her shop today for her to jeopardize a promising business connection by entering into any relationship whatsoever. He could turn out to be a lucrative customer. And she knew how a date would have gone with him anyway. He'd eventually ask, and she'd say no to that more-than-dinner proposition. Men like him were only familiar with women saying yes, and there she'd be—upsetting his perfect record.

It wasn't that he wasn't damned good-looking.

But feminist principles notwithstanding, she'd decided long ago to play it safe and not date customers. Comic book buyers were ninety percent male, and she was in business to make money.

It was all about her bottom line.

But bottom line or not, he'd managed to fire up her libido.

Not an everyday occurrence of late, when she'd been too busy to even think of sex.

She needed her therapist/best friend since grade school to cool her fevered brain, and the second he drove away, she called Megan. "You won't believe who walked in and out of my store," she breathlessly exclaimed. "Picture a totally sexy cross between Viggo Mortensen and Orlando Bloom, with a dash of —"

"It's seven-thirty," Megan grumbled. "I was at a fund-raiser until midnight last night, and the kids are still sleeping. Could this wait?"

"Sorry. Sure. But this guy was so good-looking I'm still undressing him in my mind."

"Undressing? Hey—I'm up, I'm up—my eyes are even open. Do you think he'd date a divorcée with two children, a dog, and two guppies?"

"I'll call you next time he comes in the store, and you can ask him. Although he did ask *me* out to dinner."

"Damn. Shatter my hopes at the crack of dawn."

"I turned him down."

"You're insane, of course."

"I have my rule about dating customers. Besides, he wore a shirt that said FREE MUSTACHE RIDES on the back."

"*Euwwwww.* On the other hand, you hardly leave your house, thanks to your store hours and comic book deadlines. Maybe you could ignore the T-shirt. Otherwise, you're never going to have a chance in hell of experiencing the hallowed state of matrimony."

"Do I hear you actually recommending marriage?"

"It's early. Obviously, I'm not thinking clearly."

Megan's husband had found his secretary more intriguing than his wife and family. Younger, too, Stella suspected. "Anyway, listen up. I'll make your day." And she proceeded to describe the guy in all his drop-dead-gorgeous glory from head to foot.

"Okay, you've got me panting now. What's the name of this female fantasy?"

"I don't know. I didn't ask—wait—his credit card receipt should have a name." Stella pressed a button on the cash register to roll out the drawer. "Danny Rees."

"Does he live around here?"

"I didn't ask, and it says here"—Stella squinted at the receipt—"Xzodus Software, Inc. Jeez, he's a computer geek."

"He doesn't sound like a geek."

"He's the exception to geekdom, no doubt about it." Although that might explain the Converse sneakers.

"So now what?"

"So nothing. Did I tell you he bought nearly three thousand dollars worth of comic books?"

"Not more than ten times. You should be nice to him."

"And you should go back to sleep." Megan was always telling her she should go out more. "I'm done enthusing."

"Maybe he could be the exception to your rule."

"Nah. We'd go on a date and then what? I have a business to run. I can't afford to piss off a customer."

"What makes you think you'd piss him off?"

"You didn't see him in person—he had that look . . . you know the one. He's used to ladies chasing him. And he doesn't chase them back. Charming, but detached. We've both met a few of those."

Stella and Megan had grown up next door to each other, roomed together in college, then shared an apartment their first year of teaching. In general, they could finish each other's sentences. Megan had married seven years ago, had two kids, then discovered her husband in a motel room with his secretary by accident. Which didn't say much for Chad's cleverness. The motel was right next door to his insurance office.

"One learns," Megan pointedly said.

"About good lawyers, too," Stella noted, amusement in her voice.

"True. Did I tell you Mike asked me out for dinner?"

"I don't think so, because I would have *remembered* incredibly fantastic news like that. I *hope* you said yes."

"I said I'd think about it."

"What the hell's wrong with you? Mike is great!"

"I refused him real nicely. He understood. Christ, he's a divorce lawyer. Why wouldn't he? He said he'd ask me again next week."

"That's sweet. A real Hallmark moment. We'll have to go shopping and find you a new dress. You can't wear sweats out to dinner." Megan taught phys ed, and although she looked great in sweats, because anyone who could pump a hundred pounds and run the mile in five minutes was trim and toned, there were times when even Juicy Couture sweats wouldn't do.

"Back at you, babe. Think about going out with your hunk if he promises to wear a more PC T-shirt. You've been home alone way too long. I mean it. You're too damned fussy. They're not tall enough or in tune with your world enough or God forbid, don't like the same sports teams as you. You're not going to find that perfect man. Take it from me. I know. You'll have to seriously consider the concept of casual dating."

"I don't think so. If I have to pass the evening with some stranger talking about topics I don't want to talk about just to be polite, I'd rather weed the garden. I mean it. I hate to waste my time."

"Picky, picky, picky. What's wrong with a drink and dinner and some idle chitchat?"

"I'll wait for you to set the example. You let me know how it goes with Mike."

"I'm done nagging. I don't suppose you want to go to the beach today with the kids and me? You could get Amy to come in and mind the store."

"Some other time, but thanks. I'm busy with Marky B's newest story line. Deadline's Friday."

"Damn, there goes the dog barking, which is sure to wake up the kids—oh, yeah, right on cue. I hear Lily singing her good morning song to Bob, the bunny rabbit. Gotta go, the dog just jumped on my bed."

The phone line went dead.

After her very good morning, sales-wise, Stella was tempted to go to the beach with Megan. But she wouldn't. She was pretty compulsive about her business. Not that it was a burden in any way. She really *liked* her store and comic book creation, work and pleasure overlapping with almost a zenlike perfection. She might, however, want to think about going upstairs and dressing. The store would officially open in an hour. And in the summer, with kids on vacation, she had a mob scene just about every day.

Not that she was complaining. Kids were her best customers. They religiously bought their favorite comics every week. So she kept her store kid-friendly with board games set up on tables and old comics on racks for reading. Her only stipulation in terms of decorum was no gum. She hated scraping it off the carpet and furniture.

TWO

THE MORNING OF LUMBERJACK DAYS DAWNED
sunny and bright.

Which meant there was no way a deluge or thunder-
storm was going to cancel the parade.

Stella gazed out the window with a squinty frown and cursed
the weatherman for actually being right in his predictions of
sunny skies, light breezes, and temperatures in the eighties.

Lying in bed in her airy second-floor bedroom that overlooked the river, the birds singing outside her window apparently
immune to her grumpy mood, she understood biting the bullet
was her only recourse. With a small sigh, she threw back the light
quilt and rolled out of bed.

By the time Megan called to be sure she was on schedule,
Stella was dressed, caffeinated, and resigned to her fate.

"Do you have the leaflets?"

She was tempted to say no. "They're on the front porch," she said instead, because she knew she wasn't going to break Megan of her habit of saying the obvious after twentysome years.

"What are you wearing?"

"Does it matter?"

"Of course it matters. We have to look conservative or senatorial or professional at least. I'm wearing my blue linen pantsuit."

"Oops. I guess I'd better change my bikini top."

"Don't tease, okay? I'm too nervous."

"I'm suitably attired. Everything's good. Everything's on track. Rest easy."

"I'll try. But when my polling numbers went up again last week and I began to realize I might actually have a chance of winning this election, my anxiety levels escalated."

"Everything will go smoothly, kiddo. You're on a roll. Relax."

"Thanks. I mean it, Stella. You're my rock."

Being a rock probably meant not complaining, Stella thought. "When you win this election, I will expect some suitable pork thrown in my direction. The potholes fixed on my street or something. Don't forget. Are you bringing the kids?"

"Would they miss a chance to be in a parade?"

"Duh. Stupid question. I'll bring a bag of Fizzies along."

"And a couple of those everything-but-the-kitchen-sink cookies from your store."

THE PLEASANT TEMPERATURES of morning had risen to a humid eighty-four by the time the parade began, and the crowds massed along the street were drenched in sweat despite their straw hats and sun umbrellas and various alcoholic and nonalcoholic beverages supplied by the bars and restaurants lining the historic Main Street.

Lumberjack Days always drew an enormous crowd. Stillwater's location on the river was an ideal weekend getaway, and the weather had really cooperated this year. The marching bands and floats with queens from every nearby small town, the local Boy Scouts and Girl Scouts, the troops of sundry VFW and Legions—some mounted, some marching—the motorcycle police and freshly washed fire trucks, and the clowns and mimes of every description began their progression at the north end of town, slowly moved down the eight blocks of Main Street that were literally packed to overflowing with watchers, before dispersing in a milling throng at the riverfront park. Megan and Stella ran out of leaflets a block short of the end, but by and large, people had politely accepted the campaign literature. All Stella's concerns about rude remarks or disinterest had been negated by Minnesota nice. In fact, there were enough viewers who recognized Megan from her TV interviews and gave her the high sign to make the entire long, sweaty walk worth the angst and effort.

"You're going to be the next senator from the tenth district," Stella declared, sitting down under the shade of a tree and pulling out a Fizzie. "They can stop polling now. I have a vision."

Plopping down beside her, Megan smiled. "You think? Although it did look pretty good out there, didn't it?"

Stella lifted the Fizzie bottle in salute. "To a winner."

"Gimme the Fizzie," little Ruthie exclaimed.

"Please, may I have the Fizzie, sweetie," her mother corrected.

"Here, Ruthie, you deserve it." Stella handed over the bottle. "That was a long walk for a five-year-old."

The breeze off the river was cool, and the crowds were slowly moving north in the direction of the carnival and food booths set up near the high bridge.

"Can I have a grape one?" Joey looked sweaty and hopeful.

"Let me check." Stella turned over the remaining Fizzie in her insulated bag. "This is your lucky day." She handed him a grape Fizzie.

Megan lifted her eyebrows. "I don't suppose you have a pomegranate martini in your little satchel?"

"There's martinis over there." Joey pointed to a sleek yacht docked at the riverside. The quay was lined with boats of various sizes, the slips bordering the park reserved a year in advance for Lumberjack Days weekend. On the particular yacht Joey indicated, the decks were awash with swimsuited people, several of whom had martini glasses in hand.

"Now that's the way to travel," Megan murmured. "First class all the way. Not an ounce of cellulite as far as the eye can see."

Stella smiled. "It's not allowed when you own a yacht. No cellulite is in the contract."

"That guy's waving at us."

Joey had excellent eyesight. A man wearing a captain's hat with his swimsuit stood at the rail on the highest deck, waving frantically.

"Small world," Stella murmured. "That's Buddy Morton, one of my customers. He never said he had a yacht. Although he did talk about his race horses, so I suppose I should have suspected."

Megan's gaze narrowed slightly. "I get the impression he'd like us to come over."

"No kidding," Joey said. "He's waving like crazy and screaming Stella's name. Can we ride on his big boat? Can we? Please, please, pleeeese?"

"We can at least go over and stand on it," Stella said, rising from the grass. "He may not want to lose his spot on the quay." The river was alive with boats, most waiting to dock.

"Ask him to take us for a ride!" Joey was hopping from foot to foot. "Could ya, huh, huh, could ya?"

"Remember your manners," Megan cautioned. "We can't just ask this man to take his boat out for us."

"Come on, let's go and take a look anyway," Stella said. "We'll get a chance to see how the rich and famous live."

THREE

 BUDDY MET THEM AT THE GANGWAY. "WHAT A nice surprise—in this mob of people, too. What did you think of the parade?" he asked, welcoming them onboard. "It was great, wasn't it?"

Stella smiled. "Absolutely—a perfect day for a parade. This is my friend, Megan Sullivan, and her children, Ruthie and Joey. Megan, kids, Buddy Morton."

"Wow! This is one humongous boat!" Joey exclaimed.

"Joey wants a ride," Ruthie piped up. "Really, really bad."

"Sorry about that." Megan rolled her eyes. "Kids."

"Megan's running for state senate," Stella offered. "We walked along with the parade and passed out campaign literature."

"The senate? Congratulations." Buddy glanced down at Joey and winked. "And maybe we can take the boat out later."

"Wow! Did you hear that, Mom! He said *maybe!*"

"I have to see what the others onboard want to do." Buddy made a small palm's-up gesture. "Some want to see the town and street dance, some the river. But come on—have a cool drink and check out the view."

As they followed Buddy down the gleaming deck, Megan gave Stella one of those raised eyebrow looks—you know, the half question, half way-to-go look.

Stella returned a cautionary frown, warning off any potential grilling on Buddy Morton's dating qualifications. Megan was always trying to line her up when she didn't want to be lined up or even be in the running to be lined up. Whether Buddy was married, unmarried, divorced, or in a long-standing relationship had never crossed her mind, because she didn't care. It was as simple as that.

With some men there were vibes.

With others like Buddy—none at all.

Unlike the hot stud last week who had walked into her store and taken up a prominent position—front and center—in her mind. She'd dealt with the unwanted image by consigning him to her fantasy world, letting Marky B take on a new hunky cohort in her fight for right. It was the crassest displacement of course, but highly effective. And by Friday morning, when she'd sent her latest comic to the printers, her Xzodus Software man had been relegated to six pages in *The Remarkable Adventures of Marky B,* Chapter 31.

Not that her coping mechanism would bear close scrutiny.

But then she'd understood long ago that her psychological profile wasn't anywhere near the middle of the pack. Rationalize and move on. That was her motto.

With two bartenders dispensing drinks on the top deck, Megan soon had her pomegranate martini, the kids had fruit slushies, and Stella was trying to decide between a chocolate martini and a beer that would be less apt to spill on the gently rocking boat.

"One of those," she finally said, pointing to a Belgium pilsner nestled in a tub of ice along with a dozen other kinds of beer from around the world. Buddy had financial resources, no doubt about that. Bartenders on each deck, catering staff dispensing hors d'oeuvres and picking up the mess, a buffet twenty feet long manned by servers at attention. Not to mention this yacht—definitely a seven-figure baby.

When they were supplied with drinks, Buddy gave them a guided tour, introducing them to some of the beautiful, tanned, buff, perfectly coiffed people as they moved from deck to deck. When they reached the bridge, the children were absolutely thrilled when he let them sit at the wheel in the high padded captain's chair.

"Boy, am I gonna tell Tommy about this!" Joey crowed. "Look, I'm turning the wheel! Tommy never did anything this cool—not in a million years!"

When it was her turn, Ruthie sat mesmerized by the sleek panel of lights, flipping approved switches off and on with childish glee. "Just like in a rocket to the moon," she said, beaming from ear to ear.

"I bet it goes that fast, too!" Joey exclaimed. "I just know it does!"

"If there's time, we'll take her out," Buddy offered. "I'll show you the engine room next. You'll like the twin engines, Joey. They're custom made."

A crewman entered the bridge. "One of your guests fell in, boss." He shrugged. "I think. She might have dived in."

Buddy smiled at his guests. "It's probably Kirsty, who always likes to dive after a few drinks. Make yourself at home. I'll be right back."

As Buddy walked away, Megan grinned at Stella. "Race horses and a yacht?" she whispered. "This could be your future."

"Or yours. He's not my type."

"How would you know? You don't let anyone close enough."

"I've done my share of dating. It's just not a good time for me now. I'm really busy."

"Is this great or what?" Joey cried, his nose pressed against the window. "We're practically higher than the trees. Hey, I can see tons of sandwiches on the table below!"

"And there's chocolate cake, too," Ruthie noted with a touch of longing in her voice. "Really *good* chocolate cake." She turned in the captain's chair. "And tiny little hot dogs. Can I have some more of those, too, Mom? *Please?*"

"Go on—get the kids some," Stella offered. "I'll enjoy the view out there on the back of the boat."

"The stern," Joey corrected with six-year-old expertise, thanks to his age-appropriate *Titanic* ship-in-a-bottle kit he got for his birthday.

"Right. The stern of the boat. There's a good breeze, and I'm still sweating."

"If you don't mind, I *am* starved," Megan murmured. "I didn't want to look like a pig and take one of everything when we walked by the buffet."

"No one's looking now. Go for it. Take your time. I'll try out one of those lounge chairs."

"Deck chairs," Joey said.

"Right again. Thanks, Joey."

The kids raced away, Megan following in their wake, and a few moments later Stella was stretched out on a cushioned chaise, her sandals kicked off, a breeze ruffling her hair, her last "everything" cookie in hand. Perfect. Peace and quiet. Life was good.

With luck, Buddy would be occupied for some time with the "woman overboard" and she could enjoy the river and the superfine day without having to brace herself against Buddy making a move. Her no-dating-the-customers rule had always been a matter of real diplomacy with him. The fact that he was one of her best customers made it even more dicey to say no without hurting his feelings.

"It was an awesome day for a parade, wasn't it?"

She didn't have to turn around to know the possible rule-breaker of all time was standing behind her. And if he was wearing a swimsuit like everyone else on this boat, she was going to hyperventilate big time. Count to ten, no, there's no time, turn, don't turn, could she pretend she didn't hear him? Probably not with her face turning red. Say something. *For God's sake, say something before you look like a complete idiot!* Turning, she tried not to look at you-know-what that was at eye level as he stood there in surfer swim trunks and *nothing else!* "It's perfect—I mean . . . the day—and parade—was perfect—couldn't be better." Now if she could just melt into the cushion and disappear so she didn't have to see that knowing smile, or maybe it was a seductive smile, or maybe everything about him was seductive, considering the whole package was pretty much on *full frontal display*—tropical print swim trunks notwithstanding.

"That looks good." He dipped his head and flashed his smile again as he sat down on the end of an adjacent chaise.

What looked good? What did he mean? How should she respond? A smile, a nod, something bland and all purpose?

"I saw those cookies in your store."

She felt the heat of that perfect white smile again and also felt a tiny ripple in a place she hadn't felt a ripple for a very long time. Or maybe it was the way he'd said "in your store," in a deep, silken tone that suggested something possibly *in* somewhere else. Or more likely she was hallucinating with that lean, taut body close enough to touch. "It's a family recipe," she said, her voice breathy when there wasn't a reason in the world why it should be breathy, when her grandma's "everything" cookies had never generated anything but a sigh of contentment in the past.

"Care to share?"

"Share?" Could he speak more definitively so she didn't have to feel as though she was trying to interpret a foreign language?

"The cookie," he said. The flush on her cheeks was a real turn on. "It looks good."

"Oh." Tamping down various possibilities racing through her brain—many having a sexual connotation—she thrust the cookie at him.

He reached for it.

She let go—a fraction of a second too early.

And the cookie hit the deck and shattered.

"Jeez, sorry." She blew out a breath.

"Not a problem." Leaning over, he began to pick up the pieces. "The deck's clean enough to eat off anyway." Looking up from under his unbelievably long, dark lashes, he winked. "Buddy's into antiseptic. Not that that's all bad, I suppose."

"You say it like you aren't."

"Probably not." He set the cookie pieces on the chaise. "With the exception of my car maybe."

"Your truck."

"Yeah—truck. And someone comes in and cleans my place a couple times a month. That's about it. I'm pretty middle-of-the-road. No fetishes."

She was really tempted to reply—the word *fetishes* conjuring up a wild array of pleasurable little vignettes when looking at a man like him. But then he popped a piece of cookie into his mouth, and those TV ads with all the crawly germs displaced more pleasant thoughts. "Are you sure that's wise—eating that cookie? There's a buffet to die for downstairs."

"The cookie's good. Really, the deck's clean."

"If you say so." But she wasn't going to eat any of that cookie. "How do you know Buddy?" she asked, steering the conversation onto safer ground than fetish speculation.

"We met golfing in Florida. When I found out he was a comic collector—you know how that goes. Instant rapport. By the way, *Marky B* is a real winner. I read those new issues I bought." He'd also checked out her story about not dating customers with Buddy. It was for real. But then rules were made to be broken.

"Thanks."

"You're self-published?"

"It's easy with the Internet. An international audience at your fingertips. What do you do?" If he was playing golf where Buddy Morton was playing, he must have a good job.

"Not much."

"You must do something."

"I have a small farm on the other side of the river. It keeps me busy."

Was he a drug dealer? A lottery winner? "What do you farm?" Maybe he raised Kobe beef or something really high priced.

"Mostly pumpkins. I give them away to the school kids at Halloween."

She wasn't getting much here, and short of asking to see his checkbook, she might as well drop the subject. If he didn't want to say, he didn't want to say. Then again, maybe he had a wife and kids on that farm in Wisconsin. Not that it mattered to her. She had no intention of dating him. "Are you married?" she heard herself ask, as though her self-restraint had taken the tourist train to Osceola.

"What if I said I was?" he replied with a grin.

"Then I'd figure you probably were pretty darned busy."

"I'm *not* though, and I don't have a wife—never have. How's that for full disclosure?"

"It really doesn't matter." More aptly, it shouldn't. But she wouldn't have had to write him into Marky B's adventures if she'd been able to simply dismiss him from her mind.

"Speaking of full disclosure," he murmured.

Here it came—the sordid truth. A man who looked like he did and knew people like Buddy—the Minnesota equivalent of jet-setters—probably had a scandal or two in his closet. Not that she cared; he was outside her dating pool anyway, for any number of reasons.

"We haven't actually been introduced. I'm Danny Rees."

"Stella Scott." Was it possible this man who appeared to do nothing was scandal free?

"Buddy told me."

"He didn't tell me about you."

"There's not much to tell. I've lived across the river a couple years." He smiled. "And had I known about your shop, or more aptly, its owner, I would have been in earlier."

"It's new—eleven months in business." She smiled. "I love it—not a single complaint."

"I've one." His smile was sweet and boyish, without a hint of jet-set glitterati. "I'd like you to reconsider your no-dating-the-customers policy. Although, I could stop buying comics from you if it would help—or maybe we could just not call it a date. We could call it something else."

The phrase "something else," hovered in the balmy summer air.

His meaning plain.

And damnably tempting.

She should refuse him—unequivocally. She should stick to her principles. And if he wasn't mostly nude and really buff like he worked out ten hours a day . . . not to mention one of the sexiest men she'd ever seen—she might have answered more quickly.

But she didn't.

He noticed. "Look," he said, very, very softly. "We could just give it a try. And if you don't like it—" He shrugged faintly, his pecs and biceps rippling so she was hard-pressed not to lean over and run her fingers over his sleek body. "You could say no—anytime . . . before—after—I'll understand. You won't lose a customer. I'm not that unselfish. Not when you have the best comic book collection in the Midwest." He touched her ankle with a brushing fingertip. "I'd really like to—"

"I'm back and bearing gifts—oops, sorry—I didn't know you were busy." Megan's voice faded away, and she came to an abrupt stop in the doorway. "I brought you some food. Why don't I just put this plate down, and I'll see you later."

"No, stay." Stella drew in a deep breath, feeling as though

she'd been jerked back from the brink of disaster. "Come, meet a customer of mine. Megan, this is—" She met his dark gaze and lost her train of thought.

"Danny Rees," he smoothly supplied. Not sure it was safe to stand, considering the libidinous direction of their interrupted conversation, Danny held out his hand and smiled. "A pleasure to meet you, Megan. Please, join us."

"If you don't mind," Megan murmured, giving Stella a sideways glance. "I left the kids watching cartoons in the lounge."

"We don't mind. Megan's running for the state senate," Stella explained, offering Danny a bland smile, her impetuous desires under control, thanks to Megan's opportune arrival. "We handed out campaign literature along the parade route."

"That's why we're dressed like this," Megan said, with a sweeping gesture at her pantsuit. "By the way, the woman overboard has been rescued. Crisis averted."

Danny's brows lifted marginally. "Kirsty likes spectacle."

Speaking of spectacle, Megan thought, trying not to stare at the paragon of male mojo seated opposite her. If this was the guy who'd come into Stella's store—and the description she'd heard over the phone was pretty much on target—she was going to sit Stella down and straighten her out just as soon as they left this boat. One did not turn down a body—er—man like that. There wasn't a reason in the world not to sleep with a to-die-for stud like him. Rules be damned.

"So tell me," Megan said, politely, "what comics do you collect?" She knew what comic people liked to talk about. The same things motor heads or china collectors did. Their obsession.

As far as setting Stella straight.

That would require privacy.

Megan nodded her head thoughtfully as Danny replied, giving the impression she was actually listening.

Because Stella was, she didn't have to.

She could plan her strategy instead.

Really, they were perfect together.

He was tall, dark, and handsome. Stella was tall, blonde, and beautiful.

They both adored comic books—not a match that came along every day of the week—or month or year, for that matter.

Why would Stella even *consider* saying no to a man like that defied all logic.

Luckily, she was here to dispense some straight-talking advice.

FOUR

BUDDY REAPPEARED A SHORT TIME LATER, SAT down, and participated in the comic book discussion with the enthusiasm of an aficionado. Ruthie and Joey came up searching for their mom and more slushies; a dripping-wet woman sauntered onto the scene looking dazzling—drenched hair and all—her teeny, tiny bikini and voluptuous body offsetting any possible bad hair day. Zeroing in on Danny, Miss Pink Bikini dropped down behind him on his chaise, draped her arms around his neck, and pressed her double-D boobs into his back. "Where have you been hiding, darling?" she purred.

Definitely an unsubtle this-man-is-mine signal, Stella thought. She almost felt like saying, "Relax, we're not competition." Instead, she said in a voice perhaps not entirely devoid of pettiness, "We probably should be getting along. The kids have been waiting to see the carnival."

Kirsty smiled smugly—as in victory.

"But I don't *want* to go to the carnival," Joey whined. "Buddy *promised* to take out the boat, didn't you?" He swiveled toward Buddy, looking hopeful.

"And I always get sick on the rides," Ruthie unhelpfully added. "Then I barf up all the cotton candy and pop and—"

"That's enough, sweetie," Megan interjected, taking her cue from Stella and coming to her feet. "Come, children. We've imposed long enough."

Disregarding the children's pouty expressions, Stella slid on her sandals and smiled at Buddy. "It was a pleasure to see your boat. Thanks for everything."

"Don't tell me you're going to disappoint Joey." Buddy nodded at the youngster. "Not when my twin engines can top 45 knots."

"See, Mom, see. I told you." Joey tugged on Megan's arm. "He *said* he'd take us out."

"I don't know," Megan equivocated, glancing at Stella.

She could be an ogre to a six-year-old boy, Stella thought, or she could suck it up and watch Kirsty rub against Danny Rees or maybe do worse during the time it took to show Joey top speed on Buddy's yacht. Was she an adult or what? With an inward sigh, she capitulated. "If the kids would rather stay on the boat, I'm fine with that."

"Awesome!" Joey grinned from ear to ear. "Tommy's gonna be *so-o-o* jealous!"

"Can I have another piece of cake, then?" Ruthie asked.

"Sure you can," Buddy replied, not above having an agenda of his own. "Come on kids. Anyone else wants to steer this baby, follow me," he added, rising from his chair. "And Kirsty, no diving when we're out in the river," he warned. "The traffic's too heavy. I wouldn't want you cut in half by a power boat."

"Yes, sir, captain," Kirsty replied, sultry and low. "I'll stay right here and keep Rees company." Tightening her grip on Danny's shoulders, she leaned forward and nibbled his earlobe.

Stella's stomach lurched.

A totally unwanted lurch.

Abruptly turning away, Stella followed Buddy and the children below. Not that she should take issue with whatever little Kirsty did with Danny Rees, who she couldn't possible entertain as a date anyway. Not that she should be feeling any resentment whatsoever over what he did or didn't do with the girl in the teeny, tiny bikini.

Danny Rees was outside her dating pool.

If she had a dating pool—which she did not.

So there. Case closed. Have another drink and think of more realistic possibilities than dating Danny Rees. Like world peace or saving the whales.

As it turned out, neither altruistic endeavor stood much of a chance against her strange craving for Danny Rees—who unfortunately was rarely out of sight during their entire high-speed jaunt down the river.

Stella did take small comfort though—when she shouldn't have been concerned in the least—that he seemed less interested in Kirsty than she was in him. She took even more comfort after the yacht docked once again and she saw him leave the boat alone and get into his pick-up truck. Call her bitchy, but women like Kirsty pissed her off. They were too *undressed* and too glossily beautiful. And too damned sex-kitten retro for the real world.

So, she was sour-grapes bitchy. So sue her.

* * *

"IT WAS A fun day, wasn't it?" Megan said a short time later after they'd said their thank yous and good-byes to Buddy and were strolling through the riverside park toward Main Street.

"You betcha it was! The *best* ever!" Joey proclaimed, eyes shining. "I didn't know a boat could go so *fast!*"

Megan smiled, her son's glowing face warming her maternal heart.

"Buddy said we can come again anytime," Ruthie piped up. "He really likes us."

"He does seem very nice, doesn't he?"

Stella turned to glance at her friend, not sure Megan's tone might not suggest something more than mere politeness.

"Don't look at me like that," Megan said under her breath. "Buddy *is* nice, and it's not as though I go on a yacht every day."

Stella's brows rose, and she half smiled. "Did he ask you out?"

"Not exactly." Megan shrugged. "He said he was going to the street dance tonight, and if I was there, he'd like to dance with me."

Stella grinned. "So are you going?"

"I might."

Stella's grin broadened. "Need a baby-sitter?" Buddy's taste in comics aside, he was about as normal as a comic book collector could be. And what the hell, she wouldn't turn down kinky sex with the right guy—Danny Rees coming to mind big time when she should know better.

"I already have a baby-sitter. The kids are going to my mom's."

Stella winked. "Then all you need is your dancing shoes."

"It's definitely a thought. Care to join me?"

"Probably not. I was up late last night," Stella lied. Danny might be with Buddy, and she didn't care to take that chance after having to beat down her lustful desires all afternoon. When he was in close proximity, she apparently lost whatever reason she liked to think she had. So she'd play it safe and stay away. Danny Rees was her chocolate cake, and she was on a diet. She couldn't have him.

"If you change your mind, give me a call. I won't leave until dark."

"Will do. I think we garnered a few more votes for you today," Stella added, preferring a less sexually charged train of thought. "And next week I'll design that new campaign sign so the date of your debate in the fall will be in clear view on everyone's lawn."

"What if I actually—as in the impossible dream—get elected?" Megan blew out a breath. "Just think. That would mean the Deloitte family loses their district."

"It's about time," Stella pronounced. "What's it been? Eighty years?"

"Ninety-two, but who's counting?"

"Jeez Louise. Maybe we should put *that* on the signs and say TIME FOR A CHANGE in eye-popping caps."

"Maybe we *should*."

And on the way up the hill to Stella's place where Megan had left her car, they discussed the possibilities of pointing out the Deloitte family's stranglehold on local politics. Indifferent to adult conversation, Joey and Ruthie entertained themselves by hitting each other with the foam rubber Twins baseball bats Buddy had given them. A good time was had by all.

As they parted on the sidewalk in front of Stella's house, Megan said, "If you change your mind, I'll be downtown about nine-thirty."

"Maybe. I'll see." How was that for bland evasion? "Say hi to Buddy for me if you see him."

With Megan's taillights disappearing down the street, Stella climbed the stairs to her house. Entering her store, she waved at Amy who'd come in to take her place for the day. "Thanks for holding down the fort. I expect it was quiet with everyone down at the parade."

"A ton of kids came in after the parade, but everyone went home for supper now. I sold five copies of *Marky B* to some parent who'd just heard about your comic. I think you might have a new fan."

"Hey, an extra fifteen bucks a week. Way to go. Take some of those cookies home if you like. I'll close up."

As the door shut behind Amy a short time later, Stella kicked off her sandals, picked up her sketches from the newest issue of *Marky B,* and, sinking into one of her overstuffed chairs, perused the handsome new addition to Marky B's coterie of sidekicks—namely one modern-day warrior with dark eyes and darker hair like someone she knew and a half-naked body to die for.

Damn.

It was a shame real life wasn't so easily manipulated.

If it was, she could draw one Danny Rees into her life and into her bed for a day or two and then draw him out.

The beauty of comic books was their complete disregard for reality, not to mention the satisfying conceit of viewing the world through the eyes of heroes and heroines who were larger than life—cooler, smarter, stronger, able to leap tall buildings in a single bound—and who always won in the game of life.

Ah—sweet fantasy. She flipped over a clean page in her sketch pad and reached over to the box of pencils she kept at the ready for her young customers who came to the store to learn how to draw.

Two quick strokes and a pair of shoulders took form; another sweep of her hand and one side of a lean torso appeared in a graceful, supple curve. A small smile lifted the corners of her mouth as her hand moved feverishly over the page, adding arms, hands, legs, feet, face, hair. Should she put clothes on? She grinned.

Nah.

She may not be able to have her chocolate cake in person, but right now, she could have him any way she wanted.

FIVE

SHE WAS IN THE KITCHEN FINISHING A LATE
supper when she heard a knock on her front door.

Because her friends knew enough to come around to
the back of the house, she hesitated—not in the mood to deal
with a customer who chose to disregard the prominently dis-
played store hours. She didn't want to see anyone anyway, looking like this. Her hair was pulled back into a pony tail, and she'd
changed into sweats and a T-shirt to watch the fireworks from
her porch.

"Hey Stella! Your lights are on!"

That voice instantly turned on a couple other things as well,
and she wondered if she could do a complete makeover in thirty
seconds or, better yet, have a fairy godmother transform her into
an instant Cinderella. Even her bare feet were dirty like Cinderella's; she'd picked raspberries for supper out in the backyard.

But this was one of those occasions when, liabilities aside, intellect lost out big time to pure, irrepressible, pedal-to-the-metal emotion. "I'll be right down!" she shouted, grabbing the kitchen towel to wipe her feet. Seconds later, she pulled her scrunchy free, ran her fingers through her hair, straightened her less-than-pristine T-shirt sprinkled with raspberry stains, and sprinted down the stairs to the store.

Taking a deep breath at the wide-shouldered silhouette visible through the glass-paned upper half of her door, she slowly exhaled, reminded herself that men like Danny Rees were only familiar with assent, and, throwing caution to the wind, opened the door anyway.

"I know you have your rules, but after a couple drinks at Caesar's, I thought, what the hell." He lifted a sweating Cristal champagne bottle—a very expensive bottle—the kind celebrities drank, according to the *National Enquirer* and *People* magazine. "Care to watch the fireworks with me?"

This probably wasn't the time to say she had fireworks of her own going off in various and sundry portions of her body. "I don't know—I shouldn't."

"Why not? It's just fireworks."

He didn't have to sound so adult and reasonable. He didn't have to look so luscious. She tried to shut down her dancing nerve endings and assume an equally blasé facade. "I guess—how can it hurt."

"I guarantee you it won't hurt."

"Cute. Are you telling me you're good?"

He grinned. "Are you asking?"

"Hell no. I'm staying on message. I don't date customers."

"Suit yourself. Do you want to watch from here or from somewhere else?"

The way he said it, or perhaps the way she interpreted the ambiguity in his question in terms of her own personal preferences for *something* else, *somewhere* else caused her to hesitate.

His grin broadened as though he could read her mind. "I meant should we watch the fireworks from your porch or down by the river."

"Because I'm not exactly dressed for company"—she shrugged—"let's do it here."

An abrupt silence fell.

He looked at her.

She looked at him.

Flushing with embarrassment, she stammered, "Pull up . . . the chairs—I'll find . . . some glasses." Spinning around before she said something she'd really regret like, "Let's forget about the fireworks and get into bed," she literally ran for the stairs.

"I have an opener," he called out.

As if he needed one, she thought, her mind so carnally focused every word he uttered shrieked sexual innuendo.

He wasn't thinking innuendo so much as consummation. Drawing forward a wicker chair for a better view of the river, he pulled up a small table and set down the bottle. They'd have some champagne, watch the fireworks, and go from there.

And he knew exactly where he wanted to go.

WHEN STELLA RETURNED with two flutes, she immediately sat down to keep from hurling herself into his arms and watched him deftly open the bottle. His motions were swift and sure, foil and cage taken off, the cork pulled out with a couple turns, and that small, almost nonexistent pop. A true professional. Her mind sprinted ahead to the obvious comparison of professional skills in other areas; she was apparently without censuring mechanisms in her frontal lobes tonight. In an attempt to derail the ready-for-sex-right-now locomotion racing through her senses, she silently screamed, *Stop!* According to a self-help book she'd skimmed once, that sort of internal vigilance was supposed to short-circuit one's thought process—and allow more reasonable thoughts to surface.

It did.

For a full two seconds.

And then the throbbing between her legs overwhelmed reason in a tidal wave of ungovernable impulse that took no notice whatsoever of self-help book advice. Shifting in her chair, she tried to dismiss the steady, hard rhythm centered in the core of her body. It was hot out tonight. That was it. No, *he* was hot, a little voice inside her head pointed out. And *available,* the treacherous voice went on as though she needed further encouragement when she was practically in attack mode already.

"Hey," he whispered. "Earth to Stella."

She looked up to find him smiling and holding out a champagne flute.

"I was thinking about Megan—her campaign . . . and stuff," she lied, wondering how long he'd been standing there waiting for her to return to reality. "I have to design a new poster for her debate in the fall. You know how stuff like that rolls around your head."

"I can imagine," he said, leaning against the railing.

Was that sarcasm or empathy? Did she really care when he was blocking out the moon with those really wide shoulders and lean, taut body, his dark, ruffled hair limned by silvery light? "Sit down," she said, trying to sound like a mature adult. *Stay a while,* she thought. *A couple weeks if you want,* the highly excitable, super susceptible adult entertainment zone of her body proposed.

He shook his head. "That wicker won't hold me. I'll sit here." He nodded at her railing.

"I could get another chair or something." Jeez, how was that for inane?

"Nah . . . this'll do for now."

Versus what? No, no, don't even go there. "The fireworks should start soon—they usually start by ten—or at least they always have in the past although sometimes it can be . . . later . . ." Her voice trailed off, and she glanced at her watch as if she could see it in the dim light. "Unless it rains."

What the hell was she thinking? There wasn't a cloud in the sky. "I mean sometimes it does . . . rain—although—"

"Probably not tonight." He smiled. "I saw the TV weather report while I was sitting at the bar at Caesar's. I think we're good on the weather. Relax."

Oh God, could she sink into the floor and disappear? What was this—her first date in junior high? "Sorry, I'm not usually so gauche," she muttered.

"You're just nervous because you're not sure you want sex."

"I *beg* your pardon?"

"You heard what I said."

The chauvinist message on the back of his T-shirt burned through her brain. "Maybe you should go."

"Maybe you don't really mean that."

"Maybe I do."

He smiled. "You don't *have* to have sex."

"Damn right I don't."

"We can just sit here and watch the fireworks." He grinned. "If it doesn't rain."

"Arrogant bastard."

"Uh-uh. I'm just honest with myself."

"And I'm not?"

"Vegas odds? I'd say forty to one not on this one."

"So women just fall into your arms?"

"Give me a break. This isn't war. I'd just like to get to know you."

"Meaning?"

"Meaning anything you want."

"Liar."

He smiled. "Well, I have my preferences, but I'll live either way."

"With or without sex, you mean."

He nodded. "With or without."

"That's awfully big of you."

"It's up to you, that's all I'm saying. You decide. I'll be as accommodating as hell."

When he offered carte blanche like that, it went a real long way in obliterating objections large or small. It didn't help either that the phrase, *Why don't you come upstairs with me?* had been looping through her brain since she'd answered the door. Nor that he was stretched out on her railing, looking sexy as hell, his back against one of the elaborately carved posts holding up the porch roof, his long legs crossed at the ankles, his balance superb considering he was very large and her railing was not excessively wide. And bottom line, if she was honest with herself, she had to admit he was about the best thing she'd seen since Hostess Sno-balls went pink.

"Just tell me what you want," he said, the welcome mat out in the silken softness of his voice.

"I'm thinking." She took a deep breath. "Give me a minute." She must have gone too long without sex. That was why she was damned near quivering. Or maybe he'd simply appeared at some opportune time when her hormonal stars and sexual receptors were all perfectly attuned and any red-blooded male would have inspired the same acute reaction.

Yeah, right.

If that was the case, she would have looked with interest at any number of men on the yacht this afternoon.

She hadn't.

Not to mention she was damned near salivating. And struggling to concentrate on something—*anything* other than sex.

Not an easy task with Danny Rees in all his glory close enough to touch.

Where was her commitment to the separation of business and pleasure when she desperately needed it?

"We could go to the street dance afterward if you want."

"After what?" How could he be so calm when she was being literally swamped by tidal waves of horniness?

"After whatever you want." He smiled a sweet, sexy smile that made her want to throw her arms around him and kiss him with total disregard for the imminent possibility of falling into the hydrangea bushes below. And he was clearly talking about sex—not fireworks . . . hot sex, she was thinking—that lasted all night—maybe all week, her salacious mind nimbly ran on. Which made the word *principle* in general and her own principles in particular pretty much drop off the face of the earth.

"I'm still trying to decide."

"Take your time."

She didn't even know what to say when they asked "Paper or plastic?" at the supermarket. He maybe didn't realize that.

Or maybe he did. "Wanna flip a coin?" he said with a grin.

"Wanna land in those hydrangea bushes down there?" she said with a wave of her hand.

He laughed. "Just a suggestion."

"If you don't want to wait, feel free to leave anytime."

"No way I'm leaving," he said, grinning at her. "I love fireworks."

She exhaled softly. "I'm sorry for being so indecisive, but so many of my customers are men and—hell, I don't know . . . it's complicated."

"I could make it easy."

She smiled. "Look it's a no-brainer. I'm just—I don't know—"

Picking up on her nuance, or maybe just tired of waiting for her to decide, he slid off the railing, set down his glass, and held out his hand.

Crunch time. This was where she could say no. Or she could ask for more champagne or talk about comics, or golf, or baseball and he'd answer because he wasn't the pushy type. No me-Tarzan, you-Jane stuff with Danny Rees. If she said no, he'd back off because he knew some other woman would accommodate him. A man with his looks didn't go long without sex.

So did she want sex or not?

Did she want sex with Danny Rees?

Time elapsed in final self-counsel and deliberation—ten seconds.

He hadn't moved. As if he understood. Or maybe he just understood women always said yes.

She leaned forward, placed her flute on the small table, came to her feet, and placed her hand in his. "I've decided to bend the rules tonight."

His hand closed over hers, and he grinned. "I'm grateful."

"It's purely selfish."

"Sex usually is."

She lifted her brows. "Not too selfish, I hope."

He laughed. "Just tell me what you want."

"Such confidence."

"I'm amenable—that's all."

"So I can give orders?"

His gaze narrowed infinitesimally. "It depends."

"On?"

He smiled. "Your tone of voice."

"So as long as I don't offend you, you mean."

"Something like that."

"Like that shirt you wore the other day—the one that said FREE MUSTACHE RIDES?"

"Nah. I only wore it 'cuz nothing else was clean. Did that piss you off?"

"I wrote you out of my life on the spot."

"I'm glad you changed your mind, and if it helps, I didn't buy the shirt. Some joker I know gave it to me."

"I'll bet he doesn't get laid much."

"I should probably burn it," he said with a grin.

"I'd recommend it."

"Yes ma'am."

"Cute." And he really was, in an oddly boyish way for a man who didn't have a boyish bone in his body.

"If you noticed, I'm dressed inoffensively tonight." He swept a hand downward, indicating his khaki shorts and black T-shirt. "Am I forgiven?"

"Oh, yeah—definitely."

He heard the small impatience in her voice, the horny wistfulness, too, and pulling her close, he brushed her mouth with his. "How much do you want to see the fireworks?"

"We could watch them from my bedroom." There. She'd been wanting to say that for a very long time.

Her breath was warm on his mouth, the length of her body pressed into his, her breasts softly cushioned against his chest. "Awesome."

His erection was instant and gloriously large, and if ever she might have had misgivings, they were all summarily dismissed. She wanted to feel that—it . . . his awesomeness inside her— because size really *did* matter unless you were five feet tall and ninety pounds. And now that she'd come in contact with his impressive erection, she suspected he was adored for more than his handsome good looks. "Follow me," she said—on track, in full pursuit—feeling tingly and wet and more ready for sex than she'd felt for a very long time. She really should thank her lucky stars that Danny Rees was a comic book collector.

Some people believed in destiny.

She believed in gypsy fate.

It was a family thing.

And tonight she was definitely grooving with Fate.

"I'm really glad you had a comic book store, or I might never have met you," he said as they walked from the porch into her store.

See. There. Gypsy fate smack dab in your face. "I know," she calmly said as though she wasn't remembering all those nights her grandma shuffled the cards and played solitaire to see what tomorrow would bring. As though reading tea leaves was an everyday occurrence in Stillwater. "I'm glad, too."

SIX

THEY HELD HANDS ALL THE WAY UP THE STAIRS, and their handclasp seemed natural—not awkward or clumsy. Like they knew each other forever instead of only a week . . . or only a few hours, if anyone was actually counting.

Although she certainly wasn't.

The hallway ran north and south from the top of the stairs. It was carpeted in blue-and-white rag rugs because her favorite house was the Swedish painter Carl Larson's house, even though she'd only seen it in books and he'd died about a hundred years ago.

And as if she wasn't already feeling this incredible compatibility, Danny said, "Nice rugs. Have you ever been to Sweden?"

She practically came right there, because as everyone knew, sex was sex for men, but for women sex was about some otherworldly, perhaps unexplainable *connection!*

She stopped in her tracks. Inhaled. Told herself not to blow it by coming precipitously in the hallway and then said in a breathless voice, "How did you know?"

"I've been there," he prosaically replied, like men did without a thought for mystical ramifications or female sexuality. "Your rugs remind me of Sweden."

This wasn't the time—on such short acquaintance—to explain her theory apropos male and female sexual compatibility. Or expose her slightly bizarre family, who had this tendency to give gypsy fate a great deal of relevance when no one in their right mind did. "I see," she said, tamping down all the outré thoughts in the forefront of her mind, trying to sound normal. "They're not actually from Sweden," she added, as though either of them cared.

"I like them anyway," he said, as capable of making banal conversation as she. Although, less susceptible to spiritual connections, he was damned hard-pressed not to pick her up, carry her to her bed, and have sex with her in less than three seconds.

Not a normal sensation for him—that degree of impatience and unbridled lust.

He tried to disengage from his ramming speed mentality.

Unfortunately, he'd been thinking of little else all day, and sublimation wasn't working.

How bad would it look, Stella wondered, *if I said, "I can't wait," the moment we entered the bedroom?* "I can't wait," she heard herself say as they walked into the room—her libido apparently immune to discretion. "Really, I can't wait a minute." Okay. That time it was her.

"Sweet." His voice was gruff, the word rumbling up from deep within his throat as though long repressed. And sweeping her up into his arms, he carried her to her bed without so much as

a nod to civility or a by-your-leave, which suited her just fine because she didn't want him to say another word.

Not one.

She just wanted to *feel* him—*instantly!* Sooner if possible.

He seemed to understand, or maybe he never talked during
sex—a circumstance she might investigate later—as in *after* her
orgasm.

Which wasn't in question at the moment.

In fact, if he didn't hurry, she'd have it without him.

But he seemed to understand what "I can't wait," meant and
was already kicking off his shoes as he lowered her to the bed.
His shorts and boxers were discarded a second later, and when he
looked up, she was staring.

"Wow." It was a little breathy, eyes-wide-open whisper.

A flash of a grin acknowledged her utterance. "You weren't
the only one waiting," he said, huskily, stripping off her sweats
and panties, tossing them aside, and settling between her legs a
second later in a supple flow of well-honed muscle.

Resting for an infinitesimal moment, his erection nudging her
cleft, he held her gaze. He just wanted to be sure everyone knew
what they were doing.

"Now," she breathed, "or I'm going to go on without—"
Her high-pitched cry exploded into the night air as he plunged
into her hot, dewy sleekness, accommodating her and, more
selfishly, himself.

Buried to the hilt in the sweetest of cunts, his fantasy of the
day now blissful reality, he flexed his legs and forced himself in to
the very stopped-in-one's-tracks end.

Shutting his eyes against the high-pressure jolt walloping his
pleasure centers, he choked back a gasp.

Sinking her fingernails into his shoulders, she suddenly went still beneath him and wondered why she'd ever thought about refusing him when they fit like the quintessential ying and yang of carnal pleasure.

He moved.

Shattering the perfection. "No, don't," she wailed.

"Look . . . look," he whispered, gripping her hips, pulling her closer still. "How's that?"

But she wasn't capable of answering. Her brain was exploding.

He smiled and hit his marks after that without any complaints.

They moved together in an absolute, zen-perfect rhythm, her little panting cries warming his throat on each downstroke.

Him whispering, "Here, here—take it all," as though he knew, as though he knew *exactly*.

It felt as though they'd done this a thousand times before.

Which made her seriously consider the paranormal, because in the end, it took her less than two minutes to come like it was old home week.

Five seconds later he came, although he wasn't entertaining any possibilities of otherworldly phenomenon when he'd been wanting to come in her since he'd first met her. Firmly planted in reality—a very lush, soft reality—he was damned glad he'd taken a chance and driven over tonight. Dropping a kiss on her forehead, he blew out a breath and smiled. "Sorry about that warp-speed performance. You've been on my mind. I'll take it slow next time."

She smiled. "I couldn't wait, either. You must have been on my mind, too." It wouldn't pay to add to his more-than-adequate ego by telling him the truth: that she'd been thinking of him more or less twenty-four, seven.

"So," he murmured, moving inside her. "Any requests for the second act?"

Ohmygod. He was huge again—or still huge—or whatever he was, she could feel the hard length of him on every shimmering, wet, randy, intemperate surface of her vagina. "When it feels this good, I'm not fussy," she whispered, raising her hips to draw him in more deeply. "More of the same will do just fine . . ."

"But not so fast . . . okay?" he breathed, sliding his hands under her bottom and lifting her up as he slowly drove forward.

Her breath caught in her throat.

Pleasure streaked up and out, coiled deep inside her and made her conscious of the very huge thank you she owed Buddy. If he hadn't recommended her store, she might not be lying here right now, impaled by the most sensational cock and so near orgasm again, she could already feel it racing downward.

"Hey," he whispered as she began to whimper. "Not so fast."

"Too late," she panted, and a second later her scream exploded, her body exploded, every nerve ending in her body shouted hallelujah and whatever fireworks were taking place outside were incidental to those detonating in her.

He met her in climax as if he were on the same hair-trigger orgasmic schedule, and barely breathing hard afterward, he gazed down at her rosy cheeks and closed eyes and smiled. She was hotter than hot, and it was still early. He had a real good feeling about the rest of the night.

Her eyes opened, and she smiled back. "I'm making up for lost time."

"Lucky me."

She grinned. "As long as you're suitably grateful."

"Definitely. I'm composing a sonnet in my head."

"I was thinking more along the lines of a series of additional orgasms."

"So you're more practical than romantic." He raised himself up on one arm, pulled his T-shirt over his head, switched arms, tossed his shirt aside, and settled back on his elbows.

"Practicality can be"—she swiveled her hips ever so slightly, all those taut, flexing muscles really turning her on—"much more *satisfying*."

He grinned. "I'm with you there," he murmured, driving in deeper. "And here." His lower body swung back, then forward. "And *here*," he softly growled, moving that infinitesimal distance forward.

She gasped, raw bliss flooding her senses, every brain cell and nerve ending focused on the shimmering path to ecstasy.

Wanting more, she moved her hips.

And he accommodated her, adept at reading female arousal, more adept at making women come. He took his time—or made the attempt, he thought with amusement, and as she began to race toward another orgasm, he withdrew marginally and said, "This time we're doing it my way."

"No!" She was already peaking.

"Yes," he whispered.

Which only aroused her more—male authority a distinct turn-on in the throes of passion—that dominant-submissive association like X-rated flashing neon. A score of carnal images instantly flooded her mind—triggering another climax.

A mind-blowing one.

"I don't know, Stella baby," Danny softly drawled a few moments later. "If you don't start listening—I might have to spank you . . ."

The lazy words hovered on the fringes of her largely unfocused mind, the husky amusement in his voice drifting through
her glutted senses. She thought about opening her eyes and saying, "Thank you very, *very* much," and she would just as soon as
she could make the necessary connections from brain to vocal
cords to tongue. And when she was mentally alert again, she
might take him up on his enticing proposal—being spanked by
him was likely to trump feminist principles any day of the week.
But right now, all she wanted to do was wallow—in the better-
than-Krispy Kremes, Shangri-la of pleasure with this sweet, sweet
man who seemed to know exactly where she most liked to feel
him—like ohmygod . . . *there!*

She came. Again. Just like that.

As if he knew exactly where to push her G-spot, or O-spot, or
hot spot.

Then he did it again—with some magical sense of place.

And then *again!*

She hoped he wasn't some vampire who would eventually
suck out her soul, but right now she didn't really care. Time
enough to get out her silver cross and wooden stake when she
couldn't come anymore.

Having earned his wings in the practice-makes-perfect school
of sex, Danny kept it simple, getting her off ultimately in his
self-interest.

Not that he hadn't climaxed more than enough in the process
to bring a smile to his face. But he was thinking long term with a
hot fuck like Comic Book Girl.

But there came a time when she whispered, "Stop, stop . . .
please, please . . . I can't come anymore . . ."

"You sure?" he murmured, braced on his elbows, his voice

mild as though sexual marathons were an everyday occurrence on his side of the St. Croix River.

"You must be popping Viagra." Half breathy, half pettish, she gazed up at him.

He grinned. "Maybe in twenty years."

For some ungodly reason that made no sense, she found herself resenting his last-for-hours expertise. It had to do with other women, of course. "Sorry," she muttered, recognizing the idiocy of being jealous of women she didn't know. "I should be thanking you instead of being bitchy."

"The pleasure was all mine," he said, urbanely. "And if that was being bitchy, be sure you call me up when you're in a sociable mood."

She laughed. "We did have a certain rapport."

He grinned. "Oh, yeah. That kind of rapport could run the generators in New York for a week."

"Oh, good. I'm glad you enjoyed yourself."

He laughed so hard he almost rolled off the bed.

"Hey!" She shoved at his chest.

Catching himself, he relinquished his hold on her and, still chuckling, hung in limbo half on and half off the bed. His gaze on the floor, he abruptly went quiet, an array of studly comic book heroes staring back at him from the pages scattered under the bed. Reaching down, he swung around and tossed a full-color, inked drawing on the bed. "Who the hell's this?"

Oops, she thought, her mind racing to come up with some suitable subterfuge to explain a comic book hero who bore a remarkable resemblance to the man frowning at her. "Marky B's new sidekick," she said in what she hoped was an offhand manner.

So some of her comic book sketches happened to be in a mess under the bed.

So some of them might bear a resemblance to persons living or dead.

She was an artist. The genesis of creativity was obscure.

"That guy looks like me."

She came up to a seated position, grateful she hadn't had time to take off her T-shirt. "It's just a coincidence," she said, pulling down her shirt hem over her crotch, as though sudden virtue might be a defense against his critical gaze.

"Fucking A it's a coincidence." His gaze was laser sharp. "And what's with all the other guys?"

He thought she was some nutcase. There really was a deep gulf between Mars and Venus. "You want to know their names?"

"No. Just whether they've slept here. Whether you're keeping some fucking record."

She wasn't sure she liked his tone. "I didn't know you had a problem with records." She could be snappish, too. "But then every man does, doesn't he? For your information, they're comic book characters, friends of Marky B."

"Or you."

"Does it matter?"

It took him only a second when she was looking at him like that to understand he had more to lose than gain by this conversation. So she'd slept with them. So what. It didn't affect his fun and games tonight. "Sorry. It took me by surprise, that's all."

"Maybe you have that superhero look."

He grinned. "Maybe you've been smokin' something. Nice artwork though." The sketches were in brilliant color, a couple of Marky B as well, flying through the air, her various cohorts at her side, the perspective flawless, the realism flesh-and-blood authentic. "How long does it take you to finish one of those drawings?"

"It depends." Her bland civility was as selfish as his. "Not too long. A couple hours at most."

"I'm impressed."

She glanced at his erection. "So am I. No pharmaceuticals. How do you do it?" What with the inherent Mars/Venus differences, the sooner they got off the subject of her superhero sketches, the better.

"You just need the right incentive," he drawled.

"Is that a compliment?"

"A very large one."

"Speaking of large—"

He lazily stretched. "Ready again, are we?"

"If you'd rather not. I wouldn't want to be demanding."

"Look, darling," he murmured, rolling on his side, running his finger up her thigh and sliding it into her wet slit. "You can have whatever you want."

"Mmmmm. It almost makes one greedy." He was stroking her in a really delicious way.

He looked up and grinned at her. "*More* greedy?"

"Are you complaining?"

"Hell no."

"Just checking," she cooed.

"Check this out." Tumbling her backward, he dipped his head and added his talented tongue as adjunct to his deft fingers.

The beauty of having your own personal superhero licking your clit gave new meaning to the phrase *sexual fantasy*. That he was a veritable virtuoso of oral sex only confirmed her longheld belief that if you wish hard enough, dreams really do come true.

The fact that a great deal of experience was needed to acquire his particular finesse was relegated to useless speculation.

She felt way too good.

Her climax lasted so long that time she couldn't decide if she was grateful or mildly resentful of his competence. A short debate as it turned out. She was walking-on-air grateful.

And it was only polite to return the favor.

Or so she told herself to offset the incurable lust incited by his really beautiful, perfectly formed erection. It was wondrous in every respect—width, breadth, length, and best of all . . . indefatigability.

Less prone to introspection, Danny only welcomed her interest and lay back, prepared to enjoy the experience. Although if pressed he would have had to admit, when her mouth closed over his cock, he felt a kick-ass jolt unlike anything he'd ever felt before. It was flame-hot electrifying, and if he didn't know better, he might have bought into that touchy-feely sappiness about soul-stirring affinity. But that they both had a passion for comics probably didn't matter as much as her passion for cock. And he had a real weakness for tongue action like that and a woman who liked sex as much as, if not more than, he did.

Now that was compatibility. Screw soul-stirring vibes.

The phone rang and then some damnable answering machine kicked in, the mike on. "This is Buddy! I see your truck outside!"

Stella began to lift her head.

"It can wait." Danny held her head in place.

But it turned out to be a major distraction, because Buddy kept talking and talking like drunks did.

But not a *total* distraction—this close to orgasm. Danny tightened his grip.

Stella's options were limited. Although, in her current shameless rut, being held captive did predictable things to her libido. Go figure. You have a hunky, wet-dream kind of man in your bed, and you're not thinking about hearts and flowers.

Aware of the continuing drone of Buddy's voice, but equally selfish, she swayed her hips in a small, frenzied rhythm as she sucked and licked his rock-hard penis, her thighs gripped together tightly to augment her rising pleasure. And sweetheart that he was, he noticed, slipped two fingers up her cunt, and in the best multitasker fashion, brought her to climax in a perfectly matched orgasm.

They lay panting afterward, the ridiculous sound of Buddy's unending monologue echoing in the room, his party-on message persistent.

Meeting her gaze, Danny grimaced. "Why me?"

"Us," Stella gasped.

"I don't suppose—you feel like turning that off?"

"Not . . . this—instant."

"Shit." The sound of a car door slamming came in through the open window. "That better not be them," Danny growled.

"We're takin' off for your place," Buddy's drawling cadence went on through the scratchy speakers, followed by a list of companions who would be joining him at Danny's.

"Not me." Stella recognized Megan's voice in the background.

"I'll be there!" The sex kitten resonance was audible even through the poor speakers of Stella's aged answering machine.

"See you at the farm—chop, chop. Over and out," Buddy declared in his slightly slurred intonation. The machine finally stopped, the roar of a motor punctuated the night, and the room went silent.

"So much for any plans we might have," Danny muttered.

"What happens if you don't show up?"

"God only knows. When Buddy's half lit, he's a bulldozer. He sure as hell will call again at least twice, and he might even decide to show up here and give us trouble. So the sooner I get home, the less chance there is of him making a scene in your neighborhood." Danny blew out a frustrated breath. "You're welcome to come along. If you're tired though," he added, glancing at his watch, "I understand."

She wouldn't be a member of the female gender if she let a first-class stud like Danny Rees go partying with Kirsty and her double D's. Not that she was necessarily planting her personal flag on him and taking territorial possession after a few hours in bed. It was more about thwarting that smug look in Kirsty's eyes. You know the one—*I'm drop-dead gorgeous, and my double D's have pretty much gotten me any man I've ever wanted.*

That fucking look.

So call her a shrew, but Stella wasn't in the mood to hand over one studly Danny Rees just because Kirsty thought she was top dog.

Then again, maybe it had nothing to do with peer position. Maybe it had more to do with the position that put Danny Rees' big cock in very close proximity to her happy-camper cunt.

Wasn't there a saying about sex making the world go round?

Or was it love?

Whatever.

Tonight—for her—it was definitely sex. "I'd love to come over," she replied in one of those slightly overplayed soap opera voices that the sweet female character always used. "But why don't I follow you over in my car so you're not inconvenienced."

She smiled and hoped her sweet-as-sugar thingee was flying. Because the inconveniencing was more about her than him.

She wanted to be able to leave when she wanted.

Like a Marky B–type woman.

Take what you want and then fly off. Or in her case, get in her Jetta.

Leaving after sex wasn't *exclusively* a male prerogative.

Except—shit . . . that meant leaving Kirsty behind.

She'd have to think about that.

SEVEN

STELLA LEFT AFTER DANNY, BUT HIS DIRECTIONS
were simple enough. And in less than a half hour, she was
turning into a gated gravel drive with a grassy center.

Every old farm in the vicinity had Douglas firs bordering the
drive, and Danny's place was no exception. The only problem
was that the carriages and wagons that once traveled the drives
were narrower than modern vehicles; some new owners had cut
down the trees rather than scratch the finish on their cars. Danny
hadn't, and she navigated the tunnel of towering trees very
slowly. Not that her Jetta was new; it wasn't. But it had to last her
a few more years.

Another gate was open at the entrance to the farm yard, the
house to the left, the barn and outbuildings to the right, and
from the sound of blaring music, it appeared as though the party
was in back.

She debated briefly whether she wished to pierce her eardrums or call it a night. Curiosity got the better of her—along with a reluctance to give up the possibility of another few hours of hotter-than-hot sex. So she'd put Kleenex in her ears if the sound was out of hand. What she had in mind didn't require much talk anyway.

Parking beside Danny's truck, she followed the music and a flagstone path around the side of a white clapboard farmhouse with a wraparound porch outfitted with wicker furniture. The reason, no doubt, Danny understood the limits of wicker. Window boxes decorated the first floor windows, the spicy scent of geraniums pungent in the air. Through the lighted windows she saw a cottage-feel interior with bright-colored furniture, book shelves everywhere, and—jeez—flowers in a vase on the kitchen table. The *Midwest Country Living* atmosphere made her suspicious of a possible wife or—God willing—only a decorator. This place definitely didn't look like a bachelor pad.

Nor did the screened-in pool she saw when she came around the corner.

Nor the pool house and strategically placed lighting that illuminated the water and the artfully planted garden bordering it.

Christ—maybe Martha Stewart was a relative. It looked that good.

"Hey—over here!"

Somehow Danny was able to make his voice heard over the Grateful Dead's "Casey Jones," or maybe she was reading his lips. Either way, he seemed glad to see her. Which made her gladder still, considering Kirsty was doing her usual up-close-and-personal style of conversation with him.

She saw him dip his head and say something to Kirsty, then turn and walk toward the screen door that faced the house.

He met her halfway—by a flowering jasmine plant in a over-sized pottery urn that hadn't come from Wal-Mart. Sicily proba-bly, or Tuscany.

She was beginning to think "drug dealer" again when he leaned in close, kissed her cheek, and whispered, "Come and make nice for ten minutes and then I'll show you my bedroom."

Really—with an invitation like that, little discrepancies of occupation could be overlooked. Didn't heads of state make agreements with people of less-than-stellar reputation for reasons of expediency—like trade or politics or the greater good of mankind?

In this case, it would be *her* greater good.

And it wasn't as though she was bringing him home for din-ner to meet the folks.

"I'll be nice as can be for a reward like that," she whispered back.

His grin was wolfish. "We'll be nice to each other. And *my* bedroom has a lock on the door so these yahoos can stay out."

She wanted to ask why he had a lock on his bedroom door, but under the circumstances, his assurance of security overcame curiosity or scruple. "I should be able to last ten minutes." She held his gaze. "Although, I can't guarantee it."

"With incentive like that, I might drag you away in five minutes."

"Hopefully before my eardrums burst."

"Stay here. I'll turn it down."

And like a chivalrous knight, he sprinted away to serve his damsel in distress. It was charming really, modern-day gallantry so rarely in evidence. She experienced a warm little glow—a nonsexual one . . . almost a sentimental one.

Regaining her wits a second later, she reminded herself that 1, she'd known him for twelve hours tops; 2, sentiment had nothing to do with sex; 3, he wasn't the boy next door despite his looks—not with a spread like this and no apparent source of income; and 4, one-night stands were by definition not based on tender feeling.

When he returned, she was perfectly composed and once again capable of acting like a mature adult. She'd even reconciled herself to being civil to Kirsty, who had taken off her jacket to expose a little white tank top and her huge breasts. Even from a distance, that improbable combination looked like a catastrophe in the making—the white Lycra stretched to the limit.

"The volume's down now. Your eardrums are safe. Come, have a drink."

"Maybe just a Coke. I have to drive home."

"You don't *have* to go home."

"The store doesn't open till eleven on Sunday, but even that seems early after a late night."

"Can't you call someone to cover for you?"

"At one o'clock?"

"Right. Okay. We do this hello and good-bye in record time. And ignore Kirsty if she says anything rude. She can run off at the mouth."

"I noticed."

Sarcasm like that. He'd better cover his ass. "We're just friends."

"I'm guessing maybe you haven't always been just friends."

"Like those guys under your bed." Some had been nude sketches.

"Not really. I just have a good imagination."

Back up a minute. Had he heard that right? "I'm the exception?"

"You're exceptional in every way," she murmured.

"That sounds like one smooth-talkin' line."

"Word of God."

He laughed. "Back at you, babe." Line or no line, no way was he going to piss her off by pushing the point. Her sex life was none of his business. "Do you want lime with your Coke? Or a twist of lemon? Cherries?"

"I want *you* with my Coke." There was no point in being coy on a one-night stand.

He shot a glance at his guests, took a deep breath, and said, "Hold that thought. We'll make this fast." Taking her hand, he walked to the screen door, opened it, and drew her into the pool area. "She made it," he said to the group standing at a granite topped bar. "Who needs a refill?"

Buddy came over to give her a hug, she was introduced to Brian Larson, and Kirsty nodded, *coolly.*

Stella started counting down from ten minutes—hoping for five.

She also hoped looks couldn't actually kill, or she was in trouble. Kirsty was shooting daggers at her, and what had been no more than a hackneyed cliché took on sinister implications. No way was she going to stand close to Miss Blonde Bombshell with those little plastic daggers for olives and cherries in a cup on the bar.

Buddy talked about Marky B's newest issue from cover to cover, which saved Stella from having to do more than nod and smile. With her thoughts pretty much focused on the post-ten-minute activities, actual conversation was a stretch.

After passing around the requested drinks, Danny came to stand by Stella. "Take the Coke with you," he murmured, slipping his arm around her waist. "I'll show you the house." He smiled at his guests. "See you in the morning. You know where everything is."

"Aren't we going to skinny-dip before we call it a night?" Kirsty lasered Danny with a meaningful glance. "We *always* do."

Buddy decided diplomacy was in order. "It's getting late," he suggested.

Kirsty gave Buddy a disgusted look. "Since when do we go to bed before dawn when we're partying at Rees's?"

It went quiet; you could suddenly hear the frogs croaking in the marshes.

A three count went by.

"I had enough swimming today," Danny said. "Count me out."

"I remember not too long ago when you *loved* skinny-dipping," Kirsty purred.

Danny didn't move a muscle, no blink . . . nothing. "Not tonight." His voice was neutral as hell. "If anyone gets hungry, there's food in the pool house kitchen." He turned to Stella. "Ready?"

About ten minutes ago. "Sure. Whenever."

Kirsty stepped forward, blocking their path, her boobs leading the parade. "You're not being very sociable, Rees."

"Sorry. Some other time, Kirsty. I'm expecting an early call in the morning."

Her gaze narrowed, a sullen scowl marred her perfect brows. "If I'd known you were going to be a recluse, I wouldn't have come."

"I could call you a cab." A get-off-my-back coolness in his voice.

Kirsty's baby blues gave off little resentful sparks. "Marisa says you can be hard to handle. I'll have to tell her she's right. And I don't need a cab. Brian will give me a ride home."

So some girlfriend thought he was hard to handle—not that Stella was laboring under the delusion Danny Rees was a monk. But he'd better not make any more comments about her sketches when he was living *la dolce vita.*

"You have yourself a great night," Danny said, as though he was immune to resentful women and, moving around Kirsty, he guided Stella toward the door, not sure he was home free, but hopeful. With Kirsty, one never knew. She was into tantrums.

"She looked real unhappy," Stella murmured as they moved out of earshot.

"Kirsty can be a prima donna."

"That must be why you like her around."

He wasn't going there. "She's Buddy's friend more than mine."

"She seems to like *you* though."

"Could we not talk about Kirsty?" There was no point in arguing about a woman he'd never slept with for a reason. Prima donnas weren't his style.

"We could make a deal I suppose."

He turned and met her gaze. "I'm sure we could." He grinned. "Where do I sign?"

"You're very trusting. You hardly know me."

"Hardly?" He smiled. "I envy the guy who knows you better."

"Perhaps in time you'll be fully enlightened," she said, perjuring herself just for effect. He was too sure of himself.

"What the hell does that mean?" He knew what it meant; he just wasn't sure he cared to think about it.

It worked. What a frown. Sweet. "Nothing. I shouldn't have said it," she murmured, wondering how to look blasé and worldly.

He hesitated, not sure if he was pissed off or not. What the fuck was wrong with him? He wasn't pissed off—okay? Where was he? Oh, yeah, not talking about Kirsty. "Okay," he said. "So what's your deal?"

"Do you like being tied up?"

He shot her a glance. "You don't seem the type." He'd just fucked her every which way. Call it instinct.

"What type is that?" Jeez. Could he see the not-real-experienced-with-bondage girl beneath her bluster?

"Usually a little more in-your-face." He shrugged. "You know, more—"

"Assertive?"

He was thinking hard core, not that that was all bad.

"I can be assertive. Didn't I create Marky B? She's assertive as hell."

"Don't tell me you like whips, too." Marky B was good with a bull whip. He had a feeling she wasn't. Call it a hunch.

"What if I said I was?"

He smiled. "*That* I'd like to see."

"I *could* be good with a bull whip."

"I could knit doilies, too, but it's not likely."

"Hmpf. For your information, it's *crochet* doilies."

Now *her* sulkiness was sexy as hell, in contrast to Kirsty's, which was just annoying. "Knit, crochet." He shrugged. "Whatever. Look, sweetheart, if you say you're good with a bull whip, I believe you. Really. I can picture you in leather."

"You're just saying that." But her heart was pumping overtime because he'd said "sweetheart" in the *sexiest* way possible—all intimate and hushed and sort of endearing.

She had a little-girl openness that was damnably charming. And unusual in the women he knew; he was charmed to the bone. "Show me tomorrow. I happen to have a bull whip in the barn."

"What for?"

Those big grass-green astonished eyes. He probably didn't have to worry about being tied up tonight. "It was here when I bought the place," he said in lieu of telling the truth. This wasn't a night for full disclosure. Very few of his nights were. "Are you hungry?" he asked to change the subject, opening the back door and waving her into the kitchen. "I could make you a sandwich or something."

"I'll take the something," she said with a smile. "I'm on this train that's only going one way tonight."

He grinned. "I've been enjoying the ride, too. Care to check out the next stop?"

Leaning into him, she gazed up and smiled. "I'd be real happy to have you show me."

If they didn't have guests outside, he'd show her right here in the kitchen. With her, patience wasn't a viable concept. Full steam ahead was his only speed. "That way," he murmured, nodding in the direction of a shadowed hallway, taking her hand in his and moving toward a doorway between open shelves neatly arranged with dishes, glasses, pots, and pans.

"You cook?"

"On rare occasions."

"It looks like you cook. I've never seen so many copper pots." Stella started totting up the prices in her head; one of her personal dreams was to own even a fraction of this array, so she knew prices. That drug dealer label popped into her head again. Although, lottery winner was a possibility as well . . . outrageous odds notwithstanding.

"Stay overnight and I'll cook you breakfast."

"Ummm . . . tempting. If only I didn't have to make a living."

"I could make a personal buy tomorrow that might cover your daily sales."

Her eyes widened.

"Think about it. Your comic inventory is prime. There's lots of stuff I need. And we could sleep in."

She made a moue. "I'd have to see Kirsty in the morning."

"She and Brian might leave, and if they don't, I could serve you breakfast in bed."

"What are you—Santa Claus and Prince Charming rolled into one?"

"I'm enjoying myself. I'm selfish as hell. Humor me, and I'll make it worth your while," he said with a grin. Reason had taken a trip around the world; he was operating on sex drive alone.

"Jeez . . . I don't know." She smiled. "The hotel package is damned tempting."

"We're running a weekend special for Lumberjack Days. A personal masseuse, breakfast in bed, mimosas if you like. And all the sex you can handle."

"Okay. You got me on that last item. The store can open late, and I'll apologize if anyone's waiting at the door."

"Deal." Half a loaf was better than none. And he had this curious need to wake up with her in the morning. He must be drunker than he thought.

The hallway was dimly illuminated, and as they walked by an

open door, a dazzling display of flashing lights brought her to a stop. Turning, she gazed at a room that looked like the Pentagon war room—electronic equipment by the score—a half dozen computers and monitors, two huge plasma screens, and several unfamiliar machines with lights and screens, buttons, and knobs.

"My office," he said.

"For?"

"Computer stuff."

"No shit. So you *do* have a job."

"Sort of. I design video games." He didn't say he'd designed the most popular video game in history when he was still in college and sold it five years later for mega-millions. He never offered up that information.

"You can make a living doing that? Duh. I guess you can," she said with a wave. "This is a very nice farm."

"Thanks. I like it. I'll show you the creek and tire swing in the morning." He pulled the office door shut and continued walking, preferring not to talk about his business. His friends like Buddy knew he had enough to live on, but he never discussed his finances.

"I *love* tire swings."

Jesus, she was appealing—fresh as dew and hotter than hell. "You can go first then," he said with a grin.

"You're awfully sweet."

"Not really."

"Allow me to disagree."

"I'm on my best behavior."

"Because you want sex."

Because I want you, he thought. Sex he could have anytime. "Something like that," he said with a faint smile.

"This is going to be a memorable sleepover."

He laughed. "I don't plan on sleeping. In here," he murmured, pushing open the door to his bedroom.

She stood arrested on the threshold. "You must have a decorator." She was pretty sure about the no wife after one look. The room didn't contain a hint of a woman—with the exception perhaps of the decorator's sense of color. The space was coordinated from the paint on the walls to the rugs on either side of the bed. And not a stick of furniture cost less than a grand, including that footstool with the needlepoint image of a black lab.

"My sister," he said. "She works for the Sierra Club. I think we have a nature theme going here."

Along with an opulent, gentleman's retreat motif, the furniture was antique, English probably, Ralph Lauren maybe, the carpet a muted green, the large four-poster bed covered with a tailored egg-shell-colored linen quilt. A museum-quality tall-boy stretched across one wall; a bow-front desk occupied another; and upholstered chairs were arranged on either side of a fireplace, their size commensurate with their owner's proportions, their color a startling blood red and dandelion yellow stripe overlay with a fish design. Numerous prints on the walls depicted fishing scenes as well.

"Do you like to fish?"

"Every once and a while. Libby does though. My sister," he added.

"Ah." Stella swung her arms gently at her sides.

"Enough conversation?"

"Was I being rude?"

"I'm not really in the mood to talk, either."

She smiled. "It must be karma. Or maybe it's because we both collect comics; I've never been so obsessed before."

"Could be." He didn't know, either, but whatever it was, he wanted to keep it going. Shutting the door, he drew her to the bed, lifted her up, and sat her down on the pristine linen cover. "Where were we?"

"When we were so discourteously interrupted? I think we'd both just come."

He grinned. "Something different."

"Something really fine. And a word of warning. I'm afraid I'm addicted. You may have a junkie on your hands."

"It must be my reward for brushing after meals."

"I suppose you say that to all the women."

"Nope."

"So I'm unique."

She said it with a flourishing sweep of her arms and a grin, and drama aside, damned if she wasn't.

"Like a unicorn, babe. The one and only."

"I just adore flattery. However . . ." She gave him a significant look in a significant area.

"Gotcha. No more talk."

"Take note of how I dressed for success tonight." She pulled her chartreuse sleeveless sweater over her head, kicked off her sandals, and wiggled out of her green-stripe capris in five seconds flat.

He grinned. "It works for me." She hadn't worn underwear.

"Now if you please." She tapped her wristwatch and offered him the most innocent expression . . . as though she were asking for a traffic report instead of sex.

He was even faster at discarding his clothes. But then he'd had lots of practice. "Do you have any requests—other than speed?" he quickly added, already familiar with the drill.

"Nope. That's about it."

He was laughing as he settled between her legs. "You're easy to please."

"And you're my drug of choice tonight," she purred, sliding her arms around his neck, pulling her knees up, making it easier for point A to meet point B.

"Waitin' for that first rush?" He slid the head of his cock up her wet slit.

"Oh, yeah . . ." Arching her hips upward, she reached for nirvana.

"Showtime," he whispered, sliding into her, shutting his eyes against the warmth and exquisite tightness, pushing against her yielding flesh until her pubic hair met his and there was nowhere else to go.

The world disappeared in that first rush of pleasure, the heated surge melting through their bodies—ecstasy inundating their senses.

Her pulsing tissue sent a thousand little messages of bliss to her brain and skin and tantalized receptors. And like any addict would, she said, "More—give me more."

"How much?"

Something in his voice, something raw and capricious, brought her gaze up. But his eyes when she saw them were amused, softened by his smile, and her moment of apprehension vanished. "Don't tease," she whispered. "I'm too unstrung."

She wasn't the only one operating on the edge. He'd almost gone over when she'd asked for more, his libido working overtime tonight with the insatiable Miss Stella who wanted cock almost as much as he wanted to give it to her. "Just let me know when to stop," he said, husky and low. "Holler if I don't hear you."

He settled into a hard, driving rhythm, giving her what she wanted, bringing her to climax fast like she liked it, following her a millisecond later, knowing even as he came that it wasn't enough. She was whimpering, asking for more—as though they were both in sync tonight . . . on some headlong race for the ultimate in sensation.

Impelled by an unquenchable lust, he was more than willing to give her whatever she wanted—no questions asked and rock-hard as if he'd never come. He pounded, hammered, and met her stroke for stroke. It was as if a mute and voiceless where-have-you-been-all-my-life sexual spin of the wheel had brought them together, and bent only on slaking their raging desires, sexed up and horny as hell, they found orgasmic heaven together again and again.

More focused perhaps, or in some mindless attack mode, he didn't notice her hitting his chest and shouting "Stop" until she held her hand over his mouth and nose. The word *stop* was suddenly audible. "Christ," he whispered. "I'm sorry." And rolling off, he tried to catch his breath.

It was as if he'd come awake from some killer weed where you could last all night and the next day, too. But he was straight; his hallucinogen tonight was one voluptuous lady with a smokin' appetite for sex and a soft, welcoming cunt.

That had apparently reached its limit.

He turned his head. She was staring at him. Oh, fuck.

Stella arched one tawny brow. "You need to check your hearing."

"I'm sorry—really. Did I hurt you?"

She shook her head. "Overload that's all. Break time."

"You can hit me or something."

She smiled. "I'll try the something next time."

Shifting onto his side, he smiled back. "I really am sorry, but if we're talking drugs of choice tonight," he murmured, brushing a fall of hair from her forehead, "no way Pfizer can compete with you. I was in the zone." And then he kissed her gently, without a hint of fever or randiness.

It unnerved her momentarily, a kiss like that, all softness and honey-sweet languor. One of those split-second debates about letting yourself care about a guy like him raced through her brain. She pulled back.

He was leaning over her, his gaze close. "What?"

She glanced at the clock on the bedside table. "Nothing." How do you say you're freaked 'cuz his kiss was too nice? He'd think her more looney than he did already. "I could use a drink of water," she said, needing one of those down moments to get her brain unscrambled.

He did a double take, then said, "Ice, bottled, tap?" like her request hadn't come out of the blue.

"Tap's fine."

She watched him walk to the bathroom, or what she assumed was the bathroom, and did some fast talking to herself. It didn't take long to understand that she was in a position to have some of the better sex of her life tonight. Now wasn't the time to question anything so innocuous as a kiss. He probably kissed all the women he knew that way. It didn't mean a thing. Problem solved.

She stretched and looked around: high-quality prints on the wall—nice; a worn leather jacket tossed on a chair back, a couple shirts in a pile on the floor—he wasn't a neat freak; she glanced at the books on a nearby shelf—mostly nonfiction; and then she caught a glimpse of something metallic half buried under some magazines on the table by the fireplace. When her cognitive functions correctly identified the item a second later, she jumped out of bed, walked across the room, and pushed aside the magazines.

Picking up a pair of handcuffs, she turned around to find Danny standing in the bathroom doorway, a glass of water in his hand.

"Do these fit you?" she asked.

"Don't know."

That more or less told a story. "Wanna try?"

He hesitated.

"Consider it payback," she murmured, grinning, "for you being hard of hearing."

He shrugged. "I guess I owe you one."

There was something about his reluctance that turned her on. Or maybe just looking at him, nude and ready for action like he was in training for stud of the year was the turn-on. "I'll be gentle," she teased.

His dark lashes lowered infinitesimally. "Good idea."

That look. It sent a little shiver down her spine. Sweet kiss or not, Danny Rees was more familiar with being in the driver's seat. Not always a bad thing, she reminded herself, her body revving up at the memory of his recent compelling performance that had given her numerous orgasms. "Whenever you're ready," she said, waving the handcuffs toward the bed, already in tune with her sexual readiness.

He moved toward her, his erection hard against his stomach, the engorged shaft oscillating faintly with his stride.

His standing tall penis drew her eye, another ripple of arousal sliding up her vagina. She didn't know how he did it without Viagra, but clearly he did. That was one massive hard-on.

"Drink?" he said upon reaching her, holding out the glass.

Her gaze came up and met his smile. "Don't look so smug."

"Sorry." When he clearly wasn't. "Do you want this?" He lifted the glass.

Taking it from him, she took a sip and set it down next to the magazines.

His brows flickered up and down. "Not too thirsty?"

"Is that a problem?"

"Not for me."

"Good."

He laughed. "You and Marky B have a lot in common." He gave her a raking glance. "Including your great bods. Let me know when you're rested up."

"You have to pay penance first."

"Whatever you say."

Ignoring the hint of irony in his tone, she nodded toward the bed.

Well-mannered, he complied, and moments later he was seated with his back against the headboard. "Like this or lying down?"

"Lying down." She climbed onto the bed.

"Do you know how to work those?" he asked, his gaze flicking toward the handcuffs.

"I think so. Is there a key?"

"In the drawer." He indicated the bedside table with a nod.

His tone was like "Let's get this over with," and for a fleeting moment she considered saying, "What the hell, let's just fuck." After all, that was the point, wasn't it? Climaxing. Or at least it was her ultimate goal—or goals, plural, in this case with Danny Rees and his continuous hard-on.

But she decided she'd prefer the tantalizing prospect of him handcuffed and at her mercy. As if. But that's what games were all about. Make believe.

Leaning over, she took the key from the drawer, opened the cuffs, and snapped one and then the other on Danny's wrists. They were a tight fit; he wasn't exactly average sized. But mission accomplished a few moments later, she stretched his arm upward toward one of the bed posts. Scratches circled the mahogany finish on the spiral upright—handcuff marks unless she missed her guess. Not that it was any of her business. Snap—one wrist secure. Stepping over him, she lifted his other arm and fettered the second wrist to a post.

Moving to the foot of the bed, she surveyed her shackled centerfold.

Nice.

More like perfection, from the top of his ruffled black hair to the bottom of his tanned feet with everything in between hard muscle and raw virility. The term *mouth-watering* came to mind—a definite thought. Although not just yet; she was too selfish to opt for that right away.

"You look like you're glad to see me," she murmured.

"You're my type, babe."

"Female and breathing you mean."

"Uh uh. We like comic book girls."

"How much?" she teased, when it was patently apparent.

"More than you know." Which was the honest-to-God truth, not that he was going to elaborate.

"So there might be a second act?"

He grinned. "Plan on a long run."

"I wish I had more patience," she murmured, moving closer, intent on that first act.

"Why? When we both want the same thing." In fact, if he could have moved, he would have taken over about now. He was pretty much in attack mode around Stella Scott.

She eased one leg over his thighs and, straddling him on her knees, positioned herself over his pulsing cock. "You're going to spoil me for the real world," she said with a smile.

He flexed his hips and grinned. "Our pleasure, babe."

"How nice. Are your wrists okay?" Although she was focused on sensation more than his reply, centering the head of his erection for easy entry, wiggling a little to ease it in a fraction.

"I'll survive," he murmured, sucking in his breath as she began to lower herself.

Shutting her eyes against the exquisite friction, inhaling slowly on her descent, she sighed as she came to rest—blissfully impaled. Moving her hips faintly, she groaned, bewitched by the heady pleasure.

Intent on more fevered sensation, Danny arched his spine, flexed his quads, and thrust upward.

Stella gasped, every sweet spot awash in ecstasy. "Do that again," she breathed.

"Say please."

A distinct tone of command underlaid his words. Looking up, her gaze flicked to his wrists, then back to him. "Why would I?" She took orders poorly.

He gave a nod downward. "For practical reasons."

"I can climax without you moving."

"Maybe." A wicked grin lifted his mouth. "I could think of rotting corpses or something and go limp."

She debated less than a second. Maybe he would and maybe

he wouldn't, but why take the chance? "In that case—by all means—please," she sportively replied.

His smile had warmth now. "You're easy."

"I never argue about great sex." She lifted her shoulder in the faintest of shrugs. "I prefer going for the brass ring."

He laughed. "Definitely a Marky B quality." He winked. "And loveable as hell. Hang on, babe. The merry-go-round is about to start."

It was one of those lush, salacious games with her hanging on and him accommodating her and both of them holding their breath on every powerful upstroke when he crammed her full— maybe even the faint sound of calliope music keeping time in their unconscious. Her pink-tipped breasts bounced on each upthrust, and flexing his fingers, he wished he could touch them. She rode him with abandon, her head falling back, exposing her silken throat, her wild craving so provocative he could have stayed hard for days.

She felt like a sex fiend with him, like she could never get enough, like she would die if he wasn't inside her.

He was thinking he'd found the perfect nymphet for the satyr in him, and beyond that he wasn't thinking at all.

No one said it was a match made in heaven.

But the feeling couldn't be discounted.

Finally sated, she collapsed on his chest, his cock still inside her.

Sated wasn't an operational concept for him, but he could re-strain himself if she needed some rest.

Her head was lying on his shoulder, her hair brushing his chin. "You're unbelievable," she murmured. "I'm seriously considering mystical intercession of some kind."

"Hey, babe, forget mystical and unsnap these cuffs."

"Oh, sorry." After all he'd done for her. Quickly moving off him, she reached for the key on the bedside table.

The air was suddenly cool on his penis, although his libido was still fired up and on the prowl. He glanced at the clock. How long did courtesy demand he wait for a rerun?

"I can't get the key to turn," she muttered a second later, struggling with the lock.

"It goes left."

She gave him a look.

"What? They're mine. I should know."

Of course he should know. She didn't even understand why she should care how many women he'd shackled to his bed to have the posts scratched so badly. And she didn't. Really. Not one speck. "I can't get this key to move. Let me try the other wrist."

"Never mind." Slamming one cuff against the wood post, he split open the latch. "They're break-aways," he said, wacking the second cuff against the post.

She scowled. "Why didn't you say so."

"I didn't want to spoil your fun."

"*Hmpf!*"

"Don't be mad." He pulled off the cuffs and tossed them on a chair across the room, his aim perfect. Turning back, he reached over, took her face between his hands, kissed her on both cheeks, and smiled. "Why don't I let you pick out some Kama Sutra pages you like? As atonement."

"Maybe I don't like the Kama Sutra," she said, although anyone in their right mind knew the Kama Sutra and Danny Rees would make a dynamic duo.

He grinned. "I could probably convert you."

"You're very annoying," she sniffed.

"We could play cards if you like."

"Are you serious?"

"What do you want to do then? You tell me."

There was a point when being pouty was impractical. She fell back on the bed and stared at the ceiling. "There might be a couple Kama Sutra things I like," she said.

He could barely hear her, she'd spoken so quietly, but he knew when tact was called for. "Which ones?" he asked, like she wasn't being sulky.

"I can't remember their names."

At least she was talking. "Let me grab my book," he offered. "You can find them."

And wouldn't you know, he had a copy under his bed. If the edition hadn't been such a beautifully illustrated version, she might have been more likely to persist in her sulkiness. But it was really difficult to remain angry with—you know—the man's sexual nonchalance when that little throbbing was beginning to warm her sex as she surveyed one after another full-color, lascivious depiction of men and women screwing.

And since when was she averse to nonchalant sex?

Especially with a first-class, A-number-one, mega-well-endowed man like Danny Rees.

"How about this one?" she finally said, pointing to an illustration.

"Sure," he said. Just like that. Like he could do anything.

It turned out he could.

And very well at that.

EIGHT

STELLA WOKE UP WHEN SOMEONE DOVE IN THE
pool at what seemed the crack of dawn. The clock on the
mantle disabused her of that notion; it was nine-thirty.
She had time to get home, shower, and dress before store hours.
Call her Type A, but she loved her store. Not that she didn't really
love the sex with Danny Rees. But let's face it, her store would be
there long after he had moved on.

Easing out of bed, she picked up her clothes and shoes and
tiptoed to the door. She'd dress in the hall and not take a chance
of waking Danny. Fortunately, they'd not locked the door;
they'd had other things on their mind, which worked out fine for
her—no loud metallic sound of a tumbler dropping would inter-
fere with her sneaking outta here. She turned the knob with the
caution of a safe cracker, ever so slowly, glancing at the bed
occasionally—nervous she might be found out yet determined to

leave. Apparently that one-track-mind thing worked for more than sex, and she wanted to go home.

A moment later she was standing in the hall, nude and hopefully alone.

A quick look. Yep.

She swiftly dressed and walked to the front door, which was closer to her car and farther from the bedroom *and* the pool house. The last person she wanted to see had platinum blond hair and the evil eye.

Standing on the porch a moment later, she inhaled the fresh morning air. It was a beautiful day. Sunny, warm, the birds singing their little hearts out, the fragrance of flowers wafting in the breeze. Of course, her gratifying mood may have had more to do with a night of countless, blissful orgasms than the morning sunshine and chirping birds.

Oh, oh—*that* wasn't a flower scent.

She needed a shower.

HE WOKE UP with a hard-on, which wasn't out of the ordinary, considering the nature of his dreams starring Stella Scott and every feel-good impulse known to man. He might have even experienced that earth-moving thing last night.

Maybe. Possibly.

He smiled and, still half dozing, reached out to bring his dream girl closer to the action.

His eyes snapped open, and all the warm fuzzies disappeared in a flash.

She was gone.

His first thought was of her sketchbook with all those fucking guys.

He should have known. Any woman that good in bed wasn't a novice.

Not that he was looking for a novice. But he wasn't sure he wanted to be number one thousand and fifty, either.

Shit.

It took him a few minutes to cool down and a few minutes more to remind himself that he'd walked away from a woman or two in his life. It happened. And it wasn't as though he was looking for any long-term deal. Or any deal. He liked his answer-to-no-one existence. He liked being alone. So count your blessings—last night particularly—and get on with your life.

When he padded into the kitchen after his shower, he found Buddy having an espresso and reading the Sunday paper.

"It's just the two of us, sweetheart," Buddy quipped. "Stella's car is gone."

"And Kirsty and Brian?"

"I gave up before they did. But no one else slept in the pool house, so I figure she had Brian drive her home. I slept like a baby, by the way. Thanks for putting me up."

"Not a problem. Are you done with the sports?"

Buddy slid the sports section across the table and winked. "Had a good night, did we? Your eyes are at half mast."

"A very good night." Danny set two small cups under the spouts of his espresso machine and pressed the button for a double. "How much do you know about Stella?"

"Not much other than what she's told me when I've chatted

her up at her store. I should at least have a finder's fee. You cut me out big time."

"I figured you had your chance." Danny watched the perfect crema form on the espresso. "You've known her for a while."

"True. And mostly I know she doesn't date customers." Buddy grinned. "How does it feel to be the exception to the rule?"

Danny looked up and smiled. "Exceptional." Pouring the two shots into a cup, he moved toward the table and sat across from Buddy. "Do you need a ride to your boat? Home?"

"Nah. I'll have one of my crew come and get me. They're at my slip in Afton. Come out on the boat if you like. We're going down to Lake Pepin later today."

"I'll pass, but thanks."

"You could ask Stella along."

"She's at the store." At least he assumed she was. He was sorely tempted to go over and see. Like a nicotine addiction, he was beginning to get the shakes. But he'd deal with it. He wasn't sixteen and infatuated. "What do you think about the Red Sox's pitching? It looks good."

"It should be with the money they pay Schilling."

Men didn't do blow by blows like women did.

NINE

STELLA ALMOST CALLED DANNY A ZILLION TIMES before noon. She'd looked up his phone number the minute she opened the store, and only sheer will kept her from making a fool of herself.

You didn't call up a stud like Danny and tell him what a great night you had.

Men like Danny Rees probably didn't take phone calls from women.

And despite the fact that he'd said he'd wanted her to stay for breakfast, she couldn't be sure he actually meant it or was only playing to the audience at the time.

So keep your mind on business, and forget about sex.

Not actually possible when she was already missing him.

Fortunately, she was busy most of the morning. Todd Ekhert and Jason Krantz, who were trying to make it out of seventh-grade math by passing summer school, had come in for their tutorial. They were conscientious about showing up every day, terrified they'd flunk the summer school makeup course and be held back.

She'd taught junior high math before she'd inherited the wherewithall to open her store, and she was more than happy to help. They were good kids. Just not left brain. And she'd promised them both a first edition of *Spiderman* No. 1, 1988 if they passed the course, so they were extra motivated.

She figured the math tutoring she offered at the store was her community service. Along with the remedial math class she taught during the school year one evening a week. Math was a game to her, like a puzzle where everything fell into place if you put the pieces in the right way, and she was able to make it a game for the kids, too. Within the circle of youngsters who came into her store, she was known as the Math Wizard Lady—Magic card vernacular popular at her place.

Speaking of magic, her mind automatically focused on the previous night, when pleasure had taken on an otherworldly character. How freaked out would he be if she were to call him and tell him she was deeply in love even though they weren't well acquainted? Except for the sex, of course. And in that regard, she had to think they were bosom buds.

But she didn't call. She wasn't that crazy. Not after seeing his reaction to Kirsty's less-than-subtle approach last night. There had been a distinct chill in his eyes.

But chill aside, damned it was tempting.

Maybe she could call and hang up when he answered.

At least she could hear his voice.

Psycho chick! her little voice of reason shrieked. *Don't you dare!*

Hello. Are you the one needing an orgasm? She got tough with that little voice and managed to silence it. Sex was a powerful compulsion.

But just as she reached for the phone, it rang.

Please, please, please, her lustful urges pleaded.

"Give me every little detail, or as much as you can whisper into the phone without your customers hearing X-rated material," Megan declared, foregoing a greeting.

Stella couldn't tell Megan her call was a letdown, but something in her voice must have given her away.

"The evening didn't go well? The bastard. Tell me and I'll put a curse on him, or my psychic will. She guarantees results."

"I'm not down about him—it's me. He was so perfect I'm obsessing about calling him and telling him how great he was. Tell me not to do it. Tell me to act like an adult."

"You could try, but it might be a stretch for you."

"Thanks for the vote of confidence."

"Sweetie, you're the most impulsive, disorganized, unconventional person I know. And I know an odd assortment of people because I teach in an alternative school. But listen carefully. Do. Not. Call. Him."

"I had a couple zillion orgasms last night. My body doesn't want to listen to reason."

"Would it help if I told you that calling him would be one of the most stupid things you've ever done, and that includes leaving that message on Nick Blanchich's answering machine in the eleventh grade?"

Stella groaned. "Don't remind me. His mother never looked at me the same after that."

"You shouldn't have mentioned her underwear drawer."

"He was the one who brought out that black lace nightie at the party."

"And you were the one who tried it on."

"He wanted me to."

"So you were polite. Right?"

"It might have been those couple of drinks."

Megan laughed. "Look, he was cute as hell. If he'd asked me, I probably would have done the same thing. But a word of warning: Danny Rees won't appreciate a female stalker."

"Couldn't I just say thanks?"

"And then what would you say after that?"

"Okay, okay. Point taken."

"And need I remind you that you're the lady who only a few days ago told me in no uncertain terms that dating customers was against your principles?"

"Danny Rees might be worth altering one's principles—ever so slightly."

"Let him call you. That's all I'm saying. He's used to women crawling all over him."

"You're right. I'm convinced. So did you have a good time last night? What did you think of Buddy?"

"He was nice, but it was more friendly than anything. He has money. Guys like that can pick and choose. It's just a fact. So I'm not going to start planning my engagement party."

"You *like* him. Wow. Tell me *everything!*"

"Don't get excited. It's nice, okay—not anything more. But I like that he's not into himself when he could be with his bucks, and he listens when you talk as though he cares what you're saying. He's a great dancer, too—even when he's not sober. And you know how I like to dance, not that Chad would ever dance."

"You were young. You're allowed a mistake. Forget Chad," Stella said, dismissively. "What else do you like about Buddy?"

"He's really polite, and I never thought I'd be saying anything so lame, but he opens car doors for you and orders your drink like you're some kind of special and he even asked about the kids, if you can imagine. He said he'd take the kids and me out on his boat again. So there. That's about the whole story."

"That's a real nice story. Now, tell me how much you really *do* like him, 'cuz I'm hearing something in your voice that's a notch or two up from just okay."

Megan giggled. "Maybe half a notch."

"Maybe something like say—casual affection?"

"Let's just say I'm sticking to casual right now. Don't forget, I've been practically in a nunnery since my divorce. I'm not sure my sensory receptors are even up to speed yet."

"Even then, you should have come out to Danny's last night. I wouldn't have left Buddy alone with Kirsty for a second. That lady sees every man as a potential conquest."

"I was going back to my mom's or I would have. She was expecting me to go to church with her in the morning. And Buddy said Kirsty is some kind of sixth cousin or something. She's like family. That's why she's always on his boat."

"Okay, so you're marginally safe. In my case, little Kirsty was doing her bombshell best to lure Danny away even though I was standing right there."

"Without success apparently," Megan noted.

"Without any success at all," Stella replied, the smile in her voice obvious. "And I gotta tell you, I couldn't be happier how things turned out. In fact, I'm feeling *so-o-o* infatuated this morning," Stella said, her euphoria echoing down the phone lines.

"Although I'm not sure whether it's with him or his you-know-what. He's pretty phenomenal."

"Even more reason not to call him. I expect he's been phenomenal with lots of women."

Stella sighed. "Back to the real world, right?"

"It's the only one you can count on, sweetie. Leave the love and romance for the movies."

TEN

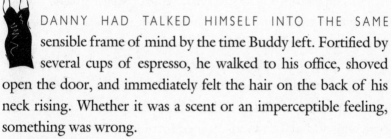DANNY HAD TALKED HIMSELF INTO THE SAME sensible frame of mind by the time Buddy left. Fortified by several cups of espresso, he walked to his office, shoved open the door, and immediately felt the hair on the back of his neck rising. Whether it was a scent or an imperceptible feeling, something was wrong.

And then he saw it.

One screen saver was out of sync in his color-coded, left-to-right sequence. If anyone tried to get into his computers, his security stopped them. But more important, he knew it. Should anyone touch his computers without his entry code, the screen-saver motion altered right to left.

Additionally, the early version hard copies of the video game he was developing had been moved. And neatly piled.

Whoever had been here was stupid enough to leave a trail.

He should have heard. He should have known someone was in the room next door.

That's what came of temporarily losing your sanity because some woman was hotter than hot.

Fuck. Fuck. Fuck.

Moving into the room, he shut the door, locked it, and methodically went through every sheet of paper on the work tables. Then he checked out the security codes on his computers. All of them had been tampered with but not breached. Not that it was likely. His security was solid as Fort Knox.

Not that he was happy that the printouts had been seen. But they were only variations on his original game and not likely to give clues to the new series he was creating.

He'd have to begin using his safe again. He'd gotten lazy when he shouldn't have—lulled into a false sense of security by his bucolic setting that could out-Mayberry the TV ideal. At least his wake-up call was relatively benign. No major damage had been done.

So—with industrial espionage rampant in his business— lock-down mode was back in effect. No way was he going to let his competitors crack the code on his next game, introduce it before him, and make a God-damned fortune.

But who the hell had broken into his office? And when?

With his fucking brain on hold all night, it could have been anytime between when Stella arrived and morning.

An outsider was a real long shot; the list of suspects was more likely those at the pool last night. Buddy wasn't a problem. He had more money than God. Brian was an unknown. Suspect number one. Kirsty? He doubted it, but maybe she wasn't as spacey as she looked. And she liked what money could buy. Nah . . . not likely. But okay, suspect number two.

Although, a certain amount of brains were required to hack into his computers, so Kirsty might be out of the lineup of likely suspects—unless she had some accomplice. Maybe Brian knew computers. He'd have to look into it.

The person he was getting twitchy about though, not only had the opportunity—if Brian and Kirsty had decamped early— but the time. And he was pretty much dead to the world this morning, thanks to the strenuous paces little Stella had put him through last night. Jesus, talk about being played for a sucker.

Sex aside, of course.

Compartmentalize to the max when it came to sex like that.

Dropping into a worn leather chair, he slid down and contemplated the injustice of finding some of the best sex this side of Bangkok and then discovering little Miss Comic Book Girl and her hot body were on a competitor's payroll.

Talk about paying a high price for a piece of ass.

Maybe. Perhaps. Definitely within the realm of possibility. Although he'd been the one who'd gone to her house. But she might have known any guy would have come to her eventually. She probably knew from past experience that all she had to do was sit and wait. Flipping back through his memory, he tried to recall whether Stella had shown any surprise at his unannounced arrival. She'd done that little I'm-not-sure-I-want-to-screw number, but come to think of it, she hadn't indicated any surprise. As for that little fiction about no sex, they'd blown that one—literally . . . in more ways than one.

Which begged the question, what was real and what was make believe about the fascinating, flame-hot Stella?

He found himself smiling despite his major break-in crisis, his brain flooding with sexually explicit, between-the-sheets images of the hot-to-trot lady he'd spent the night with.

Maybe he should just chalk it up in the no-harm-done category and be more watchful and vigilant in the future. Put in a few more safeguards. Ramp up his security system. Take care not to fall asleep if he's entertaining Miss Comic Book at home.

On the plus side—and it was a very large plus—everything was secure, no fire walls had been breached, and *Universe X* was still safely within the circuits of his computer.

Although, no doubt, the time had come to use his safe for more than his custom-made Berettas and his first editions of *Spiderman*.

DANNY SPENT THE rest of the day putting every facet of his new game on disk, revising his security codes in the event he or she had gotten to first base, and finally setting up the security camera that had been sitting in its box for six months. Apparently even Mayberry country wasn't safe—electric gate or not. Not that there was any point in putting in a yard security system. The local police wouldn't get here in time if it were broached anyway.

During the course of the due diligence required to secure his office, he was able to distract his mind from its preferred focus on sex with Stella Scott. But the second after he shut the office door and locked it behind him, he was right back on that hamster wheel—reliving the nirvana of the previous night . . . wanting sex . . . wanting her. Despite the fact she was a prime suspect.

There was no explanation. Or at least no rational one.

He'd never obsessed over a woman before.

Never.

In an effort to distance himself from his fixation, he called his sister. She was always good for a nonstop monologue about her husband, kids, or the state of the environment. Maybe she could divert his mind from sex with Stella Scott.

Or then again, maybe she couldn't.

No more than two minutes into Libby's discussion of the new chickens her kids were raising for a 4-H project she said, "You aren't listening. What's wrong?"

"Chickens. I heard."

"What about Jenny's 4-H project?"

"Okay, I may not have listened to every word."

"My first impulse would be to say it's a woman, but with you I know better. Care to talk about it?"

Libby was three years older and uberheedful of her role as big sister. Not that he confided in her much, but she had this sixth sense. "It's nothing. Have you heard from Mom and Dad? I had a call last week from Nepal, but the reception wasn't great." His parents were trekking with some *National Geographic* tour.

"They called yesterday. They'll be in Beijing next week. You weren't home. They tried calling you."

"I was at Lumberjack Days this weekend. Lots of stuff was going on."

"Such as?"

"A friend of mine has a good-sized boat. We went down the river, swam, that kind of thing."

"Anyone fun in the party?"

"Fun?" he evasively replied, because she wasn't asking that.

"Like interesting."

She wasn't asking that, either. She was asking about women, and that was the last thing he wanted to talk about. "There were a few interesting people—a museum curator, a political activist for global warming I think, a couple developers who were doing green stuff. I mostly swam though," he lied.

"And then what?"

She was like a human lie detector. "And then nothing. I came home."

"No you didn't. You never just come home after a party. You always bring people with you."

"A few people came home, I guess."

"Anyone I know?"

"Jesus, are you writing a book?"

"I just thought you might have seen that bookstore owner I met at your party this spring—you know, the one with the store in White Bear."

Wrong bookstore owner, he thought. The one he'd brought home didn't talk about esoteric literature. She didn't like to talk at all. She just liked to screw. "The guy who had the boat came over and some friends of his and a woman who owns a comic book store, too." How was that for casual?

"A comic book store? You two must have hit it off. You've been collecting comics from the time you could read."

"She has a really good store—you know . . . well-stocked, comprehensive." He kept his voice bland.

"What about her? Young, old, fat, thin, married, unmarried?"

"Sort of young, not fat"—how was that for cryptic— "unmarried, I think."

"Does she have favorites like you?"

Hot sex. But his sister meant comics. "I didn't ask. She writes her own comic though, and it's not bad."

"She sounds like a match made in heaven for you, not that I'm matchmaking when I know how much you like your independence, but—"

"You always do," he grumbled.

"What's a big sister for?" she returned, undeterred in her mission. "And consider, if you don't marry until you're fifty, you'll have one foot in the grave when your kids graduate high school."

"A charming image," he drawled.

"You know what I mean."

"Yeah, yeah." This wasn't a new conversation. Libby had been talking up marriage ever since she'd married Rick ten years ago. Apparently, wedded bliss actually did exist in Sheboygan, Wisconsin.

"You can introduce me to the comic book woman in two weeks," his sister said, with altogether too much cheer. "We're coming to shop at Mall of America. And see the Ikea store and Camp Snoopy."

"Two weeks?"

"Don't sound so alarmed. I'll bring my own sheets, and the kids love your pool."

"I have sheets, okay? I just meant—it's a surprise. You usually plan months in advance."

"I'm dying to see the Ikea store. There's one in Chicago, but then you're not there. This way we can see you and the store at the same time."

"Sounds great." He sort of meant it. He liked his sister and Rick and the kids. But he was having trouble dealing with the insistent images of Stella Scott looping through his brain at the same time his sister was talking about Ikea and getting married, not to mention his libido was doing its damndest to block out everything but his insatiable craving for what he couldn't or shouldn't have.

"A little more enthusiasm if you please."

"Sorry. There was something scrolling on TV." Lie. "I'd love to see you all again. I'll get some kid food in the house. Or are you still on the no-sugar regimen?"

"I wish. That lasted about two days. The whining got so loud I had to give in."

"Good, 'cuz Count Chocula builds strong bodies and minds."

"*Plueese*. Although a man who makes a living designing video games can't be expected to act like an adult."

"What can I say? The bar's way the hell too high."

She laughed. "Okay, okay, consider my lecture over. We'll see you in two weeks."

ELEVEN

THE STORE CLOSED EARLY ON SUNDAY. IT WAS her nod to the day of rest. Not that a handful of kids didn't always whine and moan when she rousted them out a half hour after closing time. But hey, the doors would open at nine tomorrow morning, and they could hang out here again.

She had a bunch of regulars who had more time than any kid from a normal family should. Many of them preferred her store to home. With some, it was a refuge; for others, it was just a quiet place in a noisy world. Several of them were serious about writing their own comic book; a couple kids were journaling. She had a real cross-section of teenage humanity and angst at the Hot Spot comic book store.

At times she thought she would have been better off with a degree in psychology than math. Like when Ryan Kath had threatened to kill Richie Mosbak if he didn't let him buy the last copy of *Wolverine*. Tragedy had been averted when Stella had given up her personal copy. But she'd had a little talk with Ryan after that—you know the one about anger management and no knives in her store. It turned out that Ryan had a couple hundred issues going on at home, starting with his mom's new boyfriend moving in with his three kids.

Ryan had come around and turned out to be one of her best student tutors; he was some kind of math whiz or idiot savant. She wasn't sure which, but he could do algebra formulas in his head, knew every batting average of every baseball player since dirt, and had all his comics arranged in a numerical sequence based on three squared.

So he couldn't always deal with his mom's boyfriends. Who the hell could? They came and went through a revolving door. And much as Stella liked Josie Kath for her ready smile and unending optimism, Ryan did not have a Rock of Gibraltar mother going for him.

She understood. Much as she loved her mother, she'd been raised by an unconventional woman who made garden ornaments, had tried every diet known to man, and had thrown herself body and soul into every new cause that came down the pike. If Virginia Scott wasn't painting blue cats and purple frogs, she was trying to get her husband and daughter to eat cabbage soup and little else or extolling the merits of the banana-and-peanut butter diet, not to mention her higher calling crusades to save the gorillas, timber wolves, eagles, or some obscure fish in Montana or Swaziland. Take your pick.

So Stella knew about being a rock. Someone in the family had to be. Her father was a research scientist and didn't actually relate to the real world. In a way, becoming den mother, a shoulder to cry on, and the last resort before failing math for a boatload of kids wasn't a real stretch.

She'd always been the most feet-on-the-ground stable one in her family.

THE LAST KID had meandered off. They always moved in slow motion. Shuffled, slouched, walked like they were thinking about getting where they were going in the next millennium.

She stood at the door, gazing through the window etched with the excessive curlicues of Victorian fashion. It was quiet in the store, the street outside empty of traffic, the late afternoon heat curling the leaves on the pink coneflowers lining her walk.

A white pick-up turned at the corner, and her pulse kicked into overdrive. Did Danny Rees drive a Dodge or was it a Ford? A Chevy? She racked her brain.

But the vehicle passed by.

Guess it didn't matter.

Then the truck came to a stop, backed up, and pulled into her curb.

So it was a Chevy, a little voice inside her brain said. *Now what are you going to do?*

He was getting out and looking up at the house.

Jumping away from the window, she stood with her back against the wall, not exactly sure how she should respond. Should she be effusive in her greeting or blasé? Should she tell him she'd been thinking of him all day or act like an adult and keep her mouth shut? Should she pretend she hadn't been fantasizing about having sex with him a hundred different ways since she'd left him that morning? Could she carry that one off when he was closer than a mile?

She wasn't so sure. Maybe she couldn't discount her mom's passionate sensibilities entirely. Maybe genes did matter.

Before her dilemmas of conscience and maturity were solved, he was on her porch, ringing her doorbell.

Indecision aside, there was no way she wasn't going to answer the bell.

Pushing away from the wall, she walked to the door, opened it, and smiled. "Hey."

"I thought I'd wait until closing time."

For what? she thought, but she was cool enough to say, "Good timing."

For what? he thought, not entirely unsure of the answer. But he, too, knew his manners. "I thought you might like to go out for dinner."

"Not really."

He hesitated—a half second, maybe only a tenth of a second with that look in her eyes. "Would you like to do something else?"

"It's been a real long day."

"Tell me about it."

"I was going to act mature. I was thinking blasé even."

He grinned. "Don't bother. I'm more or less out of control."

"It must be a virus going around."

"No doubt." He dipped his head. "Are you going to invite me in?"

"I was thinking about it." She shrugged. "Either that or stalk you later."

He lifted his gaze from her breasts that had jiggled as she'd shrugged, inhaled softly, refocused his thoughts from expressions like "the more you get the more you want," and said in as bland a voice as he could, "Lucky I came over and saved you the drive."

Not that he actually wanted her in his house after his office had been rifled. Which was part of the reason he'd come to her — a small part. The major reason he'd driven over was his libido. "You left early this morning." Fuck. He wasn't going to show it mattered.

"I'm more obsessed with this store than I thought. Sorry."

"Not a problem." At least she hadn't left for one of those guys in the sketches under her bed—another subject he'd vowed to ignore, because the men in her life were none of his concern. Or shouldn't be. "So?" *Keep on target, man.* He glanced past her shoulder.

Moving back a step, she waved him in. "Come into my parlor, said the spider to the fly."

He shot her an amused look. "Should I be packing heat?"

She shook her head and smiled. "Nah. I just love that line."

"I warn you," he said with a quirked grin. "I won't go down easy."

"Just so long as you go down," she murmured with a smile.

She didn't mess around. Definitely his type. "Is that first on the agenda?"

"First, second, third—whatever. Did I say I've been thinking of you all day?"

"Ditto here. I tried to read, sleep, swim—" He didn't mention his security project. "Anything to get you off my mind. Without success, as you can see."

"I'm grateful you held off until now, considering I had a store full of kids until five minutes ago."

"Seven, but who's counting?"

"You've been waiting?" How sweet. Her pussy did a little dance of delight.

"I parked around the corner. I wasn't sure I could keep my hands off you, and I didn't want to mess with sensitive, young minds."

"We've plenty of time now. The store doesn't open till nine tomorrow."

He blew out a breath. "I'm not sure you should have said that."

"Consider it a warning," she said with a wink.

He grinned. "You're one of a kind."

"I like to think so." She crooked her finger and turned toward the stairway.

What was there not to like about a woman who knew what she wanted, he cheerfully reflected. "Give me a minute to lock the doors. I don't want any interruptions."

"Especially when I plan on taking out my sex toys."

"Should I have brought my whip?"

"Not unless you're a masochist." She was halfway up the stairs, and her voice drifted lightly downward. "That's not my idea of a toy."

"Gotcha." Nice ass. He watched its gentle sway as she ascended the stairs, his erection taking note as well. Only after she disappeared from sight did he turn to lock the front door, then move down the hall to the back of the store. Passing by a table and chairs painted in green and yellow polka dots and tucked into a small bay with windows overlooking the neighbor's yard, he came to a sudden stop. A folio-sized paperback lay on the table—the title burning his retinas, *Video Game Graphics and Electronics*.

Trying to ignore the danger bells going off in his brain, he picked up the book, slid his finger under one of the two pages that had been flagged, and opened the book to the marked page. Fuck. And every other profanity known to man. A set of images from his *Blizzard 9000* game filled the page, along with step-by-step instructions for drawing the characters and setting up the game. Flipping over the second tab, he saw similar images for *Blood in the Streets*. The fact that *Blizzard 9000* was the most popular game on the planet and the other tabbed game was in the top five may have motivated the reader to examine them. It was a how-to book after all, and comic book aficionados were in the same gene pool as video game enthusiasts.

If his office hadn't been searched that morning, he wouldn't have given the choices a second thought.

Unfortunately . . .

It took less than five seconds to reconcile the warring factions in his brain—maybe less considering he was literally minutes away from burying his cock in the hottest of cunts. It helped that his office was miles away and secure. Furthermore, the possibility of the lady upstairs engaging in industrial espionage tonight was pretty much nil. She'd be too busy riding him.

With all the negatives quickly disposed of, he set down the book and resumed his undertaking. Reaching the back door, he slid the chain lock into place and then glanced around the small entry as though in search of some clue to the woman who had consumed his thoughts of late and who may or may not be a hazard to his peace of mind in more ways than one. A denim jacket, frayed at the cuffs, hung on a hook, garden clogs had been tossed in a corner, a couple straw hats lay on a cubby bench, and a bright green frog apparently used as a door stop was painted with the words LOVE LIFE—in neon orange. Now there was a Stella Scott metaphor. Resplendent, irrepressible . . . with color-me-hot buzzwords.

He exhaled slowly, telling himself not to blow it by attacking her—his libido might require a choke chain in that regard. In general though, he was counting his blessings. Time enough to deal with more dicey issues tomorrow. Right now, he was going to count his blessings and fuck his brains out.

STELLA WAS CURRENTLY engaged in her own internal discourse having to do with restraint because she was so-o-o ready for sex she was nearly shaking. The last thing she wanted to do was scare off Danny Rees by coming on too strong.

An entire day of sexual fantasy starring you-know-who and his large, lovely cock was the cause—not that understanding in any way mitigated her horniness. Nor did it help that she'd been thinking more than she should about his proficiency in all those provocative Kama Sutra contortions. Apparently, there was nothing new under the sun in terms of sex for Danny Rees.

Nice.

Pulling open her bottom dresser drawer, she lifted out her favorite toys. They were all about her. She hoped he didn't mind, she thought, lining them up on the top of the dresser. Somehow, she didn't think he would.

So she was selfish. It wasn't as though he hadn't come with the regularity of Old Faithful last night. Jeez . . . she could see it now, the tantalizing memory almost enough to give her an orgasm just thinking about it. Was he prime or what? No doubt.

He was world-class, A-list sexy, and she was about to experience him up close and personal *all night long!*

"If you want to try all of that by morning, we're going to have to crank up the time table."

She turned at the soft drawl, took in the accompanying smile, and felt a delectable warmth suffuse her senses. "I'm just laying out the options. I like them all. Take your pick."

He didn't move from his lounging pose in the doorway, his expression suddenly unreadable. *How many others had been here before,* he found himself thinking, when he shouldn't have given a damn. How many others had entertained her with that prodigious display? "You decide. It's your party."

His voice was brusque; his shuttered look gave her pause. "Should I apologize for being selfish? I'm just psyched after thinking about you all day."

His smile reappeared. He was way off-base anyway. Since when did he believe in getting involved? This was sex—not Hallmark card stuff. "Psyched I understand," he murmured, back on track. Pushing away from the door jamb, he tipped his head toward the row of sex toys. "What's your pleasure?"

"You're sure now? Sometimes I'm too pushy."

He grinned. "Sometimes you talk too much." He picked up the number one vibrating dream date: the Rabbit Habit. "How about this?"

That was her absolute favorite. "You must be psychic."

"Lucky guess," he said, not mentioning the vibrator with the little rabbit ears for the clit was lots of women's favorite.

"Have you seen the Babes in Toyland online catalogue? It's really great."

His lashes lowered faintly.

"No? With all your computers, I thought you might have seen their site."

He experienced one of those two-second twinges at her mention of computers—his mental blip almost instantly overridden by more powerful sexual impulses. If she was working for his competitors, he didn't want to think about it right now. "I don't go online much," he said. "I mostly play video games."

"Aren't you getting a little old for video games?"

"Aren't you getting a little old for comics?"

"Okay, okay—point taken."

"So are we back to essentials?"

"Sex you mean?"

He held up the pink vibrator. "And this. You like toys—right?"

"And you."

"And me," he said with a faint smile. "We can argue about our arrested adolescence sometime later over tea."

"Tea? Really?"

"Sarcasm, babe."

Too bad. She was a sucker for a nice tea.

"Are we done talking, then?" It sounded like he was settling an account.

"Maybe if you say that in a different tone of voice we might be."

"Euh—feisty."

But he'd said it real softly, and it didn't hurt that he'd pulled her into his arms and held her close so she didn't miss that pertinent contour she'd been dreaming about all day. "That's for me to know and you to find out," she whispered, leaning into his hard, muscled body.

"After last night, I'm not sure there's much more to find out."

"What if I've been saving my extra-special repertoire?" she purred.

He wasn't sure he liked the thought of her extra-special anything if it involved other guys and that collection of colored silicone and latex on the dresser. So much for "live and let live" and not getting involved.

She glanced at her dresser. "You might enjoy some of those, too."

"What if I said I wouldn't?"

"I'd say you weren't very experimental." Although, after last night, she knew better.

"Don't push your luck." He set the vibrator back on the dresser, sensitive to curiously earnest feelings that had no place in this strictly sex scenario.

"What if I like to?"

"You're gonna lose, babe." His hands slid downward, curved under her bottom. "I'm bigger," he murmured, pulling her into his erection, reminding himself why he was here.

"I don't know whether to be frightened or consoled."

He gave her an assessing look. "Why don't we play it by ear?" And bending low, he kissed her, ungently, unequivocally, with a kind of machismo promise that left little doubt about who would be doing what to whom, making sure she knew what that promise meant by holding her firmly against the bulge in his jeans.

Not that she minded a bit, his erection her target zone of bliss. "Ummm . . ." She moved her hips in a slow, gentle undulation, focused, really focused on what she'd been wanting all day. Anticipation racheted up another heated notch with each brushing sway of her hips, only two layers of denim separating her from nirvana. Easing her mouth away, she murmured, "This is better than chocolate . . ."

His heated gaze warmed her clear down to her toes.

"Maybe even better than shoe shopping," she breathed.

"Too bad we don't have some chocolate syrup." He glanced at her toys. "We could try it inside . . . with whipping cream . . ."

"I could say something really cheesy."

"And unoriginal."

"Speak for yourself." She placed her palms on his chest and pushed away enough so he could see her displeasure. "We haven't all gone 'round the world a dozen times."

Was he actually pleased that she'd said what she'd said—that she had sexual boundaries? Was it possible he subscribed to the double standard after all? Were those guys she'd sketched really the result of some creative process and not a record of her busy sex life? "How many times—you know . . . have you gone—" Christ, he must be losing it, asking such a question.

"You first."

"Never."

"Liar."

Was he that transparent? "Your turn," he said, figuring a bluff was a bluff only if you didn't cave.

"Never, and unlike you, it's the truth. I lead a very quiet life."

He *had* lost it, 'cuz he liked her answer.

"How quiet?"

"What? Are you the morality police?"

"Humor me, and I'll be sure you come with every one of those fucking dildos and vibrators."

"If you must know I haven't had a date or sex or whatever you want to call it since, Christ, probably February or March. Until last night, of course. I've been busy with this store and hadn't even missed it." She smiled. "And now, thanks to you, I'm damned near a nympho. Naturally, I will expect suitable compensation for my disclosures."

He grinned—everywhere actually . . . from his toes to his probably maladjusted brain that took strange pleasure in her recent celibacy. "A promise is a promise—if you want, we'll go down the whole line of those sex toys. Although I intend to get off, too. I'm not that unselfish."

"We better not compare selfish motives, 'cuz I'm way ahead of you. In fact, I'm thinking a Bangkok quickie."

His brows rose into his hair line.

"I just read a thriller set in the red light district in Bangkok. Very enlightening. But I just meant a wham, bam, thank you ma'am would be very nice first. If that's all right?"

"Or we could use one of those G-spot dildos if you're looking for instant gratification. They're pretty intense."

Her gaze narrowed. "You must have read that in a book somewhere."

"I believe I read that same Bangkok book as you."

"Swift."

"Not always. As I recall, sometimes you like it slow and easy."

"That's it." She reached for the zipper on his jeans. "I have to come in the next two minutes, or I'm going to explode."

"No toys?"

"Only this one," she murmured, sliding the zipper down on his jeans and helping herself to what was inside his boxers. As her fingers curled around his engorged penis, she exhaled a little sigh.

Neither moved for a very long time—with the exception of

the blood rushing through their veins. He finally said on a suffocated breath, "Let go a minute."

She shook her head.

Her eyes were shut, she was trembling, and it didn't take a genius to understand there wasn't much time. Holding her around the waist, he lifted her just enough to carry her to the bed without dislodging her grip. But there was no way around it once he dropped her on the bed and he murmured, "Just a second," when she cried out at losing him. Unzipping her jeans, he jerked them off, then her panties, and shoving her thighs apart, he entered her. He felt like he was being graded for speed, but what the hell—it wasn't as though it was a hardship to give her a quickie. It wasn't as though he hadn't thought about burying himself inside her sweet cunt for most of the day. Just. Like. This . . .

His eyes went shut, his brain went retrograde in primal mode and fingers splayed, he held her hips and jammed himself in so deep he felt the jolt all the way up his spine.

"Oh, God," she whispered, shuddering beneath him, holding him in a death grip, and arching up to meet his down thrust. "Oh, God, oh, God, oh, *God!*"

She came like she did with utter stillness and an explosive scream, and he came a second later with a muffled grunt and a series of ejaculations so powerful he was thinking about screaming, too.

Long moments later, when the world had expanded beyond the orgasmic microcosm, when she was once again capable of speech, she softly sighed. "You *have* to come over more often."

"Who said I'm leaving?" he murmured into her shoulder, his weight braced on his elbows through sheer instinct, the concept of actual movement still not registering on his sensory receptors.

"You're big," she whispered. "I really like that."

"Here?" He moved inside her—ever so slightly.

"Everywhere." She ran her hands down his back, resting her palms in the dip of his spine, feeling deliciously overwhelmed by his size, inside and out. Feeling dominated in the nicest sense of the word. Feeling small when she wasn't—every feminine hormone in her body quivering in delight. "I think there's something to be said for—"

"Quickies?" He lifted his head and grinned.

"Absolutely. And also for—"

"Simultaneous orgasms?"

"Do you mind? I'm trying to be profound."

He laughed. "It might be wasted on me, but shoot."

"I was going to say for compatibility—or a connection . . . like—I don't know . . . but something's different, that's for sure. I almost blew my head off that time."

"I did. And as soon as I catch my breath, I'm gonna do it again."

Ah, the great divide. She was feeling all cuddly and wistful, and he was avoiding talking about anything but fucking. Not that she ordinarily even brought up the subject of feelings after intercourse. Every woman knew it was a major taboo. "Who says I'm going to let you do it again?" she playfully murmured, not about to lose out on the best sex she'd ever had by being too earnest. She knew when to change the subject.

"Who says I'm gonna ask?" he murmured, doing one of those mortar and pestle circles inside her vagina.

He was hard again or still hard or what the hell—perfect. There was no way she was going to argue with him when his enormous cock was touching all her quivering nerve endings with virtuoso precision. "You won't hear a discouraging word from me." She gazed up at him, flexed her vaginal muscles, heard him suck in his breath, and smiled.

Virtuoso talents were not exclusively a male preserve.

They took it slow and easy that time, like they were plowing the north forty on a hot, sultry day and there was no point in working up a sweat to get the job done.

He'd smile once in a while and kiss her, his lazy rhythm unaltered.

She drifted in that never-never land of uncensored, grandiose pleasure, not sure how long she could last, but hoping forever and a day was not solely a poetic phrase.

"Tell me when," he whispered, as if she could.

She couldn't even begin to form a sentence.

And long moments later—or was it hours later—he breathed, "Now," as if he could fine-tune the synapses in her brain, as if he could do anything. Instantly, an incredible rush of pleasure inundated her slippery vaginal flesh and overwrought senses, flooded her brain, and melted through her body.

And neither one made a sound that time when they came.

As though they were awed spectators at the beginning of the world.

He rolled away afterward and lay on his back, utterly still, his arm over his eyes.

Had she done something wrong? Not that she was going to ask; his silence was intimidating. At least if he was leaving, her climaxes had been so fabulous she could run off the fumes for months. She decided to just be grateful.

As the silence lengthened, a couple hundred thoughts streaked through her brain—none of which she verbalized. She hated when men shut down, like they'd moved to another universe. All that Mars and Venus stuff was for real. Women talked about their feelings—not now though, with him looking dead over there. And men never did.

Which left her lying here pretending it wasn't quiet as a tomb.

She gazed at the ceiling, looked out the window, counted the neighbor's roof shingles until she got to a hundred and lost interest. Should she get out of bed and find something to eat? Order a pizza?

She found herself fixating on her hunger. And with good reason, she decided. She hadn't eaten much today—a couple cookies and an iced tea at the store—maybe a half dozen cookies if she was counting. Okay, eight or nine, but that wasn't so much for all day. Would she sound overly gauche if she asked him if he was hungry?

Was such a question out of place in a situation like this— postcoital, with a man she didn't know very well? Other than the ultimate intimacies of hot sex, of course, which didn't help much when it came to the question of his appetite for food or the lack thereof.

She finally blurted out, "Are you hungry?" because the question had risen to her lips at least twenty times before it just popped out of its own accord.

Food was one of the basic human drives, too.

Not just sex.

Raising his arm marginally, he turned his head the smallest distance possible to see her and said with what could only be described as incredulity, "You mean food?"

She nodded her head like a bobble doll. "I was thinking about a pizza." In the postcoital hush, pizza had gained prominence in her thoughts—one of those deep-dish ones with a cheese crust, lots of mozzarella, and everything on it including black olives and anchovies. She'd burned off more than enough calories. Sex was excellent exercise.

"I'm not hungry."

Now what did she do? "I'd like one," she said. Coy wasn't one of her strong suits. She also had this tendency to obsess.

He slid up on one elbow. "Then order one."

"You don't mind?"

"Why should I mind?" What he minded and what was bothering the hell out of him were the sensations she aroused that had nothing to do with sex. Like wanting to see her outside of bed and thinking of her more or less constantly. That she might be a thief only increased the muddle in his brain. On the other hand, his not-wanting-to-get-in-too-deep reservations had to be weighed against the awesome orgasms he'd recently experienced. Not really a contest there—so what the hell. He shrugged away his misgivings.

"Could you eat some?"

Having dismissed worrisome perplexities of emotional distance or the lack thereof, his grin was instant. "Depends on what you mean."

"Cute. I'm ordering an everything pizza. Okay?"

"Fine."

"Should I order a large?"

"Go for it. There's money in my jeans' pocket."

"I can pay for it." Leaning over, she reached for the phone.

"I was going to take you to dinner. Let me."

"We could go to dinner later." She found herself considering his dinner invitation with a dewy-eyed susceptibility that must have something to do with his talented cock. She was never dewy-eyed, and her alter ego Marky B didn't know what susceptibility meant.

"If you want to." Suddenly, he wasn't sure he'd meant it, those keeping-your-distance habits of a lifetime kicking in again.

She turned her head at his gruff tone. "What was that?"

"Nothing." Christ, be civil. "Sorry."

"You sure?"

"Yeah." He smiled. "Too much caffeine today," he lied. "I get jumpy. Why don't we go to Dominic's later," he said, telling himself a dinner was just a dinner, not a one-way street to commitment. "They're open till one."

There. A normal tone. Polite. "Sounds good," she said, reminding herself not to get wrapped up in some guy she'd sworn not to look at a few days ago. A guy who had women running after him big time. No way was she going to be added to *that* disposable list.

While she was ordering the pizza, he slid from the bed and walked over to the dresser. He was here for sex. He wasn't here to make any changes in his life. Getting back on track, he lifted one toy, then another, checking them out with a quick once-over until he reached the Hitachi Magic Wand. "Where's the attachment?" he asked, half turning to glance at her as she hung up the phone.

He was nude, apparently not shy about his nakedness, and Lordy, Lordy, look at that lovely erection. With the partial turn, his arousal was beautifully profiled. She didn't know if she was in need of that G-Whiz attachment or not when she had the real thing larger than life and looking mighty available. "I must have left it in the drawer."

"Let's try the Nubby G then." He picked a clear plastic vibrator. "The pizza won't be here for a while."

His tone was neutral, like he couldn't decide if he wanted to be here or not. "You're not paying for this," she said, taking offense at all that cool equanimity. "You don't have to get your money's worth."

"I thought maybe this equipment"—he indicated the toys with a wave of his hand—"meant *you* wanted your money's worth." So he wasn't quite back on track yet.

"I'm satisfied," she said in place of "Screw you." "If you're done, you don't have to be polite. You can go home."

"Do I look like I'm done?"

He'd turned completely now, and there was no doubt he was primed and ready.

She should have said something equally rude. She should have insisted he leave. But a cock that hard and long was difficult to turn away, especially after having experienced the full gamut of its capabilities. "I don't know what the hell you're mad about." Oops, that wasn't going to get her access to that fabulous dick. On the other hand, when had she found it necessary to beg for sex? "Look, you don't look like you want to be here—other than Mr. Happy there. So . . ."

He was trying real hard to tell himself this was just another hot babe who happened to be into sex toys. He liked hot babes with sex toys. This wasn't the time to foul things up by thinking too much. "I don't feel like leaving," he said, polite now, back in the program. "If that's okay with you?"

She smiled. "So stay. I ordered a large." Her smile widened. "Pizza that is. As for you, I must have just gotten lucky."

She was switching gears, keeping it light. Anyone with half

a brain would follow suit. Right now his brains were pretty much in his dick, so ignoring knotty questions was becoming easier by the second. Lifting the Nubby G, he moved toward the bed. "Does your G-spot feel lucky?"

"I feel lucky everywhere," she said with a smile, stretching with a languid arch of her back that brought her lush breasts into prominence.

"Then open up," he murmured, back on full auto-pilot. Nudging her legs apart, he slipped the wide curved head of the vibrator into her sleek flesh. "Mr. Nubby has first pass, but I'm comin' in next."

And he did both—Mr. Nubby first and then himself—with the kind of finesse and skill she'd learned to expect and adore.

Until the pizza man rang the doorbell.

"I'll be right back," he said, withdrawing and shoving the Cherry Top glass dildo inside her so quickly she only squeaked faintly as the cool, ridged glass met her hot flesh. "Don't move."

Not likely, or not very much anyway, considering the dildo was glass and she was too lazy to actually move her arms when she had a sexual provocateur of the first magnitude at her disposal. Eyes shut, she heard the zipper on his jeans zip, heard the bedroom door open and shut, and left to her own devices, considered how fortunate she'd been to go to the parade with Megan, happen to see Buddy, and bump into Danny Rees again.

It was all about Fate.

It was all about being in the right place at the right time.

Like now.

Ummm . . . she moved her hips faintly.

Just . . . like . . . now . . .

TWELVE

DOMINIC'S WINE BAR WASN'T PACKED AT MID-
night on Sunday. But several tables still had customers,
and the bar was busy with the tail-end-of-the-weekend
crowd. People who had been on the river for a couple days and
weren't ready to drive back to the Cities yet were drinking wine
and eating tapas: a few large boat owners conspicuous for their
tans and expensive watches—some with their wives . . . others
with women too young to be their wives—or at least their first
wives; the houseboat contingent who drove SUVs instead of
Beemers and talked golf instead of racketball; a shop owner or
two from the stores on the main street who needed to wind
down after dealing with ten thousand tourists since Friday; and
the boat bunnies with exposed cleavage and styled hair that never
saw river water.

Stella wouldn't have been able to ignore the leggy women

even if she'd tried, because they swiveled around on their bar stools when she and Danny walked in and waved and shouted his name—the Pam Anderson–like bartender included.

Danny smiled and waved back while Stella tried to look poised—although she wasn't going to be able to maintain her poise for long with the level of competition at the bar. Why hadn't she put on makeup or worn something more fashionable than jeans and a super-hero T-shirt?

"Everyone knows me because I come in here a lot," Danny murmured, hoping his explanation for the obvious warmth with which he'd been greeted would fly.

"I figured."

"They're just friends."

"Right."

Not a good tone. "Would you rather go somewhere else?" He wasn't being polite; he was trying to avoid trouble. He'd slept with some of the ladies at the bar.

While Stella was debating the immaturity of answering "God-damn right," the blond bartender slid a glass across the bar and called out, "Here's your favorite, Rees! It's on the house!"

"One drink?" A query, wary in the extreme. Bolting was still an option.

If Stella had known Danny Rees for more than a two-night stand, she might have had reason to sulk. As it was, she was probably in the same boat, friendship-wise, as those ladies at the bar. So she went for maturity. Sort of. "The bartender knows your *favorite*?" she said, only half-bitchy.

Ignoring the innuendo, Danny stuck to the facts. "I mostly drink one kind of wine."

She'd bet her Barry Smith–signed *Conan* comic that he didn't restrict himself to one woman though. Those boat bunnies were really *thrilled* to see him, which pretty much extinguished the warm, cuddly afterglow from her evening of prime sex. "I suppose one drink can't hurt." Other than flounce off or throw a hissy fit, what could she say?

"Thanks." A modicum of relief. "We won't stay long." Taking her hand, he approached the bar, being sure he placed himself between Stella and the other women as they sat down. Not that his strategic placement did much good with the general tenor of the conversation that was decidedly flirtatious and filled with allusions to shared experiences. The ladies and Danny knew the same people, had spent considerable time together on the river, and apparently had participated in some fund-raiser for the city park this spring that, wouldn't you know it, had a raffle for a date with a local bachelor. Guess who was one of the bachelors?

These ladies weren't casual acquaintances, Stella realized. No one had to hit her over the head with a two by four. Drinking the glass of wine that had been sharply plunked down before her, Stella prepared to take in the newest installment of the local reality show, *Who's Going to Sleep with Danny Rees?* Each of the women were clearly intent on playing that role.

She could have been invisible for all the notice the women took of her as they teased and flirted with Danny. She could have been run over by a bulldozer and none of them would have batted an eyelash. Most irritating, they all seemed to know their way around his swimming pool and knew his sister's decorating taste down to the towels in the bathroom.

Perhaps they'd been to his house for a party, she told herself, trying to be nonjudgmental. Then again, they might have had the same personal tour she'd had, which was more likely.

While they were all laughing about some picnic on the sand-bar near Hudson, she cautioned herself to reason. The women were apparently friends of much longer standing than she. She also reminded herself that the notion of jealousy was completely outrageous when she'd known Danny for a grand total of two days. She was not a crazy person. She was a rational adult and she would act like one. Smile, look interested, be polite.

Okay, that tight-lipped smile gave him about thirty seconds to get out of this place without an explosion. Coming here had been a major mistake. Gulping down the rest of his Le Pergole red, he set down his empty glass. "Ready?" he said, not waiting for Stella to answer, coming to his feet.

"Leaving so soon?" A redhead twirled one of her bright red curls around a perfectly manicured finger and pouted prettily.

"It's getting late," Danny said, helping Stella down from the bar stool and sliding his arm around her waist.

"I left a message for you at your house," the redhead said, her voice all sultry and friendly. "Call me."

Stella eased away, thin-skinned and edgy. "Call me," meant something else entirely, like so much of the conversation that had just transpired between Danny and these ladies who knew him so well.

"Will do," he said, bland as oatmeal, pulling Stella back, counting on her not making a scene.

The redhead sat up a little straighter, bringing her near-perfect boobs into greater prominence, her halter top showing some major cleavage. "I mean it, Danny. It's important."

"Yeah, right, Marisa," the bartender interposed, giving the redhead a dubious look. "But speaking of important, Danny, don't forget Grady's party next week. His brother's rockin' band is gonna play."

"And I need my bikini back sometime if you think of it," a pretty brunette said with a warm smile. "It's a silver one."

As if there were fifty bikinis that had been left behind at Danny's, Stella disgustedly thought, feeling put upon when she had no right. But jeez—these chicks were really working it. And they were all pretty or beautiful, depending on your taste, with excellent cosmetic dental work and glowing smiles for the man they obviously knew up close and personal.

Two of them wore real jewelry with their casual clothes.

The bring-over-my-swimsuit lady for one.

As a working girl, Stella noticed multiple chunky gold bracelets and diamonds that could be used for wine bottle stoppers. As a hard working girl, she always viewed women like that—Stillwater in the summer had its share—with a mixture of envy and anarchist disapproval. Some were Minnesota's equivalent of Hollywood bimbos; others, divorcées with good settlements—all of them on the make for a rich husband in the bars and on the boats where yacht-owning men with money gathered.

And tonight, the boat bunnies who could afford it were dressed for success in expensive linen sports clothes, little custom-made sandals in colorful matching colors, and the inevitable watch with a pastel leather band that looked sporty and cost six months salary for a normal person. Why couldn't she have been born rich?

At that moment of existential dissatisfaction, Danny said, "Good night ladies," like he was leaving a church supper and didn't have a care in the world and gently guided Stella toward the door.

What the hell was that, she thought as they moved toward the exit. How often was he party to public displays of way too much affection that he could deal with it so unemotionally? Don't answer that. And don't even consider getting involved with a man who could look at all those fawning females with total indifference.

Short moments later, as they stood on the sidewalk outside, Danny said, "Sorry about that. Everyone's had a few too many drinks this time of night."

Stella bit back a rude remark. Her mother would have been proud. "They all seem to be good friends of yours." How was that? Pithy, but equivocal. Like a diplomat.

What could he say? He could lie, but under the circumstances, even the best lie would look pretty lame. "Yeah," he said. "They are. If you're still hungry we could go somewhere else." Because the pizza had gone cold at Stella's house while they had better things to do, food might be a priority for her. "I didn't feel like staying there to eat."

He probably could have eaten just about anything he wanted in there, she thought, but censured the vulgarity. "I'm not really hungry," she said. "And look, it's been great, but it's getting late and I have to open the store early. I'll just walk home from here. It's only a few blocks. Go on back in and visit with your friends." She hadn't intended to sound so bitchy. But if he wanted to be with those women, he could fucking go.

"I'll give you a ride home." He could have apologized again, but he didn't feel like it. So he dated other women. She dated other guys—her rogues gallery of a sketchbook evidence of that he was guessing.

"No thanks. Really, I'm fine." That was better. Almost polite. He could date whom he wished.

"Suit yourself." His voice couldn't have been more tactful.

She smiled. "I usually do."

"I know."

She gave him a look. "What does that mean?"

"Nothing."

"Do you have some problem?"

"You're being childish. Let me give you a ride home."

The last thing she needed after witnessing such undisguised adulation for the benefit of one male ego, was that self-centered man telling her she was childish. "Fuck you," she said really, really softly. She wouldn't want him to think she was immature enough to scream at him.

"No thanks," he said even more softly. "I'm not in the mood."

"I thought you were always in the mood." It was a contest on who could speak more quietly.

"You're thinking of yourself. I like to take a breather once in a while."

"You could have fooled me."

"I was being polite."

"Like hell." And then she walked away before she did something really childish and called him all the expletives that were piling up in her brain. Damn him. As if he was doing her a favor, the smug bastard.

DANNY ALMOST DRAGGED her back. But he wasn't completely witless yet, although two nights of mind-blowing sex with her had definitely brought him to the edge. He exhaled slowly, inhaled, and told himself to get a grip. No way was he going to get into an argument over his women friends. He glanced

at the lights of Dominic's and debated going back inside. There
was plenty of diversion there if he wanted it.

But did he?

Good question.

One he wouldn't have had to ponder a few days ago when his
tastes were simple.

What the hell. It was late. He was tired. He wasn't in the
mood for revenge sex.

But he walked down the main street before returning to his
truck, giving Stella time to get home. Don't ask him why; he
didn't have an answer. And then like a stupid kid, he drove by her
house. Christ, he must be losing it.

The house was dark; she was tucked away in bed already.

As if he cared, he told himself.

He hit the gas.

The last thing he needed was some bitch giving him a hard time.

THIRTEEN

ON HER WALK HOME STELLA HAD HAD AMPLE TIME to scrutinize her taste in men, and she'd come to the conclusion that she'd been right in the first place. Men like Danny Rees were nothing but trouble. The Reeses of the world lived thoroughly selfish, me-first lives that revolved around their every whim. And in his case, because he didn't have a *real* job, he was able to indulge himself even more than most Peter Pan men. That was another thing. Her mother would freak if she was sleeping with a drug dealer.

Let's face it: he could say all he wanted about designing video games, but if he was really making a living at it, he would have mentioned the names of the games. Not that she was familiar with game titles, but her kids at the store knew every one since the beginning of time. In fact, Ryan Kath was busy trying to design a video game and, knowing him, he might actually do it. She should ask him if he knew anyone in the neighborhood who had a hit game. Video games were like pop fiction or top ten music. If you had a winner, people knew about it. And Danny's name wasn't on anyone's celebrity list in her store.

So . . . realistically, she probably could discount that little line—"I design video games."

Also, women like Kirsty and those boat bunnies tonight were always friendly with drug dealers; what better place to score free dope? In fact, Danny's damned fabulous performance in bed probably had something to do with Ecstasy. Duh. Why hadn't she thought of that before?

By the time she reached home, she'd pretty much convinced herself that the unvarnished truth about Danny Rees didn't add up to a guy one would take home to dinner. Not that she was looking; it was pure labeling. So with all her priorities in place, now all she had to do, she reflected, climbing the stairs to her front yard, was convince her addicted senses that sexual gratification was no big thing.

Damn, though. Wasn't that the way it goes.

You think you have a hand on nirvana, and it's all an illusion.

But what the hay, she had some really fine memories—sex-wise. And that wasn't so bad.

She only thought of Danny Rees ten thousand times while getting ready for bed—down from twenty earlier in the day. She was practically cured.

Now if only she didn't have to sleep in the same bed they'd just made love in, forgetting him might be within the realm of possibility. Thank God the store opened early on week days. After the kids poured in, she wouldn't have as much time to fixate on him.

Climbing into bed, she wondered if she'd be able to sleep a wink.

But after two busy days and busier nights, she dozed off immediately, slept like the dead, and came awake to a ringing phone.

"Sorry to call so early, but you won't believe what Deloitte did this weekend. He went on TV and lied about my policy toward the so-called healthy forest logging in the state park. I could kill him! Are you there? Are you alive? Do I have the wrong number?"

"I'm here," Stella murmured, lying on her stomach, squinting at the clock. Seven-thirty. "Run that by me again. I'm still half asleep."

Megan repeated her comments along with additional phrases from the local TV talk show that she'd taped and had practically memorized since yesterday. "Where have you been? I tried calling you last night."

"I must have turned down the phone." Danny had turned it off, but she wasn't about to reveal any irrelevant details, because that relationship was over. Completely. Dead. Kaput.

"The reason I called—I barely slept last night—was that I'd like you to design my green campaign signs earlier so they could help answer these baseless charges. It just burns me that someone can outright lie about you and get away with it. I'm pissed—really pissed—and I want to refute this ass's comments from the rooftops."

"I'll do it today."

"Thanks, sweetie. Go back to sleep. I'll talk to you later. I'll come over after the kids go to their game day at the park. We can brainstorm."

Brainstorming would mean she'd have to dislodge Danny Rees's image from her brain, where it was taking up most of the space, but Stella politely said, "Come over any time. I'm here."

"Thanks. You're a rock."

"That's me," Stella blithely lied, when she found herself shaky within seconds of waking—due to an apparently mega-addiction to sex with Danny Rees. "Bring muffins and a latte." Comfort food in place of sex.

"Muffins aren't good for you. Carbs, sugar, trans fats."

"Just bring two then. I'll taper off."

As Stella stretched to hang up the phone, her gaze fell on some little pink rabbit ears peeking out from under the bed. She groaned. Reminders of last night she didn't need. Not when her addiction was requiring a serious fix. Jerking away from the edge of the bed, she rolled over and caught sight of her sketch page of Danny-cum-super hero that she'd tossed on her bedside table. Oops, not good, either. There was Danny Rees's face smiling at her. She shut her eyes, counted to ten, then twenty, trying to do that zen thing where you concentrate on the number, visualize it, and rid your brain of everything but the image of the number. As if. By the time she got to twenty-two, she was daydreaming about having sex with the man who unfortunately was also the dream date of all those women at Dominic's last night, which meant if she wanted any more action from him, she'd better get in line. And after her bitchy leave-taking last night, even getting in line might not suffice. She'd probably have to frigging apologize.

Not likely that.

She had a drawer full of sex toys. She could take care of herself.

Female pride. Rah, rah, rah.

Jumping out of bed, deliberately not glancing at the rabbit

ears, she quickly dressed and brought her Marky B drawings and a fresh sketch pad down to the store. Better to distance herself from her bedroom, rely on denial and displacement, and transpose her unwanted yearnings to Marky B and her fight for justice. Perhaps it might be time to get rid of Marky's new sidekick. Have him killed off in some heroic struggle for freedom. There was no need to be ubernasty. After all, Danny Rees couldn't be faulted for his capacity to give pleasure on demand, every which way.

Do. Not. Go. There. Recollections of inexplicable bliss were forbidden. Walks down memory lane were for those more naive than she. She was strong. She was woman. She was invincible. Damn! Where were her caffeine and muffins when she *needed them for personal and spiritual strength?*

Ryan Kath suddenly swam into her field of vision, banged on the door window as if she wasn't looking straight at him, and signaled her to open up. Her savior had appeared as if by magic—in the guise of a skinny, gawky kid with a scowl.

Opening the door, she resisted the impulse to throw her arms around him and cause him to run for his life. She smiled instead. "You're up early."

"I came over to work on that video game."

Maybe he wasn't a complete savior—what with that video game allusion. But he was a body. He could talk. Hey, it beat reviewing the constant round of Rees images looping through her brain. "That video game book's probably still on the table in the back. Did you have breakfast? Need a cookie or some instant oatmeal?"

He looked at her from under his long eyelashes—his best feature, although he wouldn't care to hear the girlie compliment. "Do I look like I eat oatmeal?"

"It's supposed to be good for you."

"Do you eat it?"

"Sometimes." She was probably ten the last time she ate it, but she always bought some just in case the urge for good nutrition struck her. "What kind of cookie do you want?"

"An everything one. Thanks."

Ryan always thanked her when she fed him or gave him some comics or helped him navigate the minefield of his home life. He didn't get effusive. It was always that single word—thanks. But she knew he meant it. She handed him a cookie and an orange juice from her cooler case. "How's it going with the game?"

"Not bad. Come look."

By the time Megan arrived, Ryan had given Stella a basic overview of the computer graphics used to construct a game. He didn't know all the sophisticated software necessary to code the action, but he was going to take a class next fall he'd said. Stella shared one of her muffins with him and left him happily ensconced in the window bay drawing characters for his game.

"Okay, give me the dirt," Stella said as she led Megan to the front of the store. "What do you want to say on your signs to screw Deloitte or make yourself a hero?"

"It's not about heroes and villains. It's about issues."

"Except when they lie about you. You gotta fight back."

Megan made a face and sat down in one of Stella's comfy chairs. "I suppose you're right."

"Damn right I am." After last night, she was in the mood for a fight. "Talk to me about this change Deloitte's pushing in the state park, and we'll try to think of some snappy slogans. And thanks for the muffins." Stella held up her latte. "And this—the miracle drug of the gods. My brain is fried."

"What *did* you do last night?"

"Not much. Took it easy." Lies, lies. "Went to bed early." Fact. "What did you do?" Avoid disclosure with a question of your own.

"The kids and I went to a Disney movie. It wasn't bad. The new animation is damned realistic. Unlike my opponent's comments, I might add."

Stella pulled out her sketchbook. "We'll have to straighten him out. What's the environmental impact here with the healthy forests law changes?"

"Our state park north of town would be devastated. The lumber companies can take out old growth wood. Some of the big money behind Deloitte is lumber industry money."

"That explains it. But if people understand, they're gonna be on your side. Who doesn't like the state park? It's packed every weekend and all summer long."

"We have to let everyone know what's going on."

"In plain language that people can remember like, 'It's the economy, stupid.'"

"Maybe we could picture some of the campers and hikers. A state park that's so heavily used should have tons of supporters."

"How about 'Preserve His World' with a picture of a kid and his dog, sitting under one of those gorgeous Douglas firs? Maybe with a fishing pole beside him, like Huck Finn?"

"That's perfect! I love it! It's apple pie and wilderness America rolled into one! You should be working for an ad agency!"

"But then I'd have to get up and go to work every morning like I did for years. No thanks. I like working my own schedule."

"I hate to even ask, but how long will it take to get ready? Deloitte's comments are going to set me back in the polls."

"I'll have it ready for the printer in a couple days."

"You're an absolute sweetheart!"

Stella smiled. "So I've been told." As recently as last night, as a matter of fact. Not that it would do her much good now.

"Did he call? Is that what you're talking about?"

"No. Just a general comment." Stella didn't want to get into the good and the bad about last night. Especially because everything was over. "What do I owe you for the muffins and coffee?"

"Are you kidding when you're designing my sign for me? I guess I can afford a couple bucks for your talents."

"I won't be able to start until tonight. The kids and the store keep me pretty busy all day. But I'll put in some time after supper."

"I'll owe you big time. Think of something I can do for you."

"Don't worry about it. You do plenty for me."

"If this thing with Danny Rees doesn't work out, you have a shoulder to cry on. Don't forget. Any time, day or night."

"I'm guessing it was a one-night stand like you said. Not that I was expecting much else. *C'est la vie* with a guy like him. He doesn't take prisoners."

"You don't sound heartbroken."

"Believe me, a night with him had nothing to do with my heart."

Megan grinned. "What was I thinking?"

"Lose that suburban mind-set, babe. Get into the fast lane. Hot bodies like Danny Rees aren't looking for romance."

"You sound sensible about it all."

"I've had time to come back to reality after my sexual nirvana. The pink cloud's gone, and here I am, happy as a clam."

"For real? You sounded frenzied yesterday morning."

"I'm over it." Stella made a thumbs-up sign. "Absolutely." She was guessing it was the caffeine that loosened her tongue and made the lies flow like water.

Megan smiled. "I'm impressed. Such maturity."

Stella was impressed, too, with her new ability to lie like a rug. How much easier than embarrassing herself and telling the truth about Danny Rees's super abundant sex life with boat bunnies et al.

The two kids she was tutoring walked in the door just then and tossed their math books on a table. "Duty calls," Stella murmured, with a nod toward the boys who were already reading comics. "Make yourself at home if you want, but I'm going to get their homework done while they're fresh." She grinned. "Less whining. I'll give you a call tonight."

FOURTEEN

DANNY WAS OUT IN HIS POLE BARN THAT MORN-
ing, polishing his '88 Lotus. It was a mindless task, but he
worked up a sweat and he needed to burn off some energy.
He'd spent a sleepless night, finally flicking on cable and watching some stupid subtitled film that had had one of the most unhappy endings. That misery hadn't helped his sullen mood, and
having given up on sleep, he'd put on some shorts and had come
out to his pole barn where he kept his cars.

He collected mostly odd cars that caught his eye. Not always
top-end models, although the company he'd founded gave him a
flashy car like a Ferrari or Lamborghini every year as a bonus. He
even drove those testosterone machines once in a while. But
mostly he kept his car collection in his pole barn and polished a
model or two when he was trying to think or trying not to think.
It was his form of therapy.

He'd recently bought the Lotus on eBay and was still infatuated with it—like a kid with a new toy. Painted bright yellow
with a black leather interior and the best stereo known to man at
the time, it was one sweet machine.

Like Stella Scott was sweet—in the carnal sense. And in a couple other ways as well. He liked her . . . and her comic book
store.

But not her quick temper.

He wasn't in the market for aggravation. No more than he was
in the market for permanence. It had been nice, but not *that* nice.

As the phone rang that morning, he'd checked out his caller
ID, not in the mood to deal with any problems from the office in
L.A. They'd have to manage without him today or punt. Produc-
tion wasn't in crisis mode right now, anyway. Whatever issues
they had could wait.

When he'd sold his company shortly after college, he'd stayed
on the board of Riverfront Games and continued to serve as
chief designer. With 160,000,000 people playing *Blizzard 9000*
at twelve dollars a month, the buyers didn't want to lose his expertise. Nor was he in the mood to throw in the towel and retire
at thirty-two.

The new game he was designing was in the fun stage at
the moment; he was still changing more than he was keeping.
Maybe in another six months, he'd have all the kinks ironed out
and he'd send it in to corporate. In the meantime, if anyone had
any questions that couldn't be answered via e-mail or phone,
they'd have to fly out to see him.

He preferred his privacy here on the farm. The land had be-
longed to his grandparents, and as a kid, he'd spent summers
here. He knew the area. He liked that no one bothered him.

At least no one had until recently.

Now with the break-in, he had a potentially hazardous situation for Riverfront Games's bottom line.

Along with the added problem of Stella Scott, who had become hazardous to *his* fucking peace of mind.

Leaning hard on the bumper, he put his shoulder into it, rubbing the sheep's wool—circle, swirl, circle, swirl, circle, circle, circle. Out damned spot, out, out, out. If only he could erase Stella's image as easily. Reaching over, he turned the volume up on the boom box at his feet. Nothing like loud music to drown out the harsh realities of the world.

He didn't hear the phone when it rang, but the flashing caller ID caught his eye. At the sight of Buddy's name, he lunged for the stereo volume button and the phone at the same time, scraping the skin off his wrist in the process. Kicking the work bench, he picked up the phone, still swearing under his breath.

"Not a good time?"

"A minor mishap. Nothing earth-shaking. What's up?" Not that Danny was fussy. Any diversion was welcome.

"I was wondering how the rest of your weekend went?"

"Can't complain." An understatement of major proportions considering the volatility of his sexual activities. It took him a second to temper his voice to a mildness he wasn't feeling. "Yours?"

"The usual. Sun, drinks, the river. What's not to like? We're golfing at Stoneridge this afternoon. Care to join us?"

"What time?" As if the polish on the Lotus wouldn't wait.

"Tee time's at one. You know Darren and Louis. Maybe we'll check out The Cat Fish Bar afterward."

"I'll meet you there."

"Sounds good."

"See ya." Danny literally breathed a sigh of relief as he hung up, although he chose to overlook that fleeting moment of desperation. He liked to golf with Buddy, he thought in the next swift synapse, obliterating rash exhalations and strung out nerves. Tossing aside the sheepskin mitt, he closed the can of polish, shut off the lights, and walked toward the house sucking on his scraped wrist. He probably should return those L.A. calls before he left, he decided, his mood on the rise. There were times when his sane counsel was badly needed in LaLa Land. And Larry, the marketing manager, had made most of those calls. It probably wouldn't hurt to eat, either. Five espressos weren't exactly the breakfast of champions.

He was even in a good enough mood after breakfast and his L.A. calls to pick up when Marisa called. He was about to walk out the door. The timing couldn't have been better. "Sorry, Marisa, can't talk. I'm on my way out," he said, picking up his golf bag.

"Just when I was thinking of coming over and keeping you company," she purred. "What are you doing that's better than a nice afternoon in bed?"

"I'm golfing with Buddy."

"I didn't know you golfed."

Because they essentially met in bed, he wasn't surprised. "I do on occasion. And Buddy's waiting, so I gotta go."

"You don't know what you're missing." A low, sultry offer of sex in every syllable.

"Maybe some other time." His voice was polite. "I'll give you a call."

"See that you do. I miss your many talents. Ciao, baby."

That was easy, he thought, hanging up the phone. Not even an argument. Not that it would have done any good, but Marisa could be demanding. Luckily, he'd had a bonafide excuse. She was probably already calling the next guy in her little black book.

FIFTEEN

JUST AS STELLA WAS LOCKING THE FRONT DOOR, her parents drove up. Had she forgotten they were coming? Had her brain turned to mush after two nights of nonstop sex? She'd tutored math for three hours today, so probably "no" on that one. But still, they didn't drop by much. Her mother had a busy social life, and when her father wasn't at work, he was holed up in the greenhouse he'd built out of old storm windows, propagating his roses and Siberian irises.

Oh, fuck. Her mother was carrying a casserole dish that was wafting steam as she walked from the car. And her father was similarly ladened. Damn, when she was looking forward to left-over pizza from last night. (Danny had expressed interest in Canadian bacon and pineapple; she'd ordered a large and then one thing led to another and most of the pizza had gone uneaten.)

On the plus side, the leftover pizza wouldn't mold in one night. Nor was the night yet over.

And knowing her mother's recipes, she'd be shocked if she could actually eat that casserole moving up the stairs toward her.

"Hi, darling! It's a beautiful day, isn't it!" Virginia Scott was perennially cheerful; at times it was unnerving. "I should have called," she said, walking into the store, "but I didn't want this delicious artichoke casserole to cool. And your father's bringing your favorite, apple crumble."

Perfect. Dessert with her pizza. Even her mother couldn't screw up apple crumble.

"We added some sweet little plums to the apples."

Okay. She could deal with that.

"And pine nuts."

What the hell was she thinking? Italian apple crumble? Since when? Jeez, pine nuts were even too small to pick out.

"And your father ran in to get a pint of Cowlick's homemade vanilla ice cream when we drove through town."

There was a God. "Perfect timing, Mom. Hi, Dad. Nice shirt." It warned: GLOBAL WARMING IS DETRIMENTAL TO YOUR HEALTH. "Come on upstairs, and I'll set the table."

"You're going to adore this artichoke casserole. Your father thinks it's better than the sweet potato succotash. Don't you, dear?"

"Much better," he said with a wink over his wife's head. Jerry Scott ate most of his meals at the diner downtown—good home-cooking, open six to ten, take out. Fortunately, he had the metabolism of a longshoreman, so eating another meal at home wasn't a problem at supper time. "You'll like the sun-dried tomatoes."

The only place she'd like sun-dried tomatoes was on her gro-cer's shelf. But she and her dad had maintained a conspiracy of si-lence over the years rather than hurt her mom's feeling. Her mother subscribed to every health food magazine in the country. It was amazing the vile combinations of ingredients that could be found in the recipes printed therein.

Luckily, Stella entered the kitchen first and had time to snatch up the Silver Bullet vibrator from the counter and shove it in the towel drawer before her parents walked in. Somehow she'd missed it. It was small though and easy enough to overlook. Easier than it was to forget the way it felt when operated by Danny Rees and his golden touch. Isn't that the way it goes. The stuff you want you can't have, and the stuff you don't want—like artichoke and sun-dried tomato casserole—is sitting right smack dab in the middle of your kitchen table.

She managed to gag down a few forkfuls of casserole—if you put the food way back on your tongue you couldn't taste it much . . . a secret she'd learned early on as a child. She hid a cou-ple more mouthfuls in her paper napkin when her mom wasn't looking and all in all managed to get through another experimen-tal meal of her mother's without ruffling any feathers.

"Doesn't it make you feel heathy eating like this?" Ginny Scott beamed at her family. "The casserole's chock full of nutrition. Another serving anyone?" she brightly inquired, a spoon poised above the casserole dish.

"It's pretty filling, Mom. Thanks, though."

Stella's father put his hand over his plate and shook his head. "Delicious, but I want to save some room for dessert."

"Everything's organic in the apple crumble. Even the pine nuts. I know you want a big serving, darling," she said, smiling at her daughter. "Apple crumble has been your favorite for years."

Regular apple crumble, Stella grudgingly thought. "Not too much, Mom. I ate a bunch of cookies this afternoon."

"All that sugar isn't good for you, darling."

"When I'm frustrated, I need comfort food."

"What in the world do you have to be frustrated about? You have your own business and that nice comic you do and this darling house Marty left you. Heavens, most girls your age would be thrilled to be in your shoes. Have you thought about meditation? It might calm you, dear. You always were a little high strung."

It must run in the family, Stella thought. Her mother's idea of relaxation was a nice jog around the park or rearranging her frog collection for the umpteenth time. "I'll try it, Mom—really."

"You're just pacifying me, I know, but someday you'll see how soothing it is."

"No, I promise, I'll give it a try." Right after she figured out how to forget about Danny Rees, who was the one making her frustrated in the first place.

"I brought some coconut ice cream, too," her dad said, stepping in to change the subject. "A scoop of each?" he asked, rising from his chair and moving toward the fridge.

"Two scoops each."

Her mother did one of those so-much-sugar-isn't-good-for-you frowns, but was interrupted from lapsing into her "sugar blues" lecture by the ringing of the phone.

For a fraction of a second, Stella hoped it might be Danny—the wish immediately overcome by apprehension that it might be and she'd have to talk to him in front of her parents. Scary thought with the gist of their rapport having to do with the intimacies of sex.

It was Megan calling—which was good and bad. Embarrassment was averted, but Megan wasn't Danny Rees, either. Trying to cope with the letdown, Stella explained that her folks were over for dinner and she'd not had time to work on the sign. But she would ASAP this evening, she added before hanging up.

"What sign?" her mother asked, scooping out apple crumble on three plates.

"Deloitte's out doing some of his dirty work, and Megan wants her campaign signs to challenge his smears and lies." Sitting down, Stella took the plate her mother handed her, gratified to see very few pine nuts visible to the naked eye. Out of sight, out of mind, she decided, her brain very accommodating when it came to apple crumble.

"That political family's been running this district long enough," her mother emphatically pronounced, turning to her husband. "Haven't they, Jerry?" Before he had time to answer, she went on, "Your father went to high school with Kyle Deloitte, who everyone knew was dumb as a post. But if you have money, apparently, it doesn't matter if you can't add two and two."

Her father set two ice cream containers on the table. "Megan's up against some pros with the Deloitte's, Kyle's mental acuity notwithstanding. He can buy all the brains he needs with his fortune." Sticking serving spoons into the ice cream, he sat down and inquired, "How's Megan's campaign doing?"

"Until yesterday, when Deloitte came out with the nasty lies, she's been steadily climbing in the polls. Motive no doubt for Deloitte's actions." Stella piled coconut ice cream on top of her apple crumble.

Her father gave her a sympathetic look. "Politics isn't for sissies."

"I know. I told her she had to fight back. I'll start on her sign this evening. I've got a great graphic design program on my computer."

"We won't stay long, dear, so you can get to work. And that thunder sounds like a storm is on its way. We should get home and let the cat in. As for the Deloittes, I for one wouldn't mind if they were retired from politics. It's been way too long."

Stella's father smiled. "My *dad* used to grumble about the Deloitte's stranglehold on local politics."

"Isn't it nice that our daughter's doing her part to unseat that uncharitable family?"

"Unseated remains to be seen, Mom."

"Well, I think it's commendable that Megan is taking it upon herself to play a role in our city and district. Especially after her husband—well, you know, some women would have been devastated. Your father heard his little affair is over already. The young lady found greener pastures. Isn't that right, Jerry?"

He nodded. When her father had vanilla ice cream handy, conversation took second place.

"How *is* Megan doing?" her mother asked with a commiserating sigh for Megan's marital problems.

"She's keeping busy. The kids are home in the summer, so she's on the go."

"Keeping active is excellent. Not that Megan hasn't always been involved in any number of clubs and community events. Politics is the natural progression for her, isn't it?"

"She wanted to make a difference. The breakup of a marriage

makes you think I suppose—about broader issues than home and family."

"What a wonderful way to meet the challenge of her divorce. Not that relationships are ever easy, but nowadays young people seem to be looking for—I'm not sure what they're looking for."

Stella didn't think it would be useful to mention that "hot sex" was high on her list. Her mother wouldn't approve. "Everyone's looking for different things. Companionship. Friendship. A big house and a yacht," she teased.

"Hmpf. As if those will bring you happiness."

The kind of happiness she'd settle for right now was pretty basic and orgasmic. Was she shallow or what? "Right now, I'm happy with this coconut ice cream," Stella said in lieu of the truth. She could think of some places she might like to put the coconut ice cream that would make her happier still.

Like get in line for *that* fantasy, with the boat bunnies and the Kirsty's of the world already at the head of the pack. Life could be so unfair.

As if on cue; as if in answer to her orgasmic prayers, the phone rang again.

Maybe, maybe, *maybe,* she found herself thinking as she walked to the phone on the kitchen wall. But the ringing stopped just as she reached it.

Shit. So much for fantasies. She checked the caller ID just in case. Unknown caller, unknown number. A telemarketer. Just her luck.

* * *

DANNY STOOD IN the hallway of the golf club, his cell phone still in his hand. He was drunk, but not too drunk to know how close he'd come to making a blunder. Blame the hours they'd been sitting in the clubhouse bar. Blame too many martinis. Blame torrid memory and a lack of willpower.

Not that any of that mattered. Stella wasn't home anyway.

Maybe she was out with some other guy.

Which shouldn't have been a problem.

In the rational part of his brain it wasn't.

As for the other part—the one propelled by rash impulse and libido—he would have preferred being the guy she was fucking tonight.

SIXTEEN

DANNY RETURNED HOME TO FIND THE POWER out and had to muscle open the gate at the end of his driveway. After parking at the house, he grabbed a flashlight from his car, entered the kitchen, and dialed the emergency number for the electric company. A message machine informed him that lightning had hit one of the relay stations east of the river; Xcel had no idea when service would be restored. One of the downsides to living in the country—no swift action after storms.

That's where his generator came in. Walking to the garage, he hit the switch on the Honda 12,000-watt generator and it roared to life. Returning to the kitchen, he flipped on the lights and turned off his flashlight.

A power outage always set his surge unit to beeping, along with screwing up all his clocks and an occasional monitor screen. He'd better check the situation in his office.

The door was half open—not a good sign. Although he may have forgotten to lock it. Not very likely; he'd become ubersensitive to security since the last break-in. A quick survey disclosed a jimmied lock, all the wood adjacent to it rough and slivered. His stomach tightened as he pushed open the door and flipped on the lights.

Jesus—the place had been torn apart.

Two of his computers had been partially wrenched from their moorings; file cabinet drawers had been pulled out and emptied; a monitor hung from a desk top, dangling by its cord, scattered papers carpeted the floor. His security codes had held—as they should—so the thief or thieves had tried to carry away the hard drives.

Not an easy task when they were bolted to the desktops; he'd been in this business long enough to understand the necessity of vigilance.

But fuck, what a mess.

Definitely not the work of professionals.

The security camera should have caught the action. Picking his way through the mess, he lifted down a heavily carved frame with an early print of Kilimanjaro. The picture had been pushed to one side and was tipped now at a crazy angle—as if he'd be stupid enough to have his safe behind it. The small digital camera mounted between the lions couchant at the top of the frame had gone undetected, the drilled hole for the lens virtually invisible in the high relief of the carving.

Extracting the small chip from the camera, he took it into his bedroom, pulled out a laptop he kept in an overnight bag in the closet, and powered up. *Come on, come on, come on,* he silently urged, impatient to discover the identity of the criminals.

As the first images came up on the screen, he saw that whether by design or chance, the thieves had arrived after the power went out. All that was visible in the frames were two shadowy figures dressed in black with black ski masks. Christ, he was watching a clichéd scene from a movie. They even wore black gloves. Were they actual amateurs or someone who wanted to appear like one in dress-up? As the action unfolded, he watched their increasing frustration as the machines remained bolted down. You'd think if they were professionals, they would have had some minimum tools to deal with the secured computers. His wasn't the only office that made it difficult to carry out the merchandise.

Their penlight flashlights weren't sufficient illumination— even had they been unmasked—to allow identification.

Okay, that was pretty much useless. He shut down the computer.

Now what? Wait for them to show up again? Put in a man trap like the landed gentry did before human rights were a consideration? Call the cops and subject himself to a painfully inept investigation by county mounties who mainly gave out traffic tickets? Sit up every night with a loaded shotgun until the crooks showed up again and shake them down for the name of their employer?

Speaking of suspects—there was one he'd like to shake down more than the others.

A whole lot more.

And if he'd been sober, he might have been swift enough to discover whether she was scamming him or not and maybe enjoy himself in the bargain. But he wasn't sober, his deductive reasoning and mental acuity weren't anywhere near prime, and he was damned tired after too many sleepless nights and martinis.

So wishful thinking about Stella Scott would have to wait—probably indefinitely. He was going to bed. No one was going to try another break-in tonight. Even amateurs weren't that stupid.

He locked up, turned out the light, climbed into bed, and thanks to plenty of Grey Goose vodka, actually slept.

SEVENTEEN

TUESDAY MORNING DAWNED BRIGHT AND CLEAR. Except for some fallen trees and the rivers running high, the storm might never have passed through. The forecast was for temperatures in the eighties and sunny skies. A perfect summer day.

Stella watched the morning news in the store with Megan. She'd come over after bringing her kids to the park for the summer rec program and was admiring the preliminary design and layout of the campaign sign.

"Where did you find that perfect photo of a boy and his dog?"

"A zillion images are available online—they're in the public domain. I had my pick. I shut down briefly for the storm, but as soon as it passed over, I turned on my computer again and finished about midnight. I'll fine-tune it tonight, and we'll send it to the printer tomorrow. By the way, my folks send their good wishes for your campaign. They're as ready as we are to see the Deloittes permanently retired."

"Thanks." Megan held up crossed fingers. "God willing."

"Along with some hard-hitting truths, babe. Be sure you send out a press release talking up your new signs."

"We're way ahead of you. Peggy's sending it out the end of the week to coincide with the signs going up."

"Perfect timing."

"Are you talking about me?"

The women turned to find Buddy coming through the door. "Of course. Who else?" Stella replied with a smile. "Here for your weekly quota?"

"What else? The new comic shipments are marked on my calendar, along with my TiVo list and my golf schedule."

"Some people work for a living," Stella teased.

"And some people have the summer off. Right, Megan?" He turned to smile at Megan.

"Thank God, after nine months of teaching squirrely junior high kids. Did the storm hit your neck of the woods last night?"

"Nothing major," Buddy said. "A few trees down. The power flickered off and on, but didn't actually go out."

"It did at my place. For a couple hours. But the kids were already in bed so TV wasn't a problem."

"No blackout here," Stella said. "Your comics are on the shelf in the back, Buddy, if you're eager."

Buddy grinned. "Takes a fanatic to know one." Comic book collectors waited with bated breath for the new installments. Age didn't seem to be a factor, nor did socio-economic considerations. "Care to go for brunch later?" he asked Megan. "I'm free, you're free, and the river view at The Fish House is picture-perfect." He wasn't asking for a date; his voice was as casual as the offer.

"Why not?" Megan asked. "The kids are at the park till three."

"Care to join us?" He looked at Stella.

"We can't all be on vacation. I'll pass, but thanks."

As Buddy turned to walk toward the back, he swung around. "I forgot to ask. Did you and Rees hit it off?"

Do fish swim? "We had a good time," Stella said, not about to tell him the truth. Not about to give Danny Rees even more reason to have a big head.

"That's what he said. You two'll have to come out on the boat again sometime."

Had Rees really said they'd had a good time? Even after their none-too-friendly parting? Damn. She'd just convinced herself she could live without him—or sort of convinced herself. Translated: if she kept real busy, she didn't have time to think of him every ten seconds. Only every twenty.

It was progress.

What was that saying about the longest journey begins with one step?

AFTER MEGAN AND Buddy left, Stella was grateful the new comics had come in. The store was more mobbed than usual; she rang up sales like crazy. And for long periods of time, she was relatively free of useless fantasies in the vein of Cinderella and Prince Charming. Now if only the new comics came in every day, there might be some possibility of continuous diversion until such a time as she could talk herself out of needing sex with one certain man.

Until that dubious day, however, she had to resort to other means.

Like killing him off in Marky B's newest adventure.

Or using her sex toys with more than a little frequency.

Or shopping for shoes she didn't need.

Thank God for sane, rational coping mechanisms.

But that's what being an adult was all about, wasn't it?

Making that choice between denial and Prozac.

EIGHTEEN

DANNY HAD CLEANED UP HIS OFFICE—A RELATIVE term—and then taken out his newest Ferrari that went from zero to sixty in 4.2 seconds. The 612 Scaglietti had a V-12 engine with 540 horsepower and a top speed of 196 miles per hour. And once he hit the freeway, he turned up the stereo and let it loose.

Pissed at the job that had been done on his office, more pissed that a woman who intrigued him might be involved, he needed solitude, speed, and the Rolling Stones to sort out the agitation in his brain. Traffic was light on a Tuesday, the radar device on the dash kept him out of jail, and he slowed down from time to time when the flashing light indicated highway patrol in the vicinity. The green rolling hills and farmland passing by went unnoticed.

He had too much on his mind.

Starting with his list of suspects that may not be anywhere

near complete. A second heist attempt so soon after the first smelled strongly of an outside operation—as in outside the state and possibly the country . . . regardless whether amateurs were involved. Whoever was financing the hit was in a hurry—and unconcerned with leaving a mile-wide trail. He made a mental list of his competitors in the incestuous world of video games; he knew most everyone. And then he began mentally ticking them off one by one, categorizing them in order of predilection and motive.

His cell phone rang outside of Eau Claire, and slowing down enough to not rate as a menace on the highway, he glanced at the caller ID. Buddy must be responding to the message he'd left earlier.

"You rang?" Buddy quipped.

"I have a couple questions you might be able to help me with."

"Shoot. If it's about Stella—"

"It's not about her," Danny interrupted, not inclined to discuss the complexities of that situation. "I've had a couple breakins lately—one last night."

"I know some PIs if you need help."

"It's probably just kids looking for electronics to pawn," Danny lied, "but in the event it isn't, I was wondering if anyone was around when I talked to you Monday morning. Anyone who might have heard you say we were going golfing. You were the only call I took that day. Except for Marisa, but hers was the usual invitation for sex. Nothing new there."

"What time did we talk?" Buddy asked.

"Ten, ten-thirty."

"Kirsty might still have been with me. She stayed over Sunday night. I'm not sure when she left. Before I headed for the club. But exactly when, I couldn't say."

"Was anyone else at your place?"

"Unlike you, I limit myself to one lady at a time," Buddy said, drolly.

Danny let that pass, not about to point out an occasion or two when Buddy hadn't. "So Kirsty might have been around?"

"It's possible. I didn't pay attention to the time until later when I was concerned with making our tee time. You don't think Kirsty was involved?"

"Nah. But she might have spoken to someone. She's the friendly type. Do you know much about Brian?"

"Kirsty brought him with her Saturday. I think he's into software like you. Or was it telecommunications? He lives large near Lake Calhoun. Good address, nice car, unattached."

"Is he from here?"

"Born here, you mean? I'm not sure. I thought Kirsty said something about transferring from somewhere. Was it L.A.?"

"You think?" Danny's grip tightened on the steering wheel.

"I thought she mentioned something about Malibu, but she might have been talking about her sister who's trying to break into acting out there. Call her and ask. Kirsty would *love* to hear from you, my man. Speaking of women you know, I saw Stella today when I went to pick up my weekly supply of comics. I asked her how you two had gotten along and she said fine. Bring her along on the boat next weekend."

"My sister and her family are coming into town," Danny lied. He wasn't about to explain the unexplainable.

"You're kidding, right?"

"No. Really. They're coming to see the new Ikea store."

"Bring them along, too. The weather's supposed to be hot."

"You don't know my sister. She has her schedule etched in stone."

"Sorry about that. But hey, I know sisters, especially if they're older than you. I'm going to invite Megan and, if it's not crowding your territory, Stella, too."

"There's no territory involved. Ask away."

"If your sister should change her mind or she buys out Ikea in time . . . you know where I'm docked. We'll leave about one."

"Thanks, but you know how it is with family. You have to look interested."

"Fortunately, my family keeps their distance in Florida or Gull Lake. Not that I don't like their company, but only in small doses. I hope you're insured on those break-ins."

"It wasn't much. It's not worth reporting." He was self-insured on his specialized equipment anyway. "One more question. Did you happen to tell anyone we were going golfing? I'm trying to figure out if someone might have known I'd be gone." He couldn't ask "Did you talk to Stella?" without sounding paranoid.

"Just Darren and Louis, but they don't know anyone you know."

"Thanks for the info."

"Not a problem. It looks like you need a bigger gate."

"I'm thinking about it. Have a good weekend."

"Same to you if it's possible," Buddy said, amusement in his tone.

The details about Brian focused Danny's attention on a man who might be related to the video game industry—Buddy's recall of a software or telecommunications background not reassuring.

He'd have Brian checked out by a retired detective he knew. Frank Stanchfield knew just about everyone at City Hall after thirty-five years on the police force.

Time to turn around and do some fact checking. Exiting the freeway at the next overpass, he crossed over the highway and headed back home.

First a call to Frank, then go online and have a night vision camera FedEx'd to his place. He should have it in place by tomorrow afternoon. In the interim, he'd stay home tonight and stand guard. The next time someone tried to break in, either he'd be there to greet them or the security camera would capture their image, light or no light.

Why hadn't he thought of Frank and the night vision camera before?

Maybe if his brain wasn't clogged with Stella Scott shoulda, woulda, coulda doubts and still drying out from an excess of Grey Goose vodka, he might be operating on more than three cylinders.

He really should stop and eat.

Food. Okay? His brain was really not cooperating.

Anyway, food would help regenerate brain cells suffering from yesterday's alcoholic overload.

There—right ahead. It must be a sign. It *was* a sign.

A billboard extolling the merits of AUNT MAE'S HOME COOK-ING, BEST PIE IN TEN COUNTIES, NEXT EXIT, 500 FEET.

He slammed on the brakes.

NINETEEN

FOR THE NEXT FEW DAYS, BOTH STELLA AND Danny gave true meaning to the phrase "throwing themselves into their work."

Between the next issue of *Marky B,* Megan's campaign sign, her math tutoring, and minding the store, Stella worked nearly around the clock.

Danny isolated himself in his office and concentrated on adding a new character to his latest video game. Strangely, or not so strangely, the action figure turned out to be a tawny-haired beauty who scrambled men's brains if they didn't get out of her way fast enough. She could stage an assault from six different angles and in four different disguises. A psychiatrist might have had something to say about the evolution of such a character.

When the new security camera arrived, Danny installed it, along with adding a better lock on his office door. He put a camera out by the gate as well. So much for the bucolic countryside.

On Friday, one of the charities Danny funded for inner-city students called to invite him to their annual picnic next month. He was smiling when he hung up, reminded of what was important in life. Not vengeance. Not sex. Positive, socially relevant action for the betterment of the community. That's what.

Callie McCann personified a community activist in spades. She was also the most upbeat woman he'd ever met. She was never down when she had a dozen reasons every day that would have brought the average person to their knees. Her main job was running a youth center that offered after-school activities for kids of all ages. She not only managed it day to day, she was also its major fund-raiser, cajoling money and merchandise from individuals and businesses to keep it afloat. Danny was one of their prime contributors; he also offered his time and expertise to the state-of-the-art computer center he'd donated to the facility.

In addition to supplying funds for everything from basketballs to Barbie dolls, he also gave college scholarships to deserving kids. To date, he'd paid expenses for two hundred six students to complete their undergraduate degrees; another fifty-four had gone on to graduate degrees, thanks to him.

He earned obscene amounts of money from what could only be characterized as a frivolous pursuit. The North Side Center was a good place to spend it.

BY DINT OF hard work and full-blown denial, Stella and Danny managed to get through the week. They even managed to convince themselves that they were over any infatuation they might have had for each other.

After all, they both prided themselves on their independence.

And on a certain detachment from affairs of the heart.

Life wasn't about romance.

Life was about more important things.

WHEN BUDDY CALLED Megan to invite her to the river Saturday, he mentioned he was going to call Stella, too. He also mentioned as an aside that Danny wouldn't be there. He had family to entertain.

As best friends did, Megan immediately called Stella. "Buddy called and invited me on his boat Saturday. He's going to call you. You have to come."

"I don't think Amy can work on Saturday." It was only half a lie; Amy had asked to work, but not until noon.

"Ask Ryan. Danny won't be there—something about his sister coming to town—but you'll have fun anyway. *Pleeeease*—I won't know anyone if you don't come."

Despite her previous disclaimers about being just friends, Stella suspected Megan liked Buddy more than she was admitting. With matchmaking intrinsic to the female gene pool, Stella considered doing her part for her gender imperative. "Okay. What time?"

"Not till one. You can always find someone to take over the store for half a day."

"Hey—Buddy's calling in. I'll call you back."

The women compared notes afterward, discussing possible wardrobes for Saturday, which sandbar to beach on, the best way to avoid Kirsty on a boat in the middle of the river.

"And she won't be the only swimsuit model onboard," Megan groused.

"Certainly not a problem for you with your two percent body fat and muscles to die for."

"But she has legs clear up to her armpits."

"She's not your competition. If Buddy wanted her, he wouldn't have asked you to join him Saturday."

"He asked you, too, and said I should bring along the kids."

"He's a nice guy. So bring the kids."

"I'd rather not, just in case . . . you know, he might be like . . . maybe a little interested?"

"You two will make a stunning couple," Stella teased. "I've got a good feeling. Wear your green suit with the cut outs, and don't worry about Kirsty or anyone else. You're going to look great, and we're going to enjoy ourselves. We'll swim, drink fruity drinks with paper umbrellas, and pig out on the buffet."

"Jeez, I forgot about the food. That's reason enough to go."

"And there'll be plenty for us, 'cuz swimsuit model types can only eat two soda crackers a day."

"I'm glad he asked us."

There was something in her tone Stella hadn't heard for a long time, not since Chad had done her dirt. Excitement. "I'm glad, too. Buddy's really nice."

"Maybe he invited someone you'll really hit it off with," Megan exclaimed. "Wouldn't that be fun?"

To which Stella replied with equal enthusiasm, "It would be fabulous." When what she really meant was, "Sorry, no one is as fabulous as Danny Rees." But she wasn't crazy enough to actually utter those words. And she'd enjoy herself Saturday—just not up to the level of superlatives.

* * *

IT WAS ONLY after she'd hung up the phone that Stella was faced with the somber thought that she would be more or less a third wheel. Not overtly, because Buddy always had a boat full of people, but there it was.

She hoped like hell there was some coconut ice cream left in the freezer. At times like this, it was the only solution to a rapidly disintegrating world.

TWENTY

WHEN SHE WOKE UP SATURDAY MORNING, STELLA looked out the window and offered up a small prayer of thanksgiving.

It was a downpour.

The kind that sluiced down the streets, clogged up the gutters, and turned the park by the river into a lake.

She was saved.

There wouldn't be any boating excursion today. She wouldn't have to pretend to be having fun. She could stay home and sulk and feel sorry for herself and in general wallow in the gloom of unrequited sex.

She called Megan early so she'd be free of her obligation and could relax. "It doesn't look like a day to be out on the river. We'll go some other time."

"Haven't you seen the forecast?" Megan asked, sounding so

chipper she could have been one of the Keebler elves. "The rain's moving into Wisconsin as we speak. Clear skies and sun within the hour."

"Great." Stella needed a couple muffins pronto, and maybe some Krispy Kremes and a bear claw from Bread Loafers, too. This kind of news required major carbs, fat, and sugar.

"I'll pick you up at twelve-thirty. It's going to be *so-o-o* much fun! I've got to get the kids ready to go to my mom's. See you soon!"

The phone went dead on that frenzied exhilaration, and Stella knew she was screwed. Maybe she could bring a book and hide out. There must be a corner on a boat that large where she could disappear. She could fill up a plate with food and alleviate her sexual frustration by pigging out. *Aaagh.* If this frustration continued much longer, she'd be twenty pounds heavier. Damn, damn, damn—what was happening to her previously unsusceptible emotions? What had happened to her comfortable, complacent, I'm-too-busy-to-think-about-men philosophy?

She wished she'd never met Danny Rees.

If there were really fairy godmothers, she would have had that little lady snapping the hell out of her wand and making him disappear.

WHEN AMY ARRIVED to take over at noon, Stella said, "I might be back early."

Amy shrugged her tattooed shoulder. "Whatever."

"I just meant in case you want to make plans."

"Everyone's out of town this weekend. I don't have any plans. Take your time." The teenager ran her hand through her orange and green hair and smiled. "I might toke up in the back room after closing and read those new mangas."

Stella put up her hands. "I didn't hear that. I'm a law-abiding citizen."

"In case you come back and wonder what the smell is, it's me, that's all."

If she came back early, she might be inclined to indulge in some mind-altering substance, too. Although in her case, she was thinking about a glass of wine and a box of truffles. "Keep an eye on Chris Hines. He takes way too many comics. I'll go one or two, but that's it. He'll have to read the rest here."

"He doesn't try that stuff with me." Amy grinned. "You're a soft touch."

Chris couldn't afford many comics. His dad had been laid off six months ago after fifteen years as a mechanic at the airlines. Things were tough. "Give him a couple cookies when no one's around," Stella said. "He likes the oatmeal raisin ones."

"Will do. And Zeke, too, right?"

Amy knew who could afford what. "Melanie needs help with her journal. You're good at that. She likes chocolate-chip cookies."

"Okay, Mother Teresa. Go hang out on your yacht, and us common folks will scrap along here."

"Thanks, Amy. There's that pasta salad you like in the frig."

"Go already. You haven't even changed, and Megan's picking you up soon."

"How do you know that?"

"She called me and told me to be sure you're ready. She's hot for this guy on the yacht. Is it the Buddy who comes in here?"

"Yep."

"He collects manga."

"Right."

"He doesn't look like he has money."

"Apparently he does."

"Sweet. Megan needs a change of pace from the loser she was married to."

"At one time she didn't think he was a loser."

"He hit on Lisa once down by the river. She practically screamed. He's really old. Don't tell Megan though. What's the point?"

Amy was nineteen going on eighty. Nothing fazed her. She spoke in a quiet monotone and spent her spare time writing a novel about her dysfunctional family. The writing was good, too, the parts Stella had seen. With any luck, that book might take her away from her nine brothers and sisters, a mom who had given up coping, and a father who was a big-time lawyer but never home. Amy's dream was to live in Greenwich Village and write. Stella had to give her credit: her dream at nineteen was a better class schedule so she could sleep in. Maybe her problem was that her dream threshold was too low.

Not her current problem, when Danny Rees was the mega fantasy in her life and about as unattainable as Brad Pitt.

Think smaller. That was the way to go.

Less chance of disappointment.

"You're zoned out," Amy said, tapping Stella on the shoulder. "Go. Upstairs. And. Change." She pointed to her pricey wristwatch. "Your pumpkin will be here in twenty minutes."

But Megan didn't come in. She parked at the curb and honked the car horn like a crazy person. Obviously she was in a hurry, Stella decided, glancing at the clock while shoving her feet into her sandals. Swimsuit or no swimsuit? Nah. The last thing she wanted to do was join the parade of swimsuit models who spent a helluva lot more hours in the gym than she did. She actually never spent any time in the gym, so any one of the leggy beauties, no matter how minimal their exercise routine, were hours ahead of her.

Megan exercised enough for both of them, anyway. She had so much equipment in her basement she could stock a store. Not that she didn't put it to good purpose. Her body was toned to perfection.

Stella had always considered her regimen as part of the balance of the universe—you know, the yin and yang of muscle power. Megan was one side of the equation, and she was the other. Diversity. That was her middle name.

"Mrs. Blythe is gonna call the cops if you don't get down to the car!" Amy shouted up the stairs. Or at least shouted as much as a monotone allowed. "Get a move on!"

Her uptight elderly next door neighbor had a close relationship with the local police dispatcher and felt it her duty to inform the local authorities about stray cats, loud noise levels, children hanging around on the sidewalk in front of her house, and skateboarders. Skateboarders were Mrs. Blythe's personal bête noire, right up there with the outrage of profanity on the airwaves.

The kids who hung out in Stella's store couldn't care less. The cops ignored Mrs. Blythe pretty much all the time. But Stella took a more politic stance and attempted to appease her neighbor when possible.

Mrs. Blythe was old. She drank a little too much of that medicinal wine she kept on her buffet. And if you were eighty and hung-over, loud noises could be painful.

"We're going to be late," Megan complained, pulling away from the curb before Stella had shut the car door.

"The slip is five minutes from here. It's twelve-thirty-five."

"Twelve-thirty-six."

"We're fucked then."

"Sorry." Megan shot her a rueful smile. "This is so bizarre. I feel like I'm fifteen and out on my first date."

Stella grinned. "Good. I like to see you excited."

"I'm probably stupid to get too involved. Buddy's single by choice. And always surrounded by tons of women."

"He looks bored when he's with them, if it's any consolation."

"Really?"

"Hey, the light's turning red!"

Megan brought the car to a screeching stop, and two pedestrians jumped back on the curb.

"Want me to drive?"

Megan shook her head. "It's only a few more blocks. I guess I'm more nervous than I thought."

"What's to be nervous about? Buddy's about as mellow as they get."

"That's what I keep telling myself."

"Good. 'Cuz it's true. Green light means go," Stella murmured, gauging the blocks to the river against Megan's current lack of driving skills.

They survived the remaining five blocks and parked.

"Stay by my side," Megan pleaded as they walked to the yacht.

"Will do." Stella smiled reassuringly. And she had every intention of doing just that. But the minute they stepped off the gang plank, Buddy was there with a smile for them both and a hug for Megan.

"Come take a look at my newest toy," he said, sliding his arm around Megan's waist. "You said you liked those reruns of *Seinfeld*. Care to take a look too, Stella?"

"I'm going to get a drink first," she said, understanding her company was no longer required.

As Buddy led Megan away, Stella scanned the crowd on the deck. The usual display of tanned bodies, expensive sportswear, and the best breast implants money could buy. Was this her crowd or what?

TWENTY-ONE

DANNY HAD MADE PLANS TO MEET FRANK Stanchfield at the St. Paul Grill for lunch on Saturday. Insurance as it were, should he be tempted to join Buddy's boat party. Also a pragmatic choice, assuming broad daylight would assure him less likelihood of a break-in while he was gone. He'd been staying home at night since the last attempt.

When Frank called to cancel, Danny's best-laid plans were nullified, but he couldn't argue with the facts. Frank's contact in criminal records had been on vacation all week. His surveillance on Brian had revealed a lot of comings and goings at his house, but Frank suspected drugs were involved, not software. And in his estimation, Kirsty wasn't more than a babe who liked men with money.

"I agree. Even if she's a go-between, it's inadvertent. Thanks for the update. We'll reschedule when your guy's back." As

Danny hung up the phone, he was overcome with a niggling sense of unease.

He hadn't planned on staying home today; he hadn't wanted to.

There was always his new video game to work on, he supposed.

Or other office tasks like getting his personal checkbook and receipts organized for his accountant, who was starting to raise his voice on the phone. Maybe he'd actually start that miserable project today. Heavy rain like this precluded outside activities.

As though in direct contradiction, the rain abruptly stopped, the sun shone brightly through his office window, and a God-damned rainbow rose over his pool. Even the frigging birds began chirping.

Calling his attention to the glorious day, in case he hadn't noticed.

Reminding him that Buddy's boat would be on the river in glowing sunshine now.

And one particular woman would be onboard.

Shoving back his chair, he surged to his feet and stalked from the office. He had to get out of here! Why not go and case Brian's place himself? Get the lay of the land, as it were. Frank had given him the address; Brian was most likely on the river today. He'd do a little reconnoitering himself.

And in the process, put thirty miles of city sprawl between himself and the St. Croix River.

IT WAS NEARLY noon by the time he reached Lake Calhoun. Parking his car on a side street, he approached Brian's home from the rear. The alley was deserted, as were most city neighborhoods on a summer weekend. Everyone drove out of town on Friday, heading north or into Wisconsin.

Cautious nonetheless, he slowly opened the back gate and eased into the yard. Not a sign of life. Perfect. The large two-story stucco house faced the lake, the backyard less used: a lap pool surrounded by well-tended grass, two chaises on one side, the tree-shaded yard enclosed by a six-foot-high fence. The usual security sign was planted in the flowers near the back door. Every home in the area had one. It didn't mean the police would respond quickly. Frank had mentioned the nearest station was twenty blocks away, and every precinct was seriously under-staffed since the city budget cuts.

Danny moved toward the house, intent on a brief look inside and a quick exit before the squad car arrived.

"He's not home!"

Danny turned at the child's voice and looked up. In the leafy branches of a large maple in the yard next door, a tree house was faintly visible. "Are you sure? Brian told me to come over."

"He's gone. I'm guarding his house."

It was impossible to see who was speaking. But the word *guard* didn't portend success in entering the house. "He's paying you?"

"Fifty bucks."

The kid was proud of the amount, and taking his job seriously. Which begged the question why Brian would need someone to guard his house. "Do you do this often?"

"What's your name?"

"What's yours?"

"I asked you first."

The kid wasn't stupid. "Tell Brian Ed came over."

"I haven't seen you before."

It was bizarre speaking to a tree. It was equally useless. "Have a nice day, kid."

"Shut the gate when you leave."

Smart-aleck. He was good, though. Maybe he should think about having him guard *his* house.

As Danny walked back to his car, he pondered various reasons for Brian's interesting security arrangement beyond the drug connection. Driving slowly down the lake boulevard awash with apartment dwellers taking advantage of the beach and green grass, he was struck by a disquieting thought. Was Brian checking out his house? He might assume as Danny had, that everyone was on Buddy's boat. Grabbing his cell phone, he punched in Buddy's number.

Buddy finally answered. "I was about to give up," Danny murmured.

"Your sister left. You're comin' out. Right?"

"No can do." An ambiguous answer because he'd lied about his sister coming this weekend. "I was wondering if Brian was on the boat."

"I think so. Did you see Brian?" he asked someone. "Megan saw him come onboard with Kirsty," Buddy declared. "Hey, man, you can change your mind anytime. Don't let Kirsty keep you away. Stella's here."

The last two words burned into Danny's brain with the impact of those branding irons in the old westerns on cable.

"Hey, you still there?" Buddy asked.

"Yeah, the traffic's heavy." A small inaccuracy that avoided a larger lie.

"Get your ass out here, or won't your big sister let you come out and play?" Buddy mocked.

"I'm in Minneapolis."

"So?"

"So I won't be out."

"In case you come to your senses, we're stopping on that sandbar on your side of the river in about fifteen minutes. Megan wants to swim, don't you, honeybun?"

Honeybun? Danny didn't know whether to be more shocked by Buddy's sugar sweet tone or his immediate erection at the news that Stella Scott would be only a few miles from his house.

"Come on out, Rees. The water's fine!"

There were giggles and laughter and an abrupt ending of the call.

I T W A S A forty-minute drive to the river and another twenty minutes over back roads to the sandbar. During that hour, Danny tried to talk himself out of going where he was going for any number of reasons. Stella could be some homegrown Mata Hari who knew how to put out the lure, reel in her catch—in this case, him—and get what she wanted. She was mouthy as hell, too, and more bitchy than he liked. And the way she'd walked off in a huff the last time. Uh-uh.

He didn't need sex that badly. And if he did, he could call plenty of other women.

If he hadn't been parking in the trees above the sandbar at that moment, the option of other women might have held some merit. As it was, he was kicking off his shoes, transferring his cell phone to his short's pocket, and surveying Buddy's yacht anchored at the end of the sandbar with fornication on his mind.

Not sex in general.

But sex with a very specific woman.

BUDDY WAS SEATED in a canvas sling-back beach chair watching Megan paddle a small kayak upstream.

"You made it," he said with a grin as Danny walked up.

"Where's Stella?"

Buddy's gaze narrowed at Danny's brusque tone, but not one to ask unnecessary questions, he said, "To be honest, I haven't seen her since she and Megan came aboard in Stillwater. She's on the boat somewhere."

"Thanks." Brisk, curt, the sound of a man in a hurry.

Buddy watched Danny take the gangway in a loping run and came to the conclusion that there was one horny bastard, a curious pose for Rees, who could always take it or leave it. On the other hand, Stella was out of the ordinary in more ways than one. She had an edge; she didn't play games. Maybe that's what Rees liked.

Buddy contemplated Rees as he moved through the throng on the main deck, speaking to one or another guest in passing, asking questions apparently. A number of them shook their heads in reply. Danny moved up to the second deck and the bridge before he returned to the main deck and disappeared down the companionway.

As Danny vanished from sight, Buddy turned back to survey Megan paddling the kayak like a pro. There was one competent woman. She made him feel like a shirker. But she was relaxing as hell, too; he felt content when she was around. He liked her kids, too—which was even stranger. He didn't ordinarily see children as likeable. Maybe he was getting old. Or maybe he was thinking way the hell too much.

Shoving his plastic drink cup into the sand, he shouted to Megan, "I'll race you to the end of the sandbar," and waded into the water.

TWENTY-TWO

DANNY HAD LOOKED IN EVERY STATEROOM, interrupting couples in two rooms who didn't appreciate being interrupted, and coming up empty in the other two. The remaining door below deck led to the galley. Hardly a likely place to find someone, but his options were down to zero.

He shoved open the door.

Startled, Stella said through a mouthful of chocolate cake, "I thought you weren't coming."

"What are you doing in here?"

She didn't need that tone, nor his scowl. "Minding my own business. What are you doing in here?"

"Looking for you."

She debated another forkful of cake, the taste out of this world. And it wasn't as though he'd come in here to apologize. What the hell. She filled her mouth with dense, fudgy chocolate.

"Do you mind?" He gestured toward the cake, his jaw clenching and unclenching.

She waved her fork over the chocolate torte and pretended she didn't know what he'd meant. "You want some?"

"I don't want any."

That was curt. "Then what the hell *do* you want?" She didn't require violins and roses, but neanderthal man she could do without.

"Could we go somewhere else? There's no place to sit."

She was seated on a kitchen stool and another was shoved under the counter, so she pulled the other stool out with her foot. "Problem solved."

Steam wasn't actually coming out of his ears, but she could visualize a comic book frame with him standing there like that, barely under control. And she'd definitely put in the steam. Swirling around his head, white, red, maybe a little cerulean. In her moment of creativity, she missed the two strides that brought him towering over her until he grabbed the fork in her hand, wrenched it away, and tossed it in the sink.

"Hey! I'm not done eating!"

"You're done."

She looked up what seemed a very long distance and met his hot gaze with an icy green stare. "I believe you've mistaken me for one of the other women you fuck," she said, her voice chill as the grave. "I don't respond to orders."

"Yeah, that's right. You like to give 'em."

"As long as we understand each other," she murmured in her best get-out-of-my-face tone. "Now I was enjoying my cake and reading this book. I'm sure you'll find plenty of women on deck to do whatever you want them to do."

"You're a fucking piece of work," he breathed, a tic fluttering across his cheekbone.

"But not *your* fucking piece of work. Is that clear?"

"It depends," he whispered.

"On what?" she snapped.

"On whether I want it to be clear or not."

"This conversation is over. I don't deal with chauvinist pigs."

"Maybe I can change your mind."

"And maybe I can knee you in the balls and end this useless discussion."

"I wouldn't recommend it."

She inhaled slowly, exhaled, and told herself to act like an adult instead of a petulant child. And then, ignoring reasonableness, said, "Fuck your recommendation."

He stiffened. "We can do it here or on a bed. Take your pick."

She whipped up her hand. "Whoa, baby. Was that some kind of an invitation I just heard?"

"I wasn't asking," he growled.

"Get the hell out of here," she said, her voice taut as a bow string. "Now. Or I'll scream so loudly they'll hear me clear to Nebraska."

He laughed. It started as a soft chuckle that rolled into a wave of chortles and before long turned into a series of full-bodied, bending over, laughing his head off, tears-rolling-down-his-cheeks guffaws.

"I fail to see the humor in—"

Waving his hands and shaking his head, he tried to speak. "Never mind . . . Foghorn Leghorn—can't—explain . . ." And then he went off on another round of laughter.

"I'm pleased I amuse you," she said, pissy-like.

"Sorry," he choked out, lifting his head slightly, trying to suppress his grin. "You just looked so 'I'm a chicken hawk' small and feisty—" Overcome by his lunatic sense of humor, he went off in another fit of laughter.

She had no idea what he was talking about, but what she did know was that—very much against her better judgment—shamefully wanton little warm fuzzies were beginning to subvert her sense of outrage. Perhaps the aphrodisiac qualities of the chocolate—a known scientific fact—were stimulating her carnal senses, or perhaps Danny Rees in close proximity or the scent of his cologne were more potent cause. Maybe it was his broad shoulders that looked broader in the narrow confines of the galley and his muscles flexing under his thin cotton knit T-shirt as he laughed that tempted her desires. Maybe it was his sheer, raw maleness and that fine line between passion and anger that had suddenly blurred and confused her. But she was definitely feeling those first small tremors of arousal. And whether to give in to those delectable ripples or resist had suddenly become an issue.

He stood upright as she was debating her options, wiped the wetness from his cheeks with his knuckles, and blew out a breath. "I'm sorry." He took a deep breath. "You drive me nuts, and that's a fact."

She knew what he meant—the "I want you, don't want you" insanity causing a traffic jam in her brain as well. But not sensible enough to accept his j'accuse–type apology for what it was worth, she had to ask, "What was so funny?"

"I don't want to get you mad again."

"What makes you think I'm not still mad?"

He looked at her, raised one brow, and smiled faintly. "Just a feeling."

"I'm not sure I like that know-it-all tone."

"Tell me what you do like," he murmured. "Then, I'll tell you and we can compare notes."

She didn't know if she was ready to forgive him completely, although her body was voting big time for amnesty. "Probably what every other woman likes about you," she muttered.

He suppressed his smile. "Would you like me to apologize again?"

"Okay."

He didn't expect that answer, but he wasn't stupid. "I'm sorry for being a jerk. I wasn't going to come today," he added, in a rare moment of introspective honesty, "but I had to if you know what I mean. And I suppose it pissed me off."

"That's an apology?" But she liked that he'd come despite himself. She knew the feeling.

"It's an explanation at least. My sister's not in town. I just told Buddy that to get out of coming here."

"And I wouldn't have come if I'd known you were here."

"So we're both childish and immature."

She smiled. "About some things." She wasn't going to give him the whole nine yards on that one after his accusations outside Dominic's.

"We do have a lot in common, though."

"Don't say sex."

"No way." He knew better than to answer in the affirmative with her looking at him like that. And at base, what was rocking his world was that he and Stella might have *more* in common than sex. For one thing, he was here because he couldn't stay away. He couldn't pretend to be disinterested. He might as well face it. "Look, for starters, we both like comics. That subculture in itself gives us a certain comfort level, world view—whatever you want to call it. And we're both small-town people—introverts maybe, not to mention we both like Swedish rugs," he said with a grin that widened when he added, "And I wouldn't discount sex entirely."

She couldn't fault him on his brief litany, sex included. And she'd been missing him like crazy if she were honest with herself. Right or wrong, good or bad, there it was. "Do you like chocolate cake?"

"Not really."

She grinned. "What the hell—we can't like all the same things."

He softly exhaled. "Are we good then?"

"Probably. Whatever that means," she said with a sigh of her own. "I've been trying to tell myself you're not my type."

"And I've been trying to stay away," he murmured, with a faint grimace. "You're taking over my brain, babe. I'm freaking out."

"Wanna freak out together?"

"Oh, yeah." His dark brows flickered. "There's not much room in here, but I'm willing to give it a try."

"What if I said that's not what I meant?"

He dragged in air through his teeth. "That's a tough one. You've been on my mind for days."

"Should we compromise?"

He laughed. "You're asking me?"

"Okay, so we know your answer."

He shifted as though to move forward, and she leaned back on the wooden stool. "Not so fast. Give me a minute."

No, he wanted to say. Not after a week of wanting you. "One, one thousand, two, one thousand, three—"

So maybe her feelings might get hurt somewhere down the line. In the meantime, the pleasure of his company would more than offset possible future unhappiness. And since when had she stopped going for the brass ring? Shutting her book, she picked it up and slipped off the stool to her feet. "Find me a bed."

"Yes, ma'am," he murmured, stepping aside to give her room to pass, reaching out to open the door. "First door on your left."

She shot him a look as she eased past him. "There better not be a bottle of wine in there."

"Wouldn't think of it, ma'am."

She grinned. "I didn't know you could be so well mannered."

"It's been a long week," he said, softly.

And in truth, she did know how well mannered he could be. He never said no to anything. He always said yes. And he did it with a smile.

Preceding him out of the galley, she moved the short distance to the next room and waited for him to open the door. She didn't want to appear anxious for some ungodly reason. Probably because he was too familiar with eager women. Or maybe she wasn't in the mood to give orders today. Maybe she was in a different mood.

As he shut the door behind them and turned the key in the lock, he nodded at the book she still held in her hand and asked, "What are you reading?"

"Do you really care?"

He shrugged. "In a way."

"In what way?" She was asking one of those compulsively female questions—wanting to know what a man was thinking when he was probably only thinking about screwing.

"You seemed interested in it when I walked in."

"It's Gorky. I reread him a lot."

"Do you like Gorky's *Sketches and Stories?*"

"My favorite."

"No shit." The phrase was only half spoken, as though he were thinking out loud. And then he seemed to find himself again and added, "I like Chekhov, too."

"What I like at the moment is more physical than cerebral."

"Then we're on the same page, babe."

"Just checking," she said with a grin, tossing the book on the built-in dresser and pulling her T-shirt over her head.

Nice bra. Some kind of green lace. *Great* breasts. There go the shorts. Whatever his reservations might have been about Stella Scott, they were no longer relevant. Time enough later to deal with possible intrigues and computer theft. Right now, he was going to screw his brains out.

"Wow."

He looked up from pulling his shirt over his head to find Stella running her hand over the sheets.

"These are *not* made in America," she said. "Italian or French."

He liked the American babe leaning over the bed, her breasts hanging like plump fruit, her blond bush getting his Made-in-America stamp of approval. "Buddy had a decorator. She went to Italy to get whatever she had to get. Those for one thing, I'd guess." His shorts and boxers slid to the floor.

"Niiiiice . . . Frette." She held a pillowcase label between her thumb and forefinger.

He'd have to get new sheets, he thought. They seemed to turn her on. His tastes were more simple. Lush cunt like that in close proximity. What more did a man need? Walking up behind her, he slid his hands around her waist and slipped his cock between her legs. "While you're getting high on those sheets, I'll see if we still fit."

There was something in his tone—the not asking—that sent a quiver through her cunt. "No, don't," she said in a low, teasing contralto. "I changed my mind."

"But I want to," he murmured, picking up as though he might have been in this game once or twice before and he knew how to improvise. His finger tightened on her waist. "I've driven a long way to see you."

"Not to see me, to have sex."

She was rubbing her slit along his cock in a enticing slow rhythm, so he was guessing words and actions were antithetical. "Why else would I come this far?"

"I thought maybe we could read Gorky together."

He smiled faintly. "You read, and I'll fuck you. That way we'll both get what we want."

"Such bluntness might not get you laid."

"With a cunt this wet, I'm guessing I'll be getting it one way or another." His erection slid back and forth with frictionless ease, her sleek labia plump and swollen.

"Maybe I'd prefer reading my book."

"Gorky's *Lost Souls*? Try again. You like to fuck too much to turn it down." He slipped a finger along her labia and found her clit. Her own little dick was more than ready—engorged and prominent. He'd bet a thousand her G-spot was ready for action, too.

"Don't do that." But her voice was breathy with need.

He'd say the game was about over. She was ready to move on

to the real thing. Her palms were braced on the bed, her bottom lifted high, and she was swinging her tush faintly, begging for surcease. Or enticing him like a temptress might.

"Are you a cock tease? I'm not sure I like that," he said, in a mock brusque tone. And for a disconcerting moment he really meant it, picturing her doing this as readily with one of those other guys he'd seen in her sketches. Quickly quashing that useless mind-fuck, he reminded himself that sex was sex, like a rose is a rose is a rose. It wasn't complicated.

"I'm sorry." She'd gone still at his harsh tone. "I didn't mean to offend you." Impatient, throbbing, feverish with desire, instant gratification a real necessity, she turned her head and met his gaze. "Please . . . do me a favor. I'm done playing . . ."

Her eyes were half-lidded, unfocused, her tawny hair tumbled around her face, her cheeks flushed. And suddenly he got the impression she didn't care who it was as long as she got what she wanted. That she'd become an insatiable hunger in his gut unnerved him, that he didn't have more self-control was disconcerting for a man who had always been able to take it or leave it. He found himself viewing her hair-trigger readiness for cock anytime, anywhere with a chafing resentment. Trying to ignore his sudden intolerance for females who were ape-shit for sex, he told himself it didn't matter so long as he got off. And if Stella hadn't feverishly pleaded, "For God's sake, McKean, hurry!" he wouldn't have jerked back and stood up.

"This is a fucking mistake." He reached for his shorts, pissed as hell he'd come after her.

"Don't you dare, dammit!" Swinging upright, she slammed her fist into his back.

Scowling, he turned around, his shorts in his hand. "The name's Rees, in case you forgot."

"I know that." She was breathing hard. "What the hell are you doing?"

"You called me McKean."

"Sorry. That's Marky B's new sidekick who looks like you."

"Sure it is. Look, I shouldn't have come." But he had, like a dog in heat, he thought, bending over to put on his shorts.

"Let's get one thing clear," she snapped, stalking past him to the door. "You came here. I didn't go looking for you." Taking the key from the lock, she tossed it into the minuscule bathroom. "You were the one who wanted a fuck. I was reading my book, eating cake, and in general getting along just fine. So if you think you're going to prick tease *me* and walk away, you've got another think coming!"

He was standing upright again, his gaze as heated as hers. "What the fuck are you going to do about it?"

"Use that briefly," she said, pointing at his erection.

"Not likely. Get out of my way." The key was in the bathroom. He needed it.

She didn't move. She didn't so much as flinch.

Some people really got bent out of shape if they didn't get laid, he thought, about to push past her.

There was no way she was going to win this shoving match. "If you leave, I'll open that porthole and scream embarrassing things about you to everyone on the beach. Like the size of your dick, for starters, and I might lie."

He glared at her. "Like hell you will."

"Watch me."

He caught her just short of the porthole. Not that embarrassment was a major issue, but there were tons of families on the beach. He spun her around, pressed her hard against the wall, and said through gritted teeth, "I don't fuck on demand."

"Then call it something else," she hissed.

He decided the fastest way out of here was through her cunt. Like a shot, he hoisted her off her feet, pushed her against the wall, held her there with his forearm, and guiding his cock into her slippery warmth, rammed upward with such force she slid up the wall another six inches.

It was a manifestly contentious act.

Sex reduced to a slam-bang.

But no one was taking sensitivity ratings.

He pumped his legs like a pile driver.

She whimpered and gasped, her arms viselike on his shoulders, her legs wrapped around his waist.

It was a welcome of sorts—an animal rutting, rank horniness assuaged, and she rained kisses of gratitude on his cheek and temples, uttering little blissful sighs each time he was buried to the hilt. She came almost immediately like she did and then over and over and over again.

He should have stopped the first time she climaxed.

If she wasn't the damned sorceress of his soul he might have.

If his cock didn't feel like a fucking lightning rod to every quivering nerve in his body he might have.

If he wasn't proposing to be satyr to her nymphomania, it might have been a possibility.

As it was, he'd seriously decided—*change of plans*.

When he finally came, he ejaculated so violently he forgot where he was for a moment. But then he felt her smile on his face and heard her whispered thank yous and understood he was in some hellish paradise.

And screwed up as that was, he planned to stay a while.

"Hey." A sweet as honey whisper.

He lifted his head and smiled. "Hey."

"I'm glad you stayed," she breathed.

"I'm glad you made me."

"Did I really?"

Her gaze was beguiling. "Sure," he lied.

"Good. Then if you're not mad, I can tell you, I'm dripping all over Buddy's carpet."

Swinging her around, he moved a few steps. "Drip on his bed," Danny said with a grin and deposited her on the center of those sheets she liked.

She didn't speak, not sure what to say, not sure he'd stay. And she'd given enough orders today as it was—not that they hadn't worked out really well—orgasm-wise. But currently removed from the throes of insane lust, she found herself uncomfortable making demands.

Grabbing a couple towels from the bathroom, Danny tossed one in her direction and dropped into a sprawl beside her on the bed. Wiping himself off, he threw the towel into the bathroom, laced his arms under his head, and exhaled softly. "That was damned good. Let me know when you need me again."

She felt like throwing her arms around him and hugging him to death, but after that casual statement, he probably wasn't looking for any heartfelt declarations. "Pretty soon, probably." Was that indifferent enough to allay any male concerns apropos emotionalism?

He turned to look at her and smiled. "There's something about you," he said.

That same prosaic tone, although his smile was—dare she think—affectionate? Not if she was smart, she wouldn't. Danny Rees wasn't into affection. "There's something about you, too, and I can measure it with a ruler."

He chuckled. "Come here." Reaching out, he pulled her into his arms and gently kissed her.

It surprised her—the tenderness. But not as much as his next words. "You remind me of my sister." At her puzzled look, he continued, "Don't get worried, I'm not a pervert. I mean taking what you want in life, going for broke. Libby has that same kind of gutsy outlook."

She smiled. "That's Marky B. I'm really a pushover."

His brows did one of those quick up and down things. "You coulda fooled me."

"Yeah, well . . . you can give orders next time."

"Swear to God?" He laughed at the sudden apprehension in her gaze. "Just teasing. I was thinking maybe I'd nibble my way down your body from top to bottom and see if you can come with just tongue."

"I can't."

"Maybe today you can."

"Don't sound so damned certain." He wasn't the only one who thought about how many there may have been before.

But maybe he had reason to sound certain.

It turned out he did.

She'd have to remember the date, like those other milestones in her life: her first orgasm masturbating; her first orgasm with someone else involved; graduating high school and college; making fudge from scratch. You know, stuff like that.

It got real hot temperature-wise and body-wise in that small stateroom. Danny opened both portholes, and that helped the room. As for their insatiable sexual appetites, they finally cooled off in the shower.

MUCH LATER, WHEN the bonfire was blazing on the beach and Stella was resting on Danny's chest in the stateroom, his cell phone rang.

"Answer it," she murmured.

"Nah."

"Maybe it's your sister."

Not likely, but he was feeling too mellow to argue. Stretching down, he grabbed his shorts from the floor, slid his phone out of his pocket, and glanced at the caller ID. Frank Stanchfield. Easing her off him, he sat up against the headboard and flipped open the phone. "Rees here."

"I forgot to tell you a couple things. I checked on the lady at the comic book store. She inherited a moderate amount of stock in Electronic Arts, Inc. I don't know how that impacts your company—whether they're direct competitors or not. But I thought you should know. Also, her mother is a close friend with a psychic who has a website sponsored by Wizards of the Coast. That's it. Take it for what it's worth."

"Thanks. I'll talk to you later." Flipping the phone shut, he set it on the dresser.

"Anyone I know?"

"Nope."

"Not your sister."

"No. Some business. It can wait."

Was it one of his drug contacts? Didn't drug dealers do more business on the weekends? Is that why he said he'd talk to him later? Shit. Just when she'd been lulled into forgetting he was more or less unemployed. "Was it about your video game?" She was hoping he'd say yes. Even if it was superweird to get a business call on a Saturday night.

"Why do you ask?" Damn, he wished she hadn't said that.

"No reason."

"It wasn't. It was a friend of a friend. Nothing that can't wait."

"My mom knows a lady who works for a video game company—or is sort of involved," she murmured. "Have you heard of Wizards of the Coast?"

Christ, why was she asking about Wizards? "It sounds vaguely familiar." As in two minutes ago familiar.

Shouldn't he know the names of video game companies if he was really in the business? "What's the name of your game?"

She probably knew already if she'd broken into his house twice. Should he answer truthfully or not? Either way, it might fuck up his plans for the night. Which involved screwing until he couldn't move. "I was thinking you haven't come for at least five minutes," he whispered, rolling on his side and easing a finger into her pouty, swollen cunt. "What'd you say?"

Maybe she could worry about good and evil later. Maybe right now, the goodness part would be more satisfying. "I'd say that feels . . . glorious . . ."

TWENTY-THREE

"ARE YOU STAYING ON THE BOAT TONIGHT?" HE was having trouble with his usual, "It's been nice. I'll call you." He didn't feel like leaving her.

"Uh-uh. You know me and my ball-and-chain hours with the store."

"Do you want company?"

She smiled. "That and a few others things, too."

He winked. "Sounds good. Let me make a call, and I'll drive you home."

Pulling on his shorts, he picked up his phone from the dresser and walked out of the room.

Jeez, just when she was happily adrift in her postorgasmic trance, he had to jar her sensibilities. And not in a good way. Who was he talking to that he couldn't talk to in front of her? What was he saying to whomever he was talking to in the corridor outside?

Did he have to get permission from someone to stay out all night? Was he running short on Ecstasy and needed a refill?

Easing out of bed, she tip-toed to the door and turned the latch slowly like a safe cracker in the movie *Ocean's Twelve*. She loved that movie. Sassy and smart and funny with a cast to die for. *Jesus—did he just say break-in?* Ohmygod. He was a drug dealer who stole from other drug dealers. This wasn't going to work out—no way. She didn't want to die in a shoot-out in some dark alley during a drug deal gone bad, 'cuz that's what always happened. One side pretended not to know the other side was cutting the dope with baking soda or something and keeping the extra cash. And then they'd pull out an AK-47 or an Uzi from the suitcase that was supposed to have the money in it. And *wham*— it was over except for the blood on the asphalt.

"Thanks, Frank, I appreciate someone keeping an eye on my place tonight."

He kept his stash at his place? Probably in that big pole barn she'd seen with the really high-class coded lock on the door. That's why he lived in the country. Everyone knew the local sheriff spent more time at Shelley's Diner than he did in his car or at the office. And everyone also knew his wife knew. But hey, if anyone understood how sex could scramble your brains, she did.

He was coming back! She made a flying leap for the bed, and when Danny entered the room, she opened her eyes slowly like she'd been sleeping.

"My time is your time. The gardener was coming tomorrow. I changed the schedule."

Like why couldn't you say that with me around? she wanted to ask. And she would have if there wasn't that small matter of her not being quite sure of what she wanted yet. Or more pertinently, how much she wanted mind-blowing sex with Danny Rees. She was trying to work out some ethical compromise that would allow her to enjoy the sex without freaking out about his actual life. *Aaagh*. Not a quick and easily solved dilemma. Especially when he was standing there in only his khaki shorts, looking like some Olympian athlete who'd just won the decathlon, and she knew what was under those shorts. "Your gardener comes on Sunday?" Would Poirot have said that a little more blandly? She'd have to practice up.

"He comes whenever. Are you ready to go?"

On one level she was ready to go to the moon with him if he'd asked. On the everyday, more prosaic level, she was debating whether he carried heat and if, perhaps, her life might be in danger. Not that he could hide a handgun in his minimum clothing, she decided. She would have heard a clunk when he threw his shorts on the floor if he'd had a 9mm in his pocket.

"Hey, babe. Are you awake?"

"Ah . . . yup . . . sure am."

"Want some help dressing?" he said with a wicked grin.

"Thanks, no."

"Why don't I tell Buddy we're going while you get dressed? I'll see you on the beach." Grabbing his T-shirt, he slung it over his shoulder. "Okay with you?"

She nodded. It would give her time to reconcile all the tumult in her brain. Maybe. Or at least give her time to decide whether the hottest sex she'd ever experienced was worth the possible risk in knowing a man who could be living outside the law.

He paused at the door and looked at her. She hadn't moved. "If you're sleepy, I'll carry you to the car."

"No . . . I'm awake. Really." She smiled brightly. After he left, she dressed and left the stateroom, sure of one thing at least. A few more hours with Danny Rees probably wouldn't make or break her life—other than setting new standards of orgasmic bliss. And that was a real plus.

As she walked up to the main deck, she was struck with a consoling thought. Danny was good friends with Buddy Morton, who certainly was legit. Although, on second thought, how many people did she know who owned a yacht and race horses? On the other hand, Buddy'd once said something about his family owning one of the early flour mills in Minneapolis, and all those old pioneer families still had tons of money. So there. Buddy was more or less unimpeachable; ergo—so was his friend. There was probably some perfectly reasonable explanation for Danny not working. And she'd probably misunderstood his phone conversation. Gardeners could work on Sunday. It wasn't against the law.

Pleased that she'd rationalized away the little discrepancies, and more pleased that she could look forward to a night in bed with Danny Rees, she was smiling when she approached the group around the bonfire. Or she was until she saw the redhead Marisa with the jewelry from Dominic's. And it wasn't their discrepancies in incomes that was bothering her now, but the fact that the wealthy bitch was wearing a bikini so small it was questionable whether any actual fabric was involved. Furthermore, she was standing so close to Danny you couldn't have slipped a piece of paper between her substantially exposed tits and his chest.

And he wasn't backing up.

The bitch saw her coming and ran a lethal-looking fingernail up Danny's cheek and purred something in his ear. He took a small step backward then; Stella had to give him credit there. But he ruined it by apparently saying something funny because they both laughed.

There must have been something in the woman's gaze that made him turn his head. On seeing Stella, he spoke a few words and turned to meet her with a smile.

"You ready to go, babe?"

She would have been happier to leave five minutes ago before she'd seen that smug look on the bikini lady. Or seen so much of her really fabulous body. Silicone or not, the rest of that bod required dedicated hours in the gym; just looking at it made her feel inadequate. "I'm ready any time," she said, trying to sound as casual as he.

"Come on Stella, sit down!" Buddy called out. "We're doing songs from the '80s!"

"Come on, Danny!" Kirsty cried. "You can't leave this early!"

"We'll sing 'Rio' by Duran Duran if you want!" Megan exclaimed, lifting her wineglass in salute. "Your favorite!"

Stella looked at Danny, not sure whether to blow off her jealousy or say something about how there was no way she was staying if those bitches were here.

"We're going to call it a night," he said. "If it's okay with you," he politely added, sliding his arm around Stella's shoulder and pulling her close.

His reply was greeted with whistles and boos and shouts of "Party pooper!" from those around the fire who were well lubricated with alcohol.

Maybe it didn't matter if she wasn't wearing enough jewelry to finance a college education or didn't have double-D boobs. Maybe she'd taken this round in the "Who's Sleeping with the

Bachelor" stakes. Maybe she could afford to be magnanimous in victory. "I'd like that," she said, polite as can be.

Taking Stella's hand, Danny waved to the crowd and moved toward the tree line bordering the beach. "You didn't really want to sing around the bonfire, did you?"

"I'd have to be drunker than I am right now."

"No kidding. I've never understood the appeal."

"It's not in my gene pool, either."

He smiled at her.

And she smiled back, feeling a serious rapport, feeling as though the night had closed around them and they were walking on the sand in some other universe.

"Do you want a drink?" he murmured.

She hadn't had one all day. "Why start now?"

"That's what I was thinking." He was stone sober. He couldn't remember when he'd been with a woman without drinking at least a glass of wine or two. This was some kind of record. In more ways than one, he thought with a smile.

They moved up the beach in a companionable silence, holding hands, the stars overhead more brilliant than usual. Or so they appeared to two people who were feeling the magic.

"Nice night," he said.

"Perfect," she said.

And then they reached his car and Stella almost had a heart attack. She dropped his hand. "Is this yours?" she said, beating down the scream in the back of her throat.

"It's not new," he said, as though her stifled query required some explanation.

"It looks new. What is it?" A shiny, silver, low-slung race car that looked like it could go a thousand miles an hour gleamed in the moonlight.

"A Ferrari."

"Really." A shocked whisper.

Now he wished he'd said a Mitsubishi or something. She might not have known, and apparently the word *Ferrari* was freaking her out. "I won't drive fast if that's a problem."

What she was worried about was being shot to death in a back alley by drug dealers who wore shiny suits or baggy clothes or T-shirts that said DRUGS KILL. Shit.

He looked at her funny. She must have sworn out loud.

"What's wrong?"

"Nothing."

He bent his head enough to look in her eyes. "Tell me. I'll fix it."

Oh, jeez. That didn't sound good—that "fix it" part. He probably fixed all kinds of stuff she didn't want to hear about. Okay, she'd just blurt it out and take her chances. "Do you really design video games?"

Crap. Just when he'd forgotten all that bullshit. His gaze went shuttered. "Why do you want to know?"

She waved at the car. "I want to know how you can afford this."

This was probably where he should tell her to go to hell. But if she was working for his competitors, she would know how he could afford this car. On the other hand, she might be playing stupid for a reason. "I design video games. I can afford this." It was her serve.

"Why didn't you say that before?" She really wanted to believe him for more reasons than not wanting to die in an alley.

"Does it matter?" He watched her closely.

Why was she feeling like a cobra was looking at her ready to strike. "I thought you were unemployed, and well . . . I didn't know how you could afford your house and everything. You don't sell drugs, do you?" Her voice trailed off and she half smiled.

He had to give her credit. She did that innocent pose to a T. But they were going to her house tonight, not his; his was being guarded by a top-notch crew, and he was going to screw her all night. His smile was warm and boyish for a very good reason. "Christ, I'm sorry. I didn't realize you were worried. Buddy will vouch for me," he murmured. "Are we good now?" It was amazing what you'd do for a phenomenal piece of ass.

She nodded. "I guess I'm more of a small-town girl than I thought."

Either that or a real life cyber-thief. "Not a problem," he said, holding out his hand. "Let me help you in. The seats are low."

She was quiet as they pulled out of the parking place, and he switched on the stereo. "Anything special you'd like to hear?"

The stereo looked like the dash on a space ship, all flashing lights and words scrolling across the screen and about ten different knobs that all must be there for a reason. "How about The White Stripes. If you have it."

"This unit holds ten thousand songs. I've got it."

And a brief moment later, the music came out of so many speakers she felt as though she were sitting in the front row at the concert. "Good sound," she said, trying not to think about the amount of money this car cost. Or the stereo, for that matter. She had a boom box from Target that played one CD at a time.

Really, maybe she was getting in too deep.

She wasn't used to luxury and the possibly illegitimate funds behind it.

He touched her hand lightly, and she turned.

"Care to give that pink rabbit some game time tonight?" he murmured.

On the other hand, he could very well be a hard-working computer person who happened to make a very good living. When faced with his offer of the pink rabbit in his very capable hands, it didn't take her more than a fraction of a second to decide.

She'd give him the benefit of the doubt.

TWENTY-FOUR

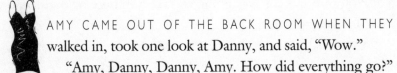 AMY CAME OUT OF THE BACK ROOM WHEN THEY walked in, took one look at Danny, and said, "Wow."

"Amy, Danny, Danny, Amy. How did everything go?" Stella asked, feeling a surge of jealousy she'd rather not feel.

"Good. Good." Amy was looking directly at Danny. "I mean, sales were good," she added, glancing at Stella. She grinned. "I'm a little high. You like comics?" she asked, staring at Danny again.

"Sure do. Stella's got a great store here. It's the best." And putting his arm around Stella, he pulled her close. "And you're the best," he murmured, kissing her lightly on the cheek.

It shouldn't have mattered that he'd been so sweet, but she felt about ten feet tall, like she'd summited Everest and found the Holy Grail at the same time. Funny thing about infatuation. It consumed you and turned your world upside down and made you consider things like drug dealers and impossibly expensive Ferraris irrelevant to wanting what you wanted.

"It was nice meeting you, Amy," Danny said, drawing Stella toward the stairs.

"Thanks, Amy. I'll pay you tomorrow."

"I'll pay her," Danny said, stopping. "What do you need?" He shoved his hand into his shorts pocket and pulled out a wad of bills two inches thick.

"Ninety-six bucks."

Peeling off two hundreds from his pile of money, he handed them to Amy. "Thanks for giving Stella a break. Keep the change."

Amy grinned. "Anytime."

He may not have had a 9mm in his shorts pocket, but that bankroll in hundreds was going to take a minute or two to rationalize away.

"Okay, babe, where were we?" Bending low so his mouth was next to her ear, he whispered, "I'll bet I can make you cry uncle with that pink rabbit."

Ohmygod. *Oh. My. God.* Then again, she was a master at rationalizing. She'd had years of practice. "You're on," she whispered back.

Hadn't someone once said about difficult choices, "There's always tomorrow"?

TWENTY-FIVE

WHEN MORNING CAME AND HER ALARM RANG, Stella groaned.

"Do you want me to open the store?"

Had she heard some miraculous voice from on high? She opened her eyes to find Danny dressed—in different clothes—holding a latte from the downtown diner in his hand and smiling like some bright, cheery person who actually liked to get up early in the morning. She groaned again, not capable of forming a coherent sentence after less than three hours of sleep.

"Go back to sleep. I can take care of things until you get up. I know comics."

He knew a ton of other really great things, too, but that sequence of thoughts would have to wait for a time when her brain cells were functioning above submarginal levels.

He gave her that finger-gun salute and walked out of the room, closing the door behind him.

Stella was sleeping again before he'd reached the ground floor.

The next time she came awake, the clock was chiming in the living room. You know how your brain automatically counts even if you don't want it to, how it keeps time with the carillon bells on Sunday? When her subconscious got to twelve, she sat bolt-upright in bed, glanced at the clock on her dresser—*noon*—and shrieked.

Right before she threw the covers aside and bolted from the bed.

Jesus Christ, the store!

And Ryan Kath and a dozen other kids who didn't have anywhere else to go when they woke up!

Not to mention the delivery guy from Bread Loafers, who had to be paid for the morning buns!

She jammed her legs into her jeans, pulled a T-shirt over her head, combed her hair with her fingers, and ran barefoot down the stairs.

"Feel like some lunch?" Danny asked, looking up from the table in the front room, as did several kids who were apparently eating lunch with him. A very wholesome, nutritious lunch comprised of whole-grain bread ham sandwiches, grapes and peaches piled in a bowl, yogurt smoothies, and best of all, chocolate cake.

"Hey." Ryan waved. "Danny said you swam too much yesterday out on the river and needed your rest. Some people just don't have stamina, right?" he teased, tossing a friendly smile at Danny that had taken her months to first see.

"Danny's telling us how to win at *Tribes*. He knows every-thing," Matt Cordell said. "Dontcha?" Another smile for the hero of the moment.

"I helped Danny figure out the cash register," Amy said. "He's a quick learner."

Now Ryan and Matt, not to mention the other three kids, were early risers. So seeing them here wasn't a stretch. But Amy didn't like to get up till afternoon. No way, no how.

That little green monster narrowed Stella's gaze. But Danny patted his knee just then, said, "Come on, sit down," and her jealousy evaporated.

"Thanks for minding the store," she said, taking him up on his offer. The feel of his arms closing around her as she settled onto his lap was pretty damned nice. Like a prize.

"Ummm, you're still warm," he whispered into her ear. "Did you sleep well?" he said in a normal tone of voice. "The kids and I have been trying to figure out if more people read *Spiderman* or *X-Men*."

"In this store it's *X-Men*."

Danny tipped his head. "You win, Ryan."

"Told ya." Ryan was beaming. "So do I get a ride now?"

Stella had forgotten about his car. Aaagh. There it was. The old demon of suspicion rearing its ugly head.

"You said whoever won. You said as soon as Stella got up."

"That I did. I'll be right back," Danny said, giving Stella a brushing kiss on the cheek.

"Eiuww," everyone at the table under fourteen breathed.

Danny grinned. "Don't knock it guys. Stella's special."

Wow. Was this what it felt like to win an Oscar? Or the No-ble Prize? Or was she just so shallow that a compliment from someone like Danny Rees could spin her head around like the girl in the *Exorcist*? She was speechless. And that hadn't happened more than twice in her life; both times she'd had her mouth full of something chocolate.

Unlike today, when being speechless was a product of sheer, unadulterated, raving-mad intoxication.

"Hey, babe, I'll be right back." Danny seemed not to notice her paralysis and, lifting her from his lap, eased her back onto his chair with a smile. Putting his arm around Ryan as they walked from the store, Danny said, "Now if you were old enough, I'd let you drive."

"I'm jealous," Amy murmured. "Lucky you."

Stella didn't know how to answer with several junior high kids staring at her. "He's really into comics," she said, hoping that would play to the crowd.

"You said it," Chris agreed. "And he's met the artist for *Superman* and for *Batman,* and he even knows Stan Lee."

"I don't believe Stan Lee," another young boy said. "He's way too big."

"He probably met him at a comic book convention," Stella noted. "I saw Stan Lee at one once."

"Saw him and know him are two different things," Matt pointedly contended.

"He knows everything." Chris's expression was awe-struck.

If only they knew, Stella reflected, Danny's expertise in several other areas was outstanding. Gold medal, first class. She might be inclined to say on occasion even better than chocolate—an encomium of the highest order.

"He must be rich if he owns a Ferrari," one of the boys said. "They cost mega-bucks."

Not an issue Stella cared to contemplate at the moment, when she was still feeling all warm and fuzzy and cared for. She didn't want to deal with the unsettling question of how Danny could afford a Ferrari.

"He creates video games," Amy explained. "They make money."

"Did he say which ones?" Stella asked.

"Uh-uh. Ryan asked him about his car and they started talking about engines."

Or maybe Danny changed the subject, Stella thought. She'd never gotten a straight answer from him when it came to the name of his game, either.

"I'm going to put him in my book," Amy said. "He's way cool. Do you know where he lives?"

For a moment Stella thought of playing dumb. But that might imply she cared when she'd be real stupid to do any such thing. "He lives over by the river," she said. "Off County Road M."

"That's not too far."

What exactly did Amy mean? But again, she chose not to consider herself a girlfriend. Danny Rees and the word *girlfriend* were mutually exclusive. *Keep everything in perspective,* she warned herself. *Keep your grip on reality.* "Pass the cake, will you?" When in doubt, reach for chocolate. It was her mantra and guiding light. It was her salvation.

SHE'D EATEN TWO pieces and was feeling much more secure by the time Danny and Ryan returned. She could even watch the delight on Amy's face without feeling more than a twinge. The euphoria occasioned by chocolate was really amazing.

Maybe instead of nuclear weapons, the defense department should consider wholesale exportation of chocolate bars. The world would be a better place. People would smile more. Americans might even forget that the interest on the deficit was costing taxpayers two billion dollars a day.

On the other hand, maybe chocolate couldn't do *everything*. Two billion dollars was a lot of money.

But it could be a start.

"WHO WANTS TO do their math now?" Danny asked.

Stella's head snapped up, she met Danny's cheerful gaze, and she immediately began to believe in karma. Not with her usual lip service. But for real. "You like math?" she said.

"I won the national math quiz in ninth grade; it was my major in college, too."

"No way."

"Word of honor."

"Are you a Boy Scout?"

"No. Are you a Girl Scout?"

Okay, never mind. She wasn't a joiner, either. "I don't suppose you like math puzzles?"

"I suppose I might."

She grinned. "Where have you been all my life?"

"Ten miles away—at least the last few years."

Oops. Why did he have to remind her that she didn't know squat about him. She didn't know where he grew up or who his parents were or where he went to school. More importantly, she didn't know if he dealt drugs and consorted with felons.

"Danny said he had some detectives guarding his place last night."

"Hey." Danny shot Ryan a sharp look. "That's enough."

"Sorry. I forgot." Ryan looked distraught. "I'm really sorry."

"Never mind. It's no big deal."

"What detectives?" Chris exclaimed, all eyes.

"They're just friends of mine. They're staying with me for a few days."

Now that story was different from the word *guarding* that Ryan had used. Fucking A it was. Her chocolate cake euphoria melted away like sugar in a rain storm.

Back to the real world, where handsome, sexy men like Danny Rees weren't likely to be your knight in shining armor. Not that she was looking for a knight, but a fellow math wizard—now that was a real dream date. That was better than a fairy tale any day. And if you added hot sex into the equation, it pretty much went off the charts when it came to a perfect match.

"Come on. Who needs help with their math homework?" Danny pointed at the kids she was tutoring and jerked his thumb toward the back room. "We'll work for a half hour and then you can have a ride in the Ferrari, too."

She'd never seen two kids move so fast in her life.

"Give me a half hour," he said, glancing at Stella. "Another ten minutes for a ride and then we'll go someplace quiet. Amy's kindly agreed to take over for the afternoon."

Amy blushed.

He was able to perform a variety of miracles. Amy rarely even showed emotion, let alone a blush like what now colored her normally unearthly pale skin. And Ryan's rare smile and the boys actually running to do their homework—no wonder she'd fallen under his spell.

He was a damned Svengali.

Be strong.

Or be afraid.

She wasn't sure which.

But by God, he could charm the birds out of the trees.

TWENTY-SIX

WHEN THE HOMEWORK WAS DONE AND THE CAR ride over, Stella and Danny left.

"Where to?" he said as they stood on her porch. "Someplace quiet preferably."

"The back room at Crystal's is quiet, and I could get a pork chop on a stick. What? I only had two pieces of chocolate cake. I need protein."

He did a two-second run through a list of other options. She was right about the quiet back room though. "What kind of tap beer?"

"Labatt's. What else?"

He grinned. "Do you think we were separated at birth?"

"I sure as hell hope not."

"Amen to that." And he waved her before him down the stairs.

She found the answer to his change of clothes tossed on the shelf behind the seats, a small overnight bag left open. "You travel prepared."

"They were left over from something or other."

Not wishing to ruin her really good mood, she had no intention of pressing for an explanation beyond his vague answer. It wasn't as though he'd been a monk before she met him.

Crystal's back room was empty at two on a Sunday afternoon in July; everyone was out on the bar's terrace overlooking the river.

The Labatt's was crisply cool, the glasses frosted, and the pork chops done to perfection on Crystal's wood grill. And a lazy lethargy, part physical, part emotional contentment, seeped into the senses of the only occupants of the room. They held hands on the table top, kissed with frosty cool lips, and smiled at each other between desultory attempts at conversation.

"My sister really is coming next weekend," he said.

"I'll see you after she leaves." She didn't even notice she was talking like a girlfriend.

He nodded and smiled. "Maybe she'll leave early." He didn't actually know what a boyfriend sounded like. That learning curve had never been explored.

"Had enough?" She offered him a bite of her third pork chop.

"Of that—yeah." He grinned. "Of other things—no. When does your store clear out?"

"Six today."

He glanced at his watch. "We might have to do it in the car."

"And where exactly would you find the necessary privacy to do that?" The town was mobbed on summer weekends.

He groaned softly.

"We could go to your place."

Obsession lent some credence to the idea. He wasn't about to fall asleep this afternoon; he could keep an eye on her. He could also call ahead and clear his house. "Why not?"

"I thought you'd never ask," she teased.

Not exactly a soothing response, but nothing he couldn't handle when he'd gone almost seven hours without screwing her. When in serious withdrawal, logic was tied up in the back room.

He paid the tab.

Stella ignored the wad of bills. She was in major denial of her own with her sexual motors revving up.

They'd almost reached the car when Danny's phone rang. After a glance at the screen, he said, "Excuse me," and walked a short distance away.

One of the guards at his house said, "We caught a man and a woman trying to get in through your gate. They say they know you. Kirsty and Brian."

"I'll be right there." Returning to Stella, he said, "Sorry, something came up. I'll take you home." And he watched for her reaction.

Jesus, he looked grim. "Is there a problem?"

"Maybe."

"Is there anything I can do to help?"

He didn't answer for a three count. "I'll let you know," he said with a tight smile, taking her arm and hurrying her to the car.

She had to practically run to keep up with him. And all her reservations came flooding back. Every TV show on drugs she'd ever seen ran like video clips through her brain. Would she see his name in the papers tomorrow? Would the headlines proclaim, MAJOR DRUG BUST IN ST. CROIX COUNTY WISCONSIN?

Shit. Why couldn't the good guys come with less baggage? Or worse, was he really not a good guy? Was he the absolute polar opposite?

Who the hell was she, he thought. Friend or foe? Was she supposed to keep him occupied while her colleagues made another pass at his office? Was hot sex her MO, and he was stupid enough to fall for it?

He didn't speak on the swift drive up the hill to her house. He was too tempted to say something rude. And if he was wrong—he'd be losing something he might not want to lose.

"Call me," she said as she got out. Although with that grim look on his face she wasn't sure he would.

"Right."

Not a smile, not so much as the slightest warmth in his voice.

She shut the car door.

He stepped on the gas—hard.

And five seconds later, her street was quiet enough even for Mrs. Blythe.

TWENTY-SEVEN

 WHEN HE REACHED HIS HOUSE, HE WAS GREETED by one of the security guards. "We found them coming across the field west of the house. They claim they climbed under the fence when they found the gate locked."

"Thanks, Zack. Where are they?"

"They're waiting in your kitchen. Stu's watching them."

"THANK GOD YOU'RE here," Kirsty exclaimed as Danny walked into the kitchen, coming to her feet, then sitting back down again after a quick look at Stu. "Tell these two gorillas we're friends."

Danny glanced at Brian, who hadn't moved from his place at the kitchen table. The guy was confident. You had to give him that.

"You don't usually come in under the fence," Danny said. "What's going on?"

"We were riding around in Brian's new car and decided to see what you were doing. The gate was locked so we decided to walk in. That's it. End of story." She jerked her head toward the guards. "Who are these guys?"

"I've had a couple break-ins. I decided to get some security." If they were involved, he wasn't giving away anything. And if they weren't, it didn't matter.

"If we were trying to break in, we would have brought a crow bar instead of a six-pack," Brian said with faint derision. "And whatever you have I don't need."

"They did have a six-pack," Zack noted.

"After Buddy docked, we were looking for something to do," Kirsty said. "We didn't think we'd be treated like criminals," she huffily added. "I've been here a hundred times."

A slight exaggeration, but he got the picture. They were still in their boating clothes, they *had* come during the day. Not necessarily a pass for them if they'd thought he was somewhere else. But still. "Sit tight. I'll be right back." He wanted to check out his office—not that they'd made it that far, but he needed assurance.

"And if we don't?" Brian challenged.

"Then Stu and Curt will have to see that you do." *Don't fuck with me,* he thought. He wasn't in the mood.

It took him five minutes to see that everything in his office was secure, and none of the little snares he'd left behind had been moved. He apologized when he returned to the kitchen, not because he necessarily believed their intentions were innocent, but because he couldn't be sure. "I've never had any problems out here before," he added. "I'm just being careful. Sorry for the inconvenience."

Kirsty puffed up her considerable chest and shot him an indignant glance. "Are we free to leave?"

"Sure. I'll give you a ride to your car."

She opened and shut her mouth, changing her mind about a temper tantrum after calculating the distance to the road. Her sandals weren't meant for walking that half-mile gravel drive.

Brian maintained his above-the-fray aloofness. Danny couldn't decide if it was machismo or something more sinister. He'd be glad when Frank's friend came back from vacation and they could see if Brian had a criminal record.

The ride to Brian's car passed in silence, the three of them in the front seat of his truck, Kirsty doing a little petulant sniff from time to time, Brian maintaining a studied nonchalance. After going through the open gate of his drive, Danny eased over to the side of the county road, caught a glimpse of Brian's car, and felt all his suspicions return.

The Porsche had been left well out of sight behind a stand of junipers. That choice of parking places didn't exactly tip the scales in favor of Brian's innocence. He could have chosen to leave his car on either side of the driveway. There was plenty of space.

Before Danny had come to a halt, Brian had the door open. His feet were on the ground before the truck rolled to a stop, and he strode away without a backward glance. Left to fend for herself, Kirsty snapped, "Thanks for nothing," and followed Brian.

Not that he cared what Kirsty thought.

But he was interested in Brian Larson.

He watched the Porsche Boxster back out of the woods and pull away, the black car gliding down the road smooth as silk. So what was that interesting experience all about? The hidden car. Brian's screw-you attitude. The fact that Kirsty never walked anywhere if she could ride. He'd just added a couple more liabilities to the increasing list of problems in his life. Fuck, he hated having problems. What had happened to his easy-going, purposely unentangled life?

Now he had cyber-thieves targeting him.

And Stella Scott burning a hole through his previously fireproof psyche.

It made one think there might actually be honest-to-God retribution for one's sins.

TWENTY-EIGHT

"MEGAN'S BEEN CALLING," AMY ANNOUNCED AS Stella entered the store. "About a hundred times."

"I'll give her a call. Thanks for keeping an eye on things. Take your wages out of the till, and leave me a slip."

Amy gave Stella a sympathetic look. "Men are undependable. Don't worry about it."

Stella looked up from straightening a pile of comics. "Am I that transparent?"

Amy smiled. "You always are. Consider yourself lucky. In a family like mine you learn to never show anything. It saves a lot of hassle."

"He left"—Stella shrugged—"not exactly angry, but something was wrong."

"Don't blame yourself. Men are so into themselves. It has

nothing to do with you, believe me. He probably got a call to go and play golf."

Stella thought of questioning Amy's expertise, but decided she'd rather not know how someone so young could be so cynical. Especially now, when her own cynicism was peaking. Dammit, though, she wasn't going to feel guilty. She hadn't done anything wrong. In fact, in terms of wrongness, Danny was probably so off the chart, she didn't want to even think about it. He had to be a drug dealer. And that was the sad and sobering truth.

After Amy left, after she'd answered four very similar questions of why she had run out of ice-cream bars, after she'd refereed a fight over who was the coolest dude in *X-Men*—Wolverine naturally—she returned Megan's call.

Before Megan had uttered more than three sentences, Stella knew she was going to need full-body armor to protect her from the giddy happiness buffeting her across the phone lines. Especially now with her own life a mess. Trying not to freak out was going to require nerves of steel.

"And besides him buying me the entire set of *Seinfeld* shows, Buddy brought the boat in early so the kids wouldn't miss the new *Lion Something* movie, and he drove them there while I made lasagna that he says is his absolute favorite," Megan breathlessly exclaimed. "And—and"—another breath was required—"you can't imagine what we're going to do tomorrow. Not in a millions years. Guess!" Apparently immune to the contradiction, she added, "You'll never guess!"

"Okay, I give up," Stella said, taking the easy way out.

"Buddy invited the kids and me to go to Valley Fair! Can you imagine?"

Actually, she couldn't, no more than she could imagine Buddy, who liked designer silk shirts and linen slacks, riding a Ferris wheel or eating a slurpee. "I can't imagine," Stella replied with complete honesty.

"Well, it's true! He asked me when he drove me home. Where have you been? I've been trying to call you!"

"Down at Crystal's."

"What for?"

"A pork chop on a stick." She wasn't going to go into the rest unless she was under torture. Not when Megan's love life was on cloud nine and her own was in the pits.

"We're going to Valley Fair at ten tomorrow!" Megan went on, reciting their entire schedule for the day with scarcely a pause for breath. "I'm so happy I could scream!" she finished.

She had been screaming, but Stella was happy for Megan. She'd had a couple bad years; she deserved good things happening to her. And if Buddy was including the children in this quasi-courtship, it could mean he was serious. "Take pictures," Stella teased. "I want a complete report of your day."

"You better believe it! I'm bringing my video camera!"

Stella laughed. "The kids must be excited."

"They're going nuts. They love Valley Fair, but you know how expensive it is. You can't run down there too often."

"Buddy can afford it."

"Don't I know it, although that's not why I like him. I would anyway. In fact, sometimes I wish he didn't have so much money. It kind of messes things up. I wouldn't want to think his income might temper my judgment."

"You're pretty stable, kid. That's why you handled all the—"

"Crap from Chad?"

"Yeah. That. So don't worry about your judgment. Look how good your kids are. That's because of you."

"They are good kids, aren't they," Megan said with a mother's pride.

"They're the best. So have a good time tomorrow, and don't worry about anything but having fun."

"Thanks for listening. I'm *so-o-o* excited."

"Not a problem. You've been there for me every time I needed you."

"How *are* things going for you and Danny?"

"Good. Fine. Couldn't be better."

"It looked that way yesterday. Hey, would you two like to join us at Valley Fair? I'm sure Buddy wouldn't mind."

"No thanks. I'm on my usual deadline. But I appreciate the offer."

"Here comes Buddy back from driving the kids! Gotta go!"

Stella didn't move for several minutes after she hung up the phone, needing some down time after being run over by that truckload of delirious joy. She was happy for Megan. Really. But she was envious, too. Especially now when nothing was going right and she was being reminded of all the negatives of a relationship with Danny Rees. You know, like *him being a criminal*.

Luckily, the store wasn't busy this time of day so she could mope unnoticed. With suppertime near, most of the kids had left. Only three or four were still lounging in the chairs in the front room, loathe to go home.

Right now, she knew the feeling. Her home had always been her haven. And now it seemed empty and comfortless without one particular man.

Not good.

Not good at all.

Maybe she'd have to take up a hobby in addition to all the other stuff going on in her life. Every time she had a quiet moment she thought of him.

Aaargh.

Ink in a black cloud over her head, she thought. This particular frame of her life wasn't going to need any bright colors.

AND THEN, AS if Stella wasn't down in the dumps enough, Megan called back no more than twenty minutes later with another news flash.

"I'm whispering," Megan said, "because Buddy's watching cartoons with the kids in the other room, but I couldn't wait to tell you something more fabulous than Valley Fair! You're going to just die!"

Because she was sliding into a slough of depression big time, obliging Megan on the dying thing might not be too difficult. "Tell me your great news," Stella said, forcing warmth into her voice. Megan's level of excitement was beyond her capabilities at the moment, but friendly was doable.

"Well, first Buddy brought a Palm Pilot home, and you know how expensive those are. And second, he's going to call some friend of his who's some media guy who runs campaigns—I mean, big-time campaigns. He's going to have this fellow give me a list of voters in my district who are interested in the environment. And best of all, Buddy's going to drive me around and help me knock on doors and show me how to punch in data on the Palm Pilot to keep track of all the voters who might vote for me. Is that like a miracle or what?"

Megan's long, breathless explanation had given Stella time to gather her composure. She was able to reply with sincerity that would have passed muster with the Pope. "Your senate seat is in the bag, sweetie. I'm so pleased."

"Isn't Buddy just the best?"

"He's a pretty nice guy." In contrast to the possible criminal type she was fixated on.

"I can't thank you enough for knowing him. Really, I mean it—if not for you, I'd never have met Buddy."

"Thank the mangas."

"The who?"

"The comics. That's how I met Buddy."

"Well, whatever, I'm so, *so-o-o* happy," Megan whispered.

"And I'm happy for you, kid. You deserve it. Keep me posted on your happiness updates. I've got a good feeling about this relationship."

"Do you think so? Do you think it could be—you know . . . an actual relationship?"

"Jeez. How many guys go out of their way like Buddy's doing?" Stella pointed out. "Calling his media friend. Asking for valuable information from him. I doubt that's going to be free."

"Oh, shit. I didn't think about that. How much do you think it will cost?"

"Don't worry. Buddy can afford it."

"But he shouldn't have to pay for my campaign stuff."

"If he didn't want to he wouldn't, believe me. I've yet to meet a guy who opens his wallet just for the hell of it—like for platonic friendship. I'm guessing you're involved in a real relationship, sweetie."

"You think?"

"Ask him."

"I couldn't. No way. Besides, I probably shouldn't be obsessing about some guy I met a week or so ago. You know . . . I should be sensible—especially after Chad."

"You never obsessed about Chad."

"I didn't?" There was a lengthy pause. "I didn't, did I?" Megan said slowly, like a mystery had been solved.

"Nope. You liked him, but you didn't obsess. You'd known Chad since grade school. It was probably one of those comfortable-as-an-old-shoe things."

"That's depressing. Oh, well," Megan whispered, brightly a second later. "It all turned out for the best."

Stella hadn't ever heard Megan say anything so cheerfully positive about her divorce—ever. "It sure looks that way," Stella remarked. "Nothing but sunshine and rainbows from now on."

"I really feel that way," Megan enthused. "Like the whole world could be mine."

With Buddy's money it probably could, Stella thought. But she said instead, "Just be sure you remember us little people once you're a big-time senator."

"You know, it almost seems possible now. Like *really* possible. I'm talking to Stella," she said in a normal tone of voice. "Are the cartoons over? I'll be right there. Buddy says hi."

"Hi back."

"I'd better get supper on the table, but I had to tell you all the unbelievable things that are happening to me—to us . . . the kids, too. Buddy's so nice to them," she added in a whisper. "I'll talk to you tomorrow."

And Stella was left with the phone in her hand and her life going in the opposite direction from the next state senator who was on the love train chugging along at top speed to Happy Town.

Megan's life was turning into a Hallmark card with a house and a white picket fence in the background, a smiling family in the foreground, and a big yellow sun above symbolizing their bright future.

She, on the other hand, was mixed up in a disaster-in-the-making, the man with whom she was obsessed so secretive she didn't even know what he did for a living.

And speculation wasn't very comforting.

Although she may have been cut from his to-call list if his mood when he dropped her off was any indication of his true feelings.

Maybe she should finally kill off Marky B's new sidekick and get it over with.

You know, like cut your losses.

Because a Happy Town ending didn't look like it was gonna happen for her.

TWENTY-NINE

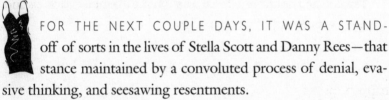 FOR THE NEXT COUPLE DAYS, IT WAS A STAND-off of sorts in the lives of Stella Scott and Danny Rees—that stance maintained by a convoluted process of denial, evasive thinking, and seesawing resentments.

Stella absolutely refused to be infatuated with a man who was most likely a drug dealer. It was not only counterproductive, but it led nowhere fast. She was a mature, sensible woman who knew enough to make informed, adult choices.

Danny had never spent more than ten minutes thinking about any one woman, and Stella Scott had tramped all over that record a couple thousand minutes ago. But the real deal-breaker had to do with her possible involvement in these break-ins. If she was working for the competition, there was no way to sugar-coat that.

If she'd stuck to her rule about dating customers, Stella

reflected, she'd be ringing up some stellar sales right now, compliments of Danny Rees's comic habit. As it was, she'd just lost a ton of money. And all for sex. How stupid was that?

Danny had tried to erase the new female character in his video game but found himself adding to her fighting skills instead of killing her off. He told himself it was all about making money with the new game; complex characters were more interesting.

Suffice it to say, neither of them were entirely sane by the evening of the second day.

Danny gave in first because he didn't have a store full of kids to marginally detract him from his lust and he'd wacked off so many times, his arm was getting sore. He didn't understand that carnal desires had anything to do with love, but then he'd never had any experience, so one could cut him some slack in that regard.

He debated briefly whether he should call or just drive over.

Gee, what would Spiderman do?

THIRTY

HIS SISTER CALLED WHILE HE WAS ON THE WAY over to Stillwater, and he almost didn't answer. He finally did on the sixth ring, because he was programed to give into her. It just went with the older sister territory.

"Did I call at a bad time?" Libby asked. "You sound like you want to rip someone's head off."

"Sorry. Road rage. Some jerk almost took my fender off." The truth wasn't an option. Libby would give him advice he didn't want to hear.

"I won't talk long if you're driving in heavy traffic. I just wanted to give you a heads-up. We're coming in a day early for a sale at Ikea."

Danny stifled a groan. Entertaining family wasn't high on his list right now. "Great," he said. So he'd put his dicey love life on hold for an *entire* three-day weekend. No problem.

"You don't sound great."

"It's the damned traffic," he lied, cursing her fine-tuned perception. She'd been the only one in the family who could understand his unintelligible toddler language; apparently that sixth sense was still functioning.

"Maybe we could meet that owner of the comic book store when we're in town."

"Why?" he asked, the muscles in his shoulders tensing.

"The kids would like to see her store. You said it was a good one. And when we talked last time you didn't say no when I mentioned it. If it's a problem—"

"If there's time," he said.

"If you'd rather not."

"Let's just see how things go."

"Did you have a fight with her?"

"Christ, Libby, give me a break. Since when do you care about my girlfriends?"

"So she's a girlfriend?"

Oops. "Girl friend, two separate words, okay? She's a friend. More like an acquaintance. We both like comics. That's it."

"Whatever you say."

He hated that tone. The I-don't-believe-you-for-a-minute tone. "That's what I have to say. I'll see you on Friday."

"Thursday night."

His knuckles went white on the wheel. "Sounds good. Thursday."

"Be careful with your driving."

"Yeah, yeah. Are we done?"

"Absolutely. Bye."

Her voice had been cheerful as hell. And he knew why. Because she was thinking she'd meet Stella in a few days, and she was think-ing there was more to Stella and him than he was saying. Not that it was likely they'd meet. For one thing, Stella might be on his shit list if she was involved in his break-ins. For another, even if she wasn't involved, their relationship wasn't exactly free of friction. Although, it had to be her fault. He'd never had this problem before.

Jeez, would they ever finish construction on the lift bridge, he grumbled, braking to a stop behind a long line of cars waiting for the flag man to give them the go-ahead. He fiddled with the ra-dio, looking for a good song, tapped his fingers on the wheel, counted the cars in front of him, checked his watch.

He wouldn't admit to nerves.

He was never nervous.

What the hell did he have to be nervous about?

"Thank you," he murmured under his breath as the flag man waved them on.

But he tensed up big time when his cell phone rang a block from Stella's and Frank Stanchfield's number came up. Now this call he'd take. Pulling over, he parked and flipped open his phone.

"What's up?" he asked.

"I have news that will eliminate some of your suspects. The first bit of news you'll read in your papers tomorrow. Brian Lar-son was just busted as part of a drug ring the feds have been watching. The Kirsty girl was with him at his house; she went into hysterics, apparently. After she was calmed down, the feds were able to question her, and she turned out to be a stupid by-stander, but otherwise innocent. I'm not saying the Larson guy is completely free of suspicion in your break-ins, but my guess is he's only doing one thing at a time. The drug ring was a pretty good size. You'll hear the inflated street prices quoted in the paper tomorrow, but it wasn't small potatoes by any means."

"So I should cross off Brian and Kirsty from my suspect list?"

"That would be my assumption."

"Okay." Danny blew out a breath. "That doesn't leave a whole lot."

"I'll keep looking. You stay buttoned up out on the farm. How are Stu and Zack doing?"

"Great. Good. Look, thanks again. I'm on my way somewhere. I'll give you a call later and get all the details."

"Sounds good."

Danny sat in his truck afterward, trying to sort through the diminishing options now that Brian and Kirsty were most likely eliminated. It was better that he'd heard the news before he saw Stella, he supposed. He slowly exhaled. Although—shit—this really complicated an already tangled, hairy-assed mess.

But complications aside, sex was still on the table.

It just went to show how fatal attractions could be addictive.

THIRTY-ONE

RYAN SAW DANNY BEFORE STELLA DID AND THEN Chris, Jason, and Zeke took up the welcome cry. He was mobbed as he came through the door.

"Give me a minute, guys. I have to talk to Stella."

"Hurry, 'cuz I want to show you my—" (iPod, game, comic, homework, new sneakers). Take your pick from the chorus.

He moved toward her, not sure whether to smile or look serious, whether he was sad or mad or just screwed up in general.

She was glad there was a counter too high to jump over, or she might have been tempted to throw herself into his arms even though he looked grim as a prosecutor in court.

"Could I talk to you?"

Defensive, elated, and every emotion in between, she went with the first one because she didn't feel like making it easy for him. "Go for it."

He nodded toward the back room. "In private?"

She didn't move.

"It's important."

"If it's about you-know-what," she cryptically said because several pairs of eyes and ears were trained on them, "no."

"It isn't. Please."

His soft appeal did a couple things to her, one good and one not so good. On the other hand, a semi-groveling man partially canceled out the not-so-good thing. "Okay, just for a minute," she said. "Ryan, you're in charge." She didn't want to lose fifty comics because Danny Rees was horny.

He stood aside so she could precede him into the back room and carefully shut the door behind them.

"If you lock it, I'm screaming."

He turned around and held up his hands. "Calm down."

A relative term with him that close, but that might have more to do with her lack of control than his. "What's on your mind?"

Other than you twenty-four seven, not much. But he had to get the dicey stuff out of the way first. And then he'd see if anything was salvageable in this emotional tailspin he was in. "Look, if you're involved in these break-ins, just tell me, and we'll deal with it. I won't press charges."

"Break-ins?" She could have been saying "Mass murders?" with the level of shock in her voice. "What the hell are you talking about?"

Her horrified look was either for real or she was a better actress than he thought. "My office has been broken into twice." He watched her for blinking. "You don't know anything about it?"

"Do I look like I know anything about it?" Not a blink. "Are you nuts?"

Okay, so the psychology of crime wasn't foolproof. "The first time it happened was the night you stayed at my house."

"So? There were other people there, too. Including Miss Kirsty," she acerbically noted, her nostrils flaring. "She's more the type to steal something if you ask me."

Don't look at her boobs when she takes a breath like that. Stay focused. "The second break-in was a few days ago when the power went out."

"I was working on Megan's campaign sign, and for your information, *my* power *didn't* go out. Rather than accuse me of this, I'd think your drug dealer friends would be more likely suspects."

"Pardon me?" Major sarcasm. His dark eyes drilled through her like an offshore oil rig. "Drug dealer friends?"

"Don't try and look all innocent and offended," she shot back, leaning forward, in his face. "You don't have a job. You live like a prince. You have cars that millionaires drive and other people only see in magazines. If you're not a drug dealer, you must have won the lottery. And the odds of that are slim to zero. So that's why I'm thinking drug dealer. And what do you have to steal anyway if you're not a drug dealer? A couple TVs?"

He stared at her like he was trying to decide if her second head was real or not.

"What? You're the fucking law-breaker, not me."

"I'm not a drug dealer."

"And I didn't fall off the last turnip truck."

"Would you like to talk to my accountant?"

"He probably only works for drug dealers. He'll vouch for you."

"What if I asked you for some proof that you didn't try to burglarize my house?"

"I'd tell you to shove it. I don't have to give you proof of anything."

He blew out a breath and scowled at her.

"Scowl all you want. I own a comic book store, not a fencing operation. And believe me, if I tried to turn to crime, Ryan and Chris would be the first ones wanting to be cut in. And probably Amy, too. And Zeke. Shit, I'd have to cut my profits twenty ways with the number of would-be juvies who hang out here."

"So maybe I was wrong." Although he was saying that for a number of reasons over and above his conditional acceptance of her statements.

"I wish I was wrong about you. So far, you haven't convinced me. Ordinary people don't drive cars like yours."

"I have fourteen of them."

"Jesus. Don't tell me that. I'll have to testify in court."

"They're all legit."

"Yeah and I'm Julia Roberts. No one in this burg is that rich."

"Have you heard of *Blizzard 9000?*"

Unless you lived in a cave you had. Even she knew it was more famous than Twinkies and Ho-Hos combined. "Yeah, so?"

"So it's my game, and 160,000,000 people around the globe pay twelve bucks a month to play it. You do the math."

"No," she said on a soft exhalation.

"Word of God."

"I couldn't possibly know anyone that rich."

"Yeah, well—hello. And that's why someone is trying to break into my office."

"Don't look at me like that. It's not me, okay? I wouldn't even know what the hell you had in your office."

"I'm working on a new game."

"One hundred sixty million times twelve times twelve. I can see why your office is popular."

"I have security guards there now."

"Good idea."

A hush descended on the room.

"I've been thinking of you," he finally said, real softly—reluctantly.

"I've been trying not to think of you, and now that you're a kazillionaire, I'm going to work even harder at not thinking about you."

If any of a dozen women he knew had discovered his financial status, they wouldn't have expressed displeasure. "I mostly give my money to charity."

"Commendable, I'm sure. But get real. A guy like you is going to be playing the field for at least another ten years. Twenty maybe. So lotsa luck. I'd better get back to my kids before they steal me blind."

"I don't play the field."

"Sure you do. You just don't admit it."

"Maybe I could stop."

"And maybe you couldn't. I don't want to be your experiment." The last few days had been rougher than hell, and seeing him now made her ache with longing. Why look for trouble? Why leave herself open for the kind of hurt she'd never understood before? The kind that meant you cared about someone more than you might wish. She had to be strong. If she wasn't, she was going to see nothing but buckets of tears for the foreseeable future. "If you'll excuse me." She walked toward the door.

He grabbed her arm. "I don't want to excuse you."

"Look, you think you want something now, but it won't last.

I know it even if you don't. Leopards and spots and all that bull-shit. There's no logical reason for you to change your way of life. And you won't—other than temporarily."

"I might."

"See—you're equivocating already."

"Don't tell me you've made up your mind long-term."

"What if I said I had?"

"I wouldn't believe you. Not a lady with a sketchbook full of former lovers."

"I never said they were lovers."

"Give me a break."

She shook his hand off.

He let her. He wouldn't have had to.

"I think we're done here." If she stayed much longer, she'd throw herself into his arms—even with that black scowl on his face.

"Could I take you out for dinner sometime?" A Hail Mary pass induced by a panic he'd never felt before.

"I think we started there."

"You told me no. We never got started."

"And then where would we go from there? You and your millions have the world at your disposal."

"I'm not going anywhere."

He'd said it softly, like he really meant it. "I sure as hell won't be going anywhere with"—she lifted her hand faintly—"this place."

"Then you might be available for dinner sometime."

"Why are you doing this?" She'd seen all the women on the boat and at Dominic's. He wasn't short of females to keep him company.

"I've missed you. Even when I thought you might be trying to steal my new video game. Even when I didn't want to."

"You missed the sex."

"Okay, I did, but I missed all kinds of other things, too. Your smart-ass mouth. Your dislike of sing-alongs. The Labatt's factor. This comic book store. The fact that I'm actually thinking about crap like soul mates. And I hate that phrase."

"Not as much as I do."

"See. It's destiny."

"You wish. It's hormones."

He could argue with her there, because hormones had pretty much governed his leisure activities for a long time. And if anyone knew the difference, he did. "I could write you a poem and explain."

"A poem? No way!"

"You think I can't write a poem?"

"Would it have Spiderman in it?"

"If you wanted it to. I'd put in Superman and X-Men, too, if it would make you change your mind. Hell, I'd throw in Storm, too, although we're talking heterosexual love here, not metrosexual."

"Did you say love?"

He felt his heart skip a beat, but there were times when one had to face the truth no matter how scary. "Yeah—I guess."

"You guess?"

"Okay, I'm pretty sure."

Hey, pretty sure was a good start. "So this would be a love poem?"

He grinned, feeling better than he thought he would after saying the word *love* and realizing he meant it. "Damn right. Although I can't do haiku. This poem might rhyme."

"It better not start out 'There once was a lady from'—"

"It won't rhyme, okay? I'll learn fucking haiku."

She took a deep breath because her world was sort of teetering on the brink. "Jeez Louise, you're getting to me."

"I could buy you some jewelry, too." He was trying to picture those ads in bride magazines that had been all over the house when his sister was getting married. There was always a picture of a man and a woman staring soulfully into each other's eyes with some huge diamond somewhere on the page. "What do you like?"

She put up her hand. "No jewelry."

"Why not?"

"'Cuz you probably buy jewelry for all the women you sleep with."

"Do not." No way he'd get that personal.

"So you'd buy me jewelry? What kind?"

He laughed. She looked amazingly young. "I don't know. You could pick something out." What did he know about buying jewelry for women? Dinner, drinks, flowers—that was the extent of his gift-giving.

"I could?"

He knew when to close a deal. "We could go now."

At that decisive moment, a loud banging on the door shattered the potential signing on the dotted line.

"Hey! Open up! I have to use the bathroom!"

"Later!" Danny barked.

"It's Chris. He has to go a lot; he drinks soda all day."

"Can't he go outside?"

Stella smiled. "Mrs. Blythe would break a leg running to the phone to call the cops. Come on, we'll finish this later."

He liked the sound of that word, *later*. He suddenly found he could relate to those scenes in movies where the clouds open up and the sun shines through. "Why don't I wait at the store until you close?"

She turned back from opening the door. "I'd like that." She was feeling the sunshine, too.

"It's about time," Chris complained, pushing into the room. "I coulda peed my pants."

Stella's and Danny's eyes met.

It was an unexpected situation in which to experience one of those earthmoving moments, considering Chris was muttering curses and giving them black looks as he barreled past.

But there it was.

There was no accounting for the timing of Cupid's arrow.

Stella giggled.

Danny smiled.

The slam of the bathroom door went unheard.

THIRTY-TWO

THE LAST FEW HOURS HAD BEEN AN EXERCISE IN evasive tactics as Stella and Danny dealt with the demands of the kids and tried to find a moment or two for themselves. They kissed once behind the door to the back room but had to jump apart when one of the kids walked in. Danny sat behind the counter with Stella and held her hand when no one was looking. This wasn't a crowd that tolerated any lovey-dovey stuff. Junior-high kids were averse to displays of affection unless it was in the form of a tussle.

Finally, the last two kids left, then Danny shut and locked the front door, and turned to Stella with a grin. "I've never watched the clock so closely in my life."

"You and me both. I was trying to think of some excuse to close early. But knowing these kids, they wouldn't listen to me anyway."

"I'm guessing this is the spot for every counterculture kid in town."

She grinned. "You noticed."

"Keeping them off the streets, are you?"

"Yeah. And out of jail. Some of the boys were hanging out and getting into trouble."

"Speaking of trouble," he murmured, advancing on her.

"Your kind of trouble I like."

"That works out then, 'cuz I'm not in the mood for a refusal."

"You're never in the mood for a refusal."

He grinned. "Something we have in common. Turn off the phone and follow me." He crooked his finger and pointed toward the stairs. "I have plans."

Maybe if Chris and Matt had left a couple minutes earlier, or if Danny had cut short the teasing, perhaps if the world was more perfect, the phone wouldn't have rung at that inopportune moment.

"Don't answer."

"I have to. I always answer the phone."

"Not always."

"Okay. But I'm not in the midst of an orgasm now. My brain is working." Stella picked up the phone without looking at the caller ID and kicked herself a second later for being so stupid.

"Is Danny there?" It was a sultry female voice, creamy smooth.

"Who wants to know?" Stella probably shouldn't have spoken so crisply, but jealousy was quirky when it came to good manners.

"*Give* Danny the phone, darling. That's a good girl. I'm parked behind his truck so I know he's there."

Stella felt like asking a million questions, but she didn't think she'd like the answers.

The flush on Stella's cheeks could mean one of her boyfriends was calling. "Who is it?" Danny asked, his voice more curt than he intended.

"One of your girlfriends," Stella replied, equally curt. Two could play that game.

"I'm not here."

"She says she's parked behind your truck. I don't think she's going to go for the 'I'm not here' bullshit. Maybe you've got yourself a stalker," Stella said, an edge to her voice.

His expression shuttered, Danny reached across the counter and took the phone from Stella. "Who is this?" He wasn't polite, but then he'd been seconds away from finally having what he'd been waiting for all afternoon—for days, actually. He wasn't in a good mood.

"This is Marisa. I have to talk to you right away."

"This isn't a good time."

"At the risk of sounding melodramatic"—she took a deep breath—"it's a life-or-death situation."

With Marisa, her interests were always important *and* often melodramatic. A wealthy divorcée, she had way too much leisure time. "I'm sure it is," he said, "but I'm busy right now."

"Someone just tried to kill me!" A hint of hysteria had entered her voice.

Jesus, had she taken one too many Vicodin with her martinis? "Calm down, Marisa. No one's trying to kill you. That's not possible."

Kill? Did he say *kill?* All Stella's drug dealer doubts came flooding back, and she called herself every kind of stupid for falling for Danny's smooth talk just because she desperately wanted sex with him. Jeez—what if sex with him turned out to be fatal! She began backing away.

He noticed and shook his head.

Which only made her more apprehensive. Was he going to do her in because she'd inadvertently become a witness to something illegal? Was her comic book store about to become the scene of a crime?

"Listen to me!" Marisa cried.

Okay, that was clear-as-a-bell hysteria.

"Someone just tried to sideswipe me on the freeway! The people who are trying to get in your house are mad at me!" She was screaming full out now. "They rammed me twice! Twice! Do you hear me?"

His spine had gone rigid. "Yeah, I hear you."

"It wasn't some bizarre mistake. I wasn't imagining it! If a police car hadn't come onto the freeway, my car would have been pushed into the river!"

Okaaay. Definitely not Vicodin talking there. That was real fear and a story to back it up. Moving to the window, he glanced out and scanned the street. It was quiet. Marisa's baby-blue Mercedes was parked right behind his truck, the driver's side definitely caved in. "Stay put. I'll come down and get you," he said.

"You're bringing her in here?" Stella exclaimed, female resentment overcoming her fear of possibly being murdered.

"There's a problem."

No shit. "Call the police. Isn't that what you do when the word *kill* comes into the conversation? If you won't call them, I will."

"Don't call the police."

His voice was like ice. His eyes were, too. Wow. He had drug dealer written all over his face. Maybe this wasn't the right time to be fearless.

"I'll take care of this," he said in a gentler voice. "Give me a couple minutes, and I'll explain."

"With her here?" Jealousy was a powerful emotion; for a moment she forgot about drug dealers and killing.

"Marisa's frightened. It has nothing to do with you or me." He blew out a breath. "Look, I have to go and get her."

And he left. Walked right out the front door as though that sketchy explanation was sufficient to smooth over a stalker woman outside her door and suggestions of killing, not to mention her drug dealing paranoia. As though she was supposed to trust him and not run away or call the cops or in general act like a normal person would under the circumstances. But she didn't move, other than sit down on the counter stool behind the cash register. So maybe she wasn't normal. Maybe she'd never been normal. Maybe that explained her *Marky B* comic and this store and all the weird kids who hung out here and depended on her to give their life some structure.

Okay. That wasn't normal. Looking to her for structure.

I rest my case.

HE GAVE HER the sweetest look when he came back in and saw her sitting there behind the counter, and when he formally introduced Marisa, who she knew perfectly well from their numerous meetings, he said, "Marisa, this is my girlfriend, Stella."

Not that being his girlfriend would wipe away a couple kilos or a truckload of pot or even a woman dripping with jewelry who looked like Marisa and was hanging onto Danny's arm like it was her only anchor in a world gone mad.

But it helped.

It made her more likely to give him a chance to explain.

"Sit down." He eased Marisa toward a chair, although he didn't sit. He leaned against the counter, his back to Stella. "Tell us what happened. Start at the beginning."

Us. That was a lovely pronoun. It conjured up a future, possibly even a rosy future. One that might even include a trip to Comic Con or Heroes Convention with someone who didn't wear an alien costume. She was beginning to elaborate a fantasy that might even require her throwing away her old sketchbook and some of her sex toys she'd received as gifts when Marisa said, "When you left me I was so angry I wanted to hurt you. Really I wouldn't have done it otherwise."

When he *left* her, as in not leaving in the morning after a one-night stand, but the other kind of leaving? That sketchbook was staying, dammit.

"Tell me what's going on here."

His voice was smooth as silk, like he hadn't even noticed Marisa had said she was angry with him for leaving her. Like that had flown right over his head

"They must have been following you," Marisa said. "That's how they knew where I lived. They stopped by one afternoon and told me they knew you and asked if they could come in and talk to me about a business proposition. They were well dressed and polite—two men—European, I think. Although everyone speaks English now with an American accent so I'm not sure where they were from. They offered me money to bring them the plans for your new game. Don't look at me like that, Rees. You had hurt me terribly."

The only way he'd hurt her was not being at her beck and call. Marisa had come out extremely well in a divorce settlement and had virtually nothing to do but spend her money and fuck. "I don't know if that's an excuse for grand larceny," he quietly said.

"I know now how wrong it was." She looked at him from under her lashes. "I'm truly sorry."

"Did you tell them you were going to disclose this to me?" He didn't believe that sorrowful pose for a second. She was leaving something out. "Is that why they're trying to kill you?"

"I think they're punishing me for not succeeding." She played with an egg-sized emerald on her finger, not about to admit that she'd tried to shake them down for more money by threatening to tell Danny.

"They must have paid you something up front." Perhaps that explained their attempt at retribution. She *had* screwed up if the attempts had really been her work. Maybe they'd found someone else.

"It was just a pittance."

"A down payment though."

She shrugged. "I suppose you could call it that."

"Did they want you to return it?"

"No one said anything. As far as I was concerned, it was good-faith money."

He doubted the money was a pittance, just as he doubted his competitors were giving away good-faith money. "So why do you think they were trying to sideswipe you?"

"I don't know. It seems completely outrageous. And terrifying."

None of what she'd said made sense, other than she was

approached and accepted the assignment. As for them trying to kill her, the only reason they'd do that was to conceal their identity. And the only reason they had to conceal their identity was if she threatened to expose them. Which probably meant she'd asked for more money and they'd refused.

This wasn't the first time industrial espionage had occurred in his business. The MO wasn't rocket science; it was common. She wasn't being honest about something—or everything. "I might be able to help you, but you have to level with me. You're not being truthful."

"I resent that!" she retorted, heatedly. "I've almost been killed!"

"You threatened them, didn't you?" He didn't want to waste a lot of time on false righteousness.

"No, of course I didn't. Good God, Rees, do I look like some common thief?"

What she looked like was some woman so put together she could have been on the cover of *Vogue,* Stella thought. From the top of her perfectly coiffed hair to the purple paint on her toes that matched her cute little purple designer dress that was so short when she crossed her legs like she was doing now, the only unknown was the color of her pubic hair. *And* whether she was actually a thief despite the ton of jewelry she was wearing.

"Has the stock market hurt your portfolio?" Danny's voice was mild.

Marisa flushed beet red.

He was getting a good feeling. He might have nailed it. "You needed money. You asked for more. They said no, and you threatened to expose them."

"No—no . . . that's not true." But she didn't meet his gaze.

"If you need money, I might be able to help you out," he said in a cool-as-a-cucumber voice.

She looked directly at him this time. "How exactly would you do that?"

"If you were willing to testify against these people, I could pay you, say a consultant's fee—for appearing in court." It was diplomacy at its finest.

A small smile formed on her glossed lips. "How much might that be?"

You had to give her credit. She was poised and guilt free. A testament to a life of always taking advantage of opportunity. Her marriage a case in point. She had been the trophy wife. Her husband had wanted a trophy. Until apparently, he'd found the company of his male assistant more interesting. It had almost been a scandal when Marisa uncovered the truth.

Her extravagant settlement had halted that possibility, of course.

But she couldn't have anticipated the tanking of the stock market.

"Tell me what you need. And I'll see what I can do." He didn't really care about the amount, relieved on a number of fronts that he'd discovered who was involved in the break-ins.

"Half a million."

"Sure."

Had he said *sure* to a half a million bucks, Stella shrieked inside her head. He really could afford all those copper pots in his kitchen.

Marisa was immediately sorry she hadn't asked for more. As she opened her mouth to speak, Danny murmured, "Don't get greedy."

"I was simply going to ask you how you intend to identify these men," she quickly improvised. "They didn't give me their names."

"Did you get cash, a check, or were the funds wired?"

"They wired the money to my account."

"Then I'll trace it." Even hacking into the Pentagon wasn't a problem, although he hadn't done that since he was a kid. "Give me your bank account number, and I'll take it from there. By the way, who was your accomplice?"

"My pool boy. But he only came along to help me out. Monty's a sweet kid."

Danny knew that tone of voice. Sweet in more ways than one he'd guess. "Is Monty going to be a problem?"

"Of course not. He thought I was playing a prank on someone."

She was amazing. No guilt, no contrition. On the other hand, his mystery was solved. Marisa's unrepentance was less than a minor issue. "It might be wise for you to disappear for a while until I can clear this up," he said, preferring her out of the way for a variety of reasons. "Why don't I have one of my security guys take you up north for a couple weeks."

"Where up north?" There were resorts and there were resorts, and Marisa didn't consort with fishermen unless they had really expensive boats.

"You name it. I don't care. Let me call Stu and have him come over to get you. I wouldn't go home if I were you. Buy what you need on the way up." Shoving his hand in his shorts' pocket, he pulled out a thick roll of bills and handed it to her.

She just loved men who didn't count their money, Marisa thought, shoving the bills into her purse, pleased to see they were all hundreds. A shame Danny seemed to be enamored with that odd woman standing behind him. The blonde, with hair that looked as though it hadn't been combed this week, who didn't have a speck of makeup on and really—a cartoon T-shirt? She must be good in bed. Rees wouldn't waste his time for any other reason.

"I'm going upstairs," Stella said as Danny punched in some numbers on his cell phone. She didn't care to wait for whomever was coming over to arrive. Marisa, the magazine-cover diva, was staring at her like she was a specimen under glass.

Danny looked up and smiled. "I'll be up soon." He was in good spirits. His piracy problems soon would be over. Most important—Stella was cleared. He was looking forward to going back to his uneventful life. "Hey, Stu, listen up. I've got a new project for you."

THIRTY-THREE

DANNY WAS OUT ON THE PORCH, WATCHING STU drive away with Marisa. She'd taken one look at the young security guard with the killer bod and made it clear she was looking forward to spending time with him up north.

He was guessing Stu wouldn't mind.

Tomorrow, he'd check out the source of Marisa's funds. Because it was slightly illegal to hack into the banking system, he'd do it himself. Then he'd call in the company lawyers and see what they could do about bringing to court whomever had hired Marisa. Right now, though, he was going to forget all that hassle and enjoy an evening alone with Stella. She was no longer a suspect—thank you, God. She was upstairs waiting for him and would no doubt bring him to the brink of exhaustion by morning. Not that he was complaining. No way, no how.

Danny walked inside, shut the door, and was just about to flip the lock when a car pulled up in front. A second later, Buddy got out, followed by Megan on her side of the car. Damn. Visitors he didn't need.

How quickly could he get rid of them was his first thought.

Could he say Stella was gone?

But then she might come downstairs and make a liar out of him.

They were walking up the steps.

Plan B. Make it a short visit. "Hey, Stella," he shouted. "We have company! Buddy and Megan!"

With her brain in tumult over one of Danny's girlfriends stopping by, not to mention his casually offered half-million-dollar payoff, Stella wasn't sure she was in a tranquil enough mood to be sociable. As if she had a choice with Megan screaming to her to get downstairs.

Dragging herself off the bed, she took a deep breath, tested a smile on her face—found it scary as hell in the mirror over her dresser—and went for unsmiling but polite.

But she couldn't help say, "Why me?" under her breath as she walked down the hallway.

"We didn't know Danny was going to be here," Megan said, waving at Stella as she came down the stairs. "But now we can share our"—she glanced at Buddy and giggled—"incredibly exciting news with both of you. *I* thought we should wait, but Buddy said, 'Why?' He's been waiting all his life, so here we are!" She looked at Buddy again with a smile. "Do you want to tell them, or should I?"

"You do it," he said, beaming back at her.

It was the same Buddy on the surface: designer linen slacks and shirt, custom shoes, spiked brown hair, and healthy tan. But something was different. The blasé nonchalance was gone. His smile was from the heart.

"We're getting married," Megan blurted out.

Stella practically mouthed the words as Megan spoke. You couldn't miss that breathless, over-the-top fervor.

"Buddy *just* asked me, and I said it's too soon, and he said he's been waiting for me all his life. Isn't that just so sweet?" She looked up at him adoringly before turning back to Stella and Danny.

Buddy had always railed against marriage—calling it a useless institution foisted on unsuspecting males to curtail their freedom. Apparently, he'd had a change of heart, Danny decided, taking in his friend's obvious delight.

How many times had Megan said she wasn't ready to marry again until maybe the sky fell or her brain went soft, Stella thought.

"Congratulations," Danny said.

"No kidding," Stella added. "Big time congratulations."

"We haven't set the wedding date yet, but Buddy wants to get married soon, don't you, darling"—another of those doting looks—"and the kids are thrilled. We're all going to Disney World for our honeymoon!" Megan added with a trilling little laugh. "Isn't that super?"

Buddy in Disney World. *Wow,* Danny thought. *There's a picture.*

"Disney World," Stella said. "Won't that be nice."

"Tell them our other big news," Buddy prompted, looking like someone who had won his tenth gold medal at the Olympics or maybe discovered the hidden treasure of the Incas.

Something to top whirlwind wedding plans? Stella braced herself.

"You won't believe this," Megan breathlessly began. "I didn't at first. But one of my campaign volunteers brought in the video and, well—it's truer than true."

The words *video* and *campaign* always made one consider the word *scandal* with a capital S. "It's good news, right?" Stella quickly said.

"Couldn't be better. It's a real news flash." Buddy nodded at Megan. "Tell them."

"Well . . ." Megan took a deep breath, squeezed Buddy's hand, and said in a rush, "George Bennet saw Deloitte stealing my new campaign signs and tossing them in his car. George was on his way home from videotaping his son's baseball game, so"—she grinned from ear to ear—"we have twenty minutes on tape of Deloitte's criminal behavior."

"I already had it sent to all the TV stations," Buddy remarked.

"And Buddy says that he can donate more to my campaign if we're married than if we're not." Megan blushed. "Not that I care about any of that."

"I told her she was crazy if she didn't take me up on my offer."

"So that's all our news," Megan said. "We're going to go and tell my mom now."

"Jeez, that's pretty great news. A state senator for sure now," Stella said, genuinely glad for Megan. "And a wedding. I'll get to wear my strappy silver shoes."

"You'll be my maid of honor, of course."

Stella smiled. "Of course." She didn't say for the second time 'cuz that would have spoiled the mood.

"And you're my best man if you're willing," Buddy said to Danny.

"Absolutely."

"We're just having a small wedding," Megan said.

"I'm pushing for next week." Buddy grinned. "But I'm getting static."

"We'll see." Megan leaned into him.

"Hey, that's a hopeful sign." Buddy gave the thumbs up. "Keep your calendar open. We're out of here, right?" He glanced at Megan. "Her mom's waiting."

"Maybe you could do me a favor on the way," Danny said. "I need Marisa's car moved. You could leave it in the McDonald's parking lot."

"Sure, no problem." No questions, no looks—male bonding at its best.

"I'll walk out with you. Be back in a minute," Danny said to Stella.

"I'll call you later." Megan waved at Stella. "We'll talk about your bridesmaid's dress," she added with a grin.

Stella laughed. "You're going to give me grief, aren't you?"

"I was thinking about orange chiffon," Megan teased, the words drifting back through the open door. "With black lace trim and lots of sequins."

THIRTY-FOUR

NOW THERE WAS A CINDERELLA STORY, STELLA
thought, standing at the door, watching the three of them
walk away. You meet someone, they sweep you off your
feet, propose marriage, and then offer to pay for your campaign.
Not that she wasn't really, really happy for Megan. Megan deserved every kind of happiness that came her way after the rough
time she'd had for the last few years. And for the years of her
marriage, too, come to think about it. Chad had never been Mr.
Faithful.

But having to consider all that perfect happiness brought her
own life into sharp perspective. Unlike Megan's fairy tale ending,
here she was mired in some craziness over a guy who was more
secretive than Fort Knox, who could say "Sure" when someone
asked for half a million dollars, and who more or less had women
lining up for him and taking a number. The women were a

problem—call her jealous; there was no way around it. And bottom line, she wasn't sure she was comfortable with someone who was so rich she couldn't remember if it was a trillion or zillion dollars a month he earned from *Blizzard 9000*.

Although, maybe it wasn't about comfort levels. Maybe she was figuring she'd be left sooner or later by a man like that.

Maybe she was just a coward.

Or realistic. Why sign up for guaranteed heartache?

When Danny came into the room a short time later, he found Stella lying on the bed in a lethargic sprawl.

She tried to smile.

"You gotta do better than that, babe." Not that he didn't expect some rankled feathers after having Marisa in the house, but he didn't mind apologizing every which way for that. "Come on, give me a real smile. Megan and Buddy are happy as clams. We're finally alone. Life's good."

She grimaced.

"Okay, spit it out. I'll listen and be understanding as hell."

"It's easy to be in a good mood when you're a kazillionaire."

It stopped him for a moment. Had he figured her wrong? Was she after money, too? "You need money?" he asked and waited, his good mood heading south.

"Don't look at me like that. No, I don't need your money. I don't want your money. In fact, I wish you didn't have any. And don't you dare say something about Megan not having a problem with Buddy's money or about buying me jewelry after seeing that bitch downstairs wearing your numerous gifts."

"I didn't buy that stuff. Marisa had a rich husband."

"Had? Did she give him up for you?"

"No. I met her after her divorce."

"Lucky her."

"I don't want to fight over Marisa."

"I don't want to hear her name, okay?" She must be more jealous than she thought. She was acting like a child.

"Sorry. I won't be seeing her again."

"Except for the trial and the depositions and all the phone calls she's going to have to make to you when she's frightened and alone. I'm thinking she's going to be needing to make a lot of calls to you before this is over." It was turning out to be harder than Stella thought to act like an adult.

"You're jealous."

"No, I'm mad." Mostly that she couldn't function without him. How stupid was that?

"Mad and jealous."

"Screw you."

He knew better than to joke back. She really meant it. "Why don't I sit down over here and we can talk about whatever you want to talk about." He took a seat in the chair across the room. No way he was messing this up at this stage when his break-ins were solved and the person he most wanted exonerated was.

"I don't want to talk."

"Wanna watch TV?"

She gave him a look.

He was going to sit here all night if necessary. The woman who had come to mean so much to him was unhappy. He had to fix it. "Was it something I said?" If it wasn't just about Marisa, he needed a clue. The money stuff couldn't be a real issue.

She shook her head.

It was a start.

"I suppose it was Mar—" She drilled him with a look and he stopped.

"It's not her, it's all of them. Plural. And I know why the crowd's so large. Besides your obvious charms, and don't go getting a big head."

"Because you've seen charms like that before," he said, testily. "Like in your sketchbook."

"This isn't about me."

"Of course it's about you. It's always about you." He couldn't help it. When he thought about all those guys fucking her, he went crazy.

She sat up, her spine stiff as a rod. "I beg your pardon?"

"Don't give me a hard time about women when you've been notching your belt with all those guys. At least I don't keep a fucking record."

"Are you telling me there's a double standard?"

"Maybe sometimes there is," he muttered.

"There isn't. There better not be."

"Because you wouldn't want to give up your smorgasbord."

"You should talk. Women follow you around in droves."

He shut his eyes, counted to ten, and opened them again. "I'm jealous. Okay? I'd like to rip up your sketchbook and burn it— along with all those damned sex toys of yours. I know, I know— women have as much right to enjoy sex as men. So sue me. I don't want you to have sex with anyone but me. And that's the way I feel."

"Ditto here."

"I won't then. Your turn." His gaze was laser sharp.

"I don't want to, either."

He smiled. "So what's the problem?"

"It's your money, too."

"I give most of it to charity. You see how I live. It's not too out of the ordinary."

She snorted. "Fourteen cars?"

"They're yearly bonuses. They're a write-off for the company."

"You don't turn them down."

"Why should I?"

She didn't have an answer. Or at least a reasonable one. "I suppose," she said.

"And I suppose I could learn to live with your sketchbook."

"Compromise and negotiation, right?"

"Isn't that what love's all about? I do stuff for you and you do stuff for me?"

"What kind of stuff?"

Her voice had shifted an octave lower, turned soft. Things were looking up. "Any kind you want," he said with a smile.

"Pink rabbit stuff?"

He laughed. "After tonight, though, I'm buying you a new one."

She sighed.

"What?"

"I don't like to feel this way—caring so much. Worried." She'd never so much as given a man a second thought. Sex was sex. This was different.

"Marry me and stop worrying. We'll have a double wedding with the love birds who just left."

"You don't mean that."

"Jeez, you sound like Amy," he said.

"What do you know about the way Amy sounds?"

"She's distrustful, although she has reason."

"How do you know she has reason? See—this is what's going to happen. I'm going to be crazy jealous all the time and ruin my life and yours. Shit. If this is love, I don't like it."

"You'll change your mind."

"Don't sound so reasonable. I hardly know you anyway."

"Well, I know you, and I know what I want. As for the rest, we'll work it out." He rose from the chair and moved toward the bed, thinking if he could formulate three hundred thousand commands to design a game, he could figure out some way to make Stella see things his way.

"What are you doing?"

"What do you think I'm doing? I'm coming to bed."

"You sure?"

"Oh, yeah. I'm real sure."

"So it really wouldn't help if I were equivocal or not."

"Nope."

"You're coming to bed anyway."

"Yup."

She smiled for the first time the way she used to. "I was just thinking."

"I know."

"No you don't."

"You were thinking I should stop here and open this drawer and bring your pink rabbit to bed with me."

She grinned. "You're a mind reader."

He winked. "Fucking A." He held up the pink rabbit. "And he's a mind reader, too. Move over. We've got things to do."

She scooted over enough so there was room for him to sit down, her senses doing a little flutter of anticipation as he tossed the vibrator on the bed, pulled his T-shirt over his head, and began stripping down for action. He could have been on a *Playgirl* calendar with his hard, taut muscles and sleek power, with that damned near-zero-body-fat factor. He had to work out, although he didn't talk about it. Not that he talked about his fourteen cars much, either.

His clothes were on the floor in mere seconds. But then he'd been on the way here for the last couple days. It wasn't as though he had to think about his next move. "So you're playing the sultana?" he said as he turned back to her. She hadn't moved in her lounging pose.

She grinned. "Roxana, I think."

"Not in that cartoon T-shirt."

"Okay, Miss Piggy. It's all about *moi*."

He didn't care what it was all about; he was real adaptable. And focused. "Let's fire up the rabbit and get him in the rabbit patch."

"I just adore a man who takes charge."

"A man? Could we be a little less general?" But he was teasing as he unzipped her shorts. He knew where he stood.

"One by the name of Rees with a body that's turning me on."

"That's better." He stripped off her shorts and panties. "You'll get preferential treatment now."

"The full spa treatment?"

He grinned. "You betcha. One happy ending coming up." Nudging her thighs apart with a sweep of his palms, he flicked the switch on the rabbit vibrator and eased the glossy rotating head into her by slow degrees until the belt of pearls at the base of the shaft was solidly against her pussy. The rotating shaft was working on her G-spot at the same time as the clit-tickling rabbit ears were stroking what they were designed to stroke.

He glanced up to check out the effect of his handiwork and smiled.

She was breathing little shallow breaths, as though she didn't want to move too much and lose the magic.

It was almost too easy with her. Not that he was complaining. They were a good match. But he was guessing she wouldn't mind another few degrees of sensation. In fact, he knew she wouldn't.

"Don't move," he unnecessarily whispered, easing her T-shirt off so quickly she didn't have time to do more than moan as a rush of pleasure bombarded her brain. The slightest motion registered in the seething pool of frenzied nerve endings caressed by the rotating shaft and rabbit ears, the possibility of sensual overload imminent.

No bra. Handy. And dipping his head, he cupped one breast, drew the taut nipple into his mouth, and gently sucked.

She cried out—the softest of whimpering sounds.

He licked the taut crest, exerted slightly more pressure, tugged on her nipple, bit little nibbling bites—not too hard, but hard enough to elicit a little moan, a squirm of her hips. It was all about self-restraint, tempered with just enough forcefulness—he stretched the pliant flesh, suckled the tender bud as though he relied on it for sustenance. Gave the pink rabbit a little nudge with his palm.

Ravished by a dizzying, raw sensation that traveled downward and upward and met in her hot, strumming core, she quivered and arched her hips upward, reaching for that singular delight.

"You can't come yet," he said, flexing his arm, sliding the pink rabbit upward the merest fraction. "You have to wait."

She tensed—from pleasure, from the husky authority in his

voice, from a kind of rarefied, stunning splendor and abruptly climaxed in a shuddering, almost noiseless, paroxysm.

He wondered for a moment if he'd done something wrong. She was always hair-trigger fast, but never so constrained. And then he saw the tears seeping from under her lashes and felt an inexpressible fear. He'd hurt her. Jesus. Flicking off the vibrator with lightening speed, he carefully removed it and swept her into his arms.

"I'm sorry," he whispered, cradling her in his lap. "Don't cry. God, don't cry."

Her lashes lifted, sparkling with tears. "It's okay. I'm happy."

"Like hell you are." He brushed away a trail of tears on her cheek.

She shook her head and offered a shaky smile. "You swept me off my feet, lover boy."

That wasn't exactly an intelligible phrase to a man with both feet on the ground. "What's that got to do with crying?"

"I'm feeling all dewy-eyed and mushy." She couldn't quite bring herself to say love, but it was on the tip of her tongue.

"Mushy?"

"Like quivering heartstrings, cooing doves, baby names."

His gaze narrowed. "You'd better not be pregnant, 'cuz I haven't known you that long."

"Excuse me. Have you heard of the pill? And unless you change that tone of voice, my mushy stuff is going to ride off into the sunset."

"Okay. I like mushy. I love mushy." He grinned. "It's my favorite word."

"Speaking of favorite things."

He blew out a breath of relief; talk of feelings made him

nervous. "This I understand. Are we talking mechanical devices or the real thing?"

"You tell me."

"The real thing."

There was really something to be said for that mind-reading concept where one knows exactly what the other is thinking. Or at least Stella was hoping it was mind reading and not—you know—that professional skill that comes from using mechanical devices in hundreds of other bedrooms. In her superfine mood, she was going to go with mind reading.

As it turned out, he even knew how she didn't like a lot of questions. He even knew how she liked it slow and easy. He was a virtuoso of rhythm, depth, and timing. He even knew that there was that moment when the real thing did what real things did and met her exactly, precisely, to the nanosecond of perfection in a mutual orgasm.

She didn't have to say one single word.

Maybe she'd have to think about retiring the pink rabbit. On the other hand, there was no need to make overly hasty decisions.

Everyone knew that decisions made in the heat of passion didn't always stand up to the cold light of day.

But of one thing she was sure.

If this was love, it was sweet.

IN FACT, LOVING someone more or less changed everything—from the color inside your eyelids when your eyes were shut to the taste of kisses. She'd never known kisses tasted at all. They were sort of a cross between Jujubes and Gummy Bears. Really nice. And then there was your skin, which had suddenly become supersensitive and tingly and susceptible to a thousand degrees more sensation. She was probably glowing from within like a firefly.

If she could do haiku, this would definitely be the time to try it out. She'd have to put in a line about her old friend the pink rabbit.

"We should read poetry," she murmured.

"Umm . . ." His mouth was sliding down her throat, and when it came to rest in the curve of her collarbone, he whispered, "Beauty alone will not account for her. No single attribute her charm explains. Hafiz. I had to read him in freshman English."

Hafiz. One of her favorites. How sweet was that? She almost came right then.

And then he rolled on his back, carrying her with him as though she were weightless.

He was so gloriously strong; that would be another great line of haiku.

Swinging her up, he placed her on his thighs, facing him. "Now we're going to talk about this marriage thing, or you can't have anymore."

"That's not fair." She tried to rise to her knees enough to ease down his upthrust erection.

"I don't feel like being fair." He held her firmly in place. "So what do you say?"

She struggled against his hold. "Let's talk about it later." When she could actually think beyond her next orgasm.

"When later?"

"Five minutes." Really, it was shocking how concentrated

one's thinking became when impelled by feverish desire—the need for orgasm swamping all else.

"After you climax again," he said.

She nodded. "I'll buy a wedding dress right after."

Whatever it took, he thought. This wasn't the time to have scruples. "Here we go, babe." He released his hold, guided himself into her silken warmth, and heard her breathy sigh as she sank down his rigid length. Some women wanted diamonds; others, trips to Club Med. His comic book girl wanted this. Was he lucky or what?

Short moments later—another orgasm later—Stella came up for air. She'd actually said wedding dress, hadn't she? Could she renege? Wasn't this all too hasty? Shouldn't two people know each other better before they made such a long-term commitment? Then again, he was lifting her upward again, slowly, leisurely, and her insatiable senses were anticipating the coming pleasure with tiny little quivers of excitement.

Maybe marriage wouldn't be so bad after all—look at Megan, going for it again.

Maybe what one lost in independence, one gained in sensational, starry-eyed, halcyon sex.

Maybe she could at least go *looking* at wedding dresses.

"Five minutes are up," he murmured, easing her downward again. "Say yes."

Her heated gaze met his. "Maybe."

He grinned. "Maybe, *I'll* have to keep this up until I change your mind."

Now that was the kind of persuasion she liked. "I gotta tell you," she said with a smile, "I can be real stubborn."

"And I gotta tell you"—he grinned—"ain't no mountain high enough."

It wasn't haiku, but it was really touching. "That sounds like dedication."

As a man, he would have called it something else, but he wasn't a fool. "Utter devotion, babe. That's me."

It was sort of looking like Marky B might keep her new hunky cohort after all, she found herself thinking. After all, one had to give credit where credit was due. Utter devotion was a concept that had real impact.

Like that—*ohmygod* . . . that was mind-blowing impact and a couple thousand inexplicable sensations more.

This definitely wasn't the time to parse the mysteries of love.

Plenty of time for that tomorrow . . .

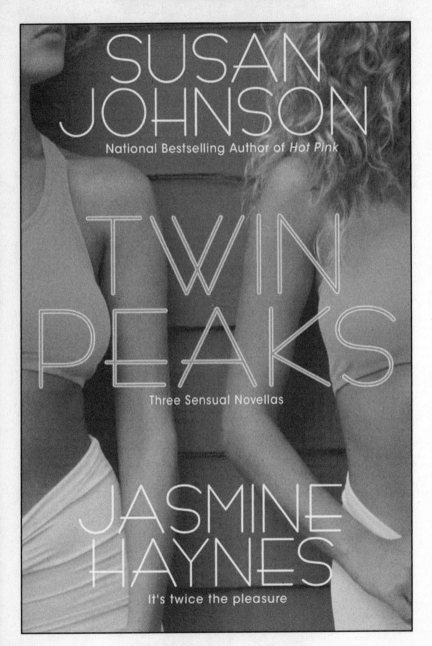